PENGUIN BOOKS
The Time Out Book of Paris Short Stories

Nicholas Royle is the author of three novels – *Counterparts*, *Saxophone Dreams* and *The Matter of the Heart* (Abacus) – and around a hundred short stories. His new novel, *The Director's Cut* (Abacus), will be published in 2000. He has edited numerous anthologies, including *The Time Out Book of New York Short Stories* (Penguin) and *Neonlit: Time Out Book of New Writing* (Quartet). He is also the editor of *Books Online* on *Time Out*'s website (www.timeout.com).

The Time Out Book of
Paris Short Stories

Edited by Nicholas Royle

PENGUIN BOOKS

PENGUIN BOOKS

Published by the Penguin Group
Penguin Books Ltd, 27 Wrights Lane, London W8 5TZ, England
Penguin Putnam Inc, 375 Hudson Street, New York, New York 10014, USA
Penguin Books Australia Ltd, Ringwood, Victoria, Australia
Penguin Books Canada Ltd, 10 Alcorn Avenue, Toronto, Ontario, Canada M4V 3B2
Penguin Books (NZ) Ltd, 182-190 Wairu Road, Auckland 10, New Zealand

Penguin Books Ltd, Registered Offices: Harmondsworth, Middlesex, England

First published in Great Britain by Penguin Books 1999
3 5 7 9 10 8 6 4

Printed in England by Clays Ltd, St Ives plc

Contents

For Alain Robbe-Grillet

The editor would like to thank the following: Peter Ayrton, Natasha Edwards and Gareth Evans for advice on contacts; Lanning Aldrich and Jonathan Cox for advice on contracts; Jean-Daniel Brèque for inside information on the language; Rhonda Carrier for her eagle eye and impeccable taste; Christopher Burns, M John Harrison and Liz Jensen for the benefit of their wisdom; Helen Constantine for her superb translations; Richard Ford for his interest and enthusiasm; Chris Quinn for his disappearing act; Lily Dunn, Peter Fiennes, Sarah Guy, Ruth Jarvis, John Oakey and Caro Taverne for professional help and advice.

Contributors

Ron Butlin, novelist, short story writer and poet, lives in Edinburgh with his wife and their dog. His books include a short story collection, *The Tilting Room*, and two novels, *The Sound of My Voice* and *Night Visits*. His work has been translated into ten languages. 'The Convalescents' is an extract from a novel-in-progress.

Michel Butor was born in Monsen-Baroeul in 1926. A novelist, essayist and prominent figure among practitioners of the *nouveau roman*, he is the author of *Passage de Milan*, *L'Emploi du temps*, *La Modification*, *La Génie du lieu* and many other works. He lives in Lucinges, France. The texts that make up 'Seven Stations in the Paris Whirlwind' appeared originally, in a different arrangement, in *Transit*; this is the first time they have been published in this format and in English.

Didier Daeninckx, born in Saint-Denis in 1949, is the author of numerous books including *Meurtres pour mémoire* (1984; published in English as *Murder in Memoriam* by Serpent's Tail, 1991), *Le der des ders* (1984; published in English as *A Very Profitable War* by Serpent's Tail, 1994), *Zapping* (1992), *Nazis dans le métro* (1996) and *Mort au premier tour* (1997). He lives in Aubervilliers, just outside Paris.

Marie Darrieussecq, born in 1969 in Bayonne, France, is the author of two novels, *Truismes* (1997; published in English as *Pig Tales* by Faber, 1997), which sold 300,000 copies, and *Naissance des fantômes* (1998). 'I Love Paris' first appeared in the French magazine *Atmosphères*. It is published here in English for the first time.

Patricia Duncker teaches writing at the University of Wales, Aberystwyth. Her first novel, *Hallucinating Foucault* (1996), won the Dillon's First Fiction Award and the McKitterick Prize. Her most recent publication is a collection of short fiction, *Monsieur Shoushana's Lemon Trees* (1997). A second novel, *James Miranda Barry*, is forthcoming from Serpent's Tail in 1999. She spends part of the year in France.

Edward Fox was born in New York in 1958 and now lives in London, where he works as a freelance journalist. He is the author of one non-fiction book, *Obscure Kingdoms: Journeys to Distant Royal Courts*, and a number of short stories published in *London Magazine* and various anthologies, including *The Time Out Book of New York Short Stories*.

Maureen Freely, born in Neptune, New Jersey, in 1952, grew up in Istanbul. She now lives in Bath with an industrial sociologist and has four children and two step-children. Her novels include *Mother's Helper*, *The Stork Club*, *Under the Vulcania* and *The Other Rebecca*. She is a lecturer on the Creative Writing Programme at the University of Warwick.

Ismail Kadare, born in 1936 in the Albanian town of Gjirokaster, studied in Tirana and Moscow. He is Albania's best-known poet and novelist. His works, including *Broken April*, *The File on H*, *The Three-Arched Bridge*, *Albanian Spring*, *The Palace of Dreams* and *The Pyramid*, have been translated worldwide. Having sought asylum in France in 1990, he now lives in Paris.

Christopher Kenworthy was born in Preston in 1968 and has lived in Bath, London and Western Australia. He ran the independent press Barrington Books and edited three original anthologies of short fiction, *The Sun Rises Red*, *Sugar Sleep* and *The Science of Sadness*. His first collection, *Will You Hold Me?*, is published by The Do-Not Press, and his début novel, *Summer in Mordor*, is due to be published by Serpent's Tail.

Linda Lê, born in Vietnam in 1963, is the author of four novels, including *Calomnies* (published as *Slander* by Nebraska Press, 1996), *Voix* (1998) and *Lettre morte* (1999). She lives in Paris.

Toby Litt was born in 1968. He grew up in Ampthill, Bedfordshire. His first two books are a short story collection, *Adventures in Capitalism*, and a novel, *Beatniks*. His new novel, *Corpsing*, will be published by Hamish Hamilton in early 2000.

Kim Newman's short stories have been collected in *The Original Doctor Shade and Other Stories* and *Famous Monsters*; a third collection, *Unforgivable Stories*, is forthcoming. His novels include *The Night Mayor*,

Jago, *The Quorum*, *The Bloody Red Baron*, *Life's Lottery* and *Judgment of Tears: Anno Dracula 1959* (aka *Dracula Cha Cha Cha*). His non-fiction books include *Nightmare Movies* and *Millennium Movies*. Born in Brixton in 1959, he lives in north London.

Michèle Roberts is half-English and half-French. She is the author of nine novels, three collections of poetry and one collection of short stories. She lives in London and in Mayenne, France.

Patrick Smith was born and grew up in Ireland but has spent much of his life in Sweden working as an architect and writer. He now lives in France. His most recent book is *An Unmarried Man* (Jonathan Cape).

Adam Thorpe was born in Paris in 1956 and brought up in India, Cameroon and England. He has published two volumes of poetry, *Mornings in the Baltic* (1988) and *Meeting Montaigne* (1990), and three novels, *Ulverton* (1992), *Still* (1995) and *Pieces of Light* (1998). He has written three plays for BBC Radio, and his first stage play, *Couch Grass & Ribbon*, was performed at the Watermill Theatre, Newbury, in 1996. His third volume of poetry, *From the Neanderthal*, will appear in June 1999, a volume of short stories, *Shifts*, in 2000. He lives in France with his wife and three children.

Erica Wagner was born in New York in 1967. Since 1986 she has lived in the UK and is now literary editor of *The Times*. Her début collection of short stories, *Gravity*, was published by Granta Books in 1997. *Ariel's Gift*, a book about Ted Hughes's *Birthday Letters*, will be published by Faber in 2000.

Marc Werner, born in 1968, has lived in Brussels, Berlin and London, and currently lives in Paris, where he works as a photographer. 'Paris Noir' is his first published short story.

Introduction

There is only one way to bring to mind everything that Paris means to you, and that is to go back there. In practical terms, it's never been easier to get to the French capital. For anyone like myself who is scared of flying and sick of sailing, the Channel Tunnel is a gift from God. But first I had to get past the HM Customs security check at Waterloo's Eurostar terminal.

A man who looks as if he's spent the last twenty minutes sucking on a particularly sour lemon asks me what is the purpose of my trip to Paris. Now, I honestly believe this is the first time I've been asked this question. 'I'm editing a book,' I tell him. 'I'm going to Paris to write the introduction.' 'Have you done any of these *books* before?' The word 'books' is pronounced with particular distaste. He spits it out as if it's a pip from one of his lemons. 'Yes, several,' I tell him. 'What? Travel books?' 'Yes, travel books and other books as well. This −' I hesitate before going on − 'is a book of short stories about Paris.'

A veil comes down over his eyes − or is it a red mist?

'Why do you need to go there to do that?' he asks me.

At times like this I wish I could lie to people like this man, figures of authority. Or adopt a bitterly sarcastic tone, at the very least a touch of irony. But I can't.

'I don't *have* to,' I say. 'I could sit at my desk in London and write it, but I'd rather go to Paris and do it. It might make it fresher, more authentic.' Well, it's certainly getting more authentic by the minute. Authentic for crossing an international frontier. Kurt Waldheim's Austrian customs men who once threw me out of a Swiss train carriage before ripping up the seat cushions have got nothing on this guy.

Things pick up considerably on the train with an offer of complimentary coffee and croissants. Henceforth it gets better and better.

If originally I had planned to go straight to the Latin Quarter, then find the right café and sit down and write this introduction, that plan was abandoned as soon as I walked out of the Gare du Nord − and kept on walking. Like Michel Butor and Marie Darrieussecq, I love

Paris. I walked all day and saw a million things about Paris that I loved – and a few that would infuriate a saint (mainly on the pavement or – dammit! too late – on the sole of your shoe). They are largely the same things that I loved (and hated) when I lived here fifteen years ago, a bored language assistant and a struggling actor and writer, with a few new things thrown in as well.

I love the rivers that run in the gutters directed by bizarre rolls of sodden carpet or old trousers, whose distribution appears random, and yet I know that if a single drain-stop were to be accidentally misaligned at a certain moment of the day, the entire network would suddenly be transformed, causing streams in the 18th *arrondissement* to flow uphill and hydrants in Montparnasse to run dry. I love the riot of scents in the streets, from perfumed ladies walking tiny beribboned dogs in the 17th to students chaining Gitanes on the boulevard St Germain (the slogans they chanted, which Edward Fox recalls in 'The Events', are unheard ghosts in the pre-millennial clamour). From the hint of melting rubber on Métro line 4 to the distinct whiff of sulphur from the deeper RER. The smell of fresh bread on every other corner and the tang of squashed fruit from busy street markets.

Since my last trip to Paris was before 31 August 1997, I feel drawn to the Tunnel de l'Alma in a way I never was before. Tributes to the passengers of the black Mercedes that is not unlike the black Mercedes in Patricia Duncker's 'Paris' are scrawled on the parapet of the bridge over the tunnel entrance and plastered over the popularly appropriated, golden Flamme de la Liberté.

A stone's throw from the place de l'Alma, on rue Georges-Bizet, I see a well-dressed man in the driving seat of a Renault Espace, his face expressionless as he studies the pictures in a pornographic magazine.

When I do finally get down to the Left Bank and check out the rue de Seine – its fruit stalls and *charcuteries* exactly as described by Michèle Roberts – I eavesdrop on a group of French tourists who are laughing and looking in the window of the Galerie de l'Europe. The gallery is showing some startling modern art that looks like nothing so much as great sheets of rusty metal. 'There's a play on in Paris called *Art*,' says one of the tourists, and I think that's extraordinary because one of the actors playing in that production is a friend of mine. I know him because fourteen years ago he directed me in a play at the Galerie 55 on the rue de Seine. The Galerie 55, a tiny theatre specialising in

English-language productions, closed down some years ago and the Galerie de l'Europe opened up in its place.

I overcome my natural timidity where exclusive galleries are concerned and go in. (I would probably never have entered the gallery in Patrick Smith's 'The Storm' for fear of being challenged and found to be wanting.) The premises have been gutted and painted white, but downstairs, where luckily the exhibition continues, I recognise one of the old stone archways under which we used to rehearse. And for the briefest of instants I detect the unforgettable smell of that damp, long-ago basement with its tiny dressing rooms and red velvet drapes. The walls might have changed but – as in Christopher Kenworthy's 'The Wishbone Bag' – the space itself has not.

While I'm in the Latin Quarter I take a close look at rue Princesse, one of the macabre sites visited in Marc Werner's 'Paris Noir', only to discover it's literally around the corner from the street where Linda Lê lives.

I see the Tour Montparnasse in the distance and I wish I had time to head in that direction and see if Maureen Freely's Rosebud bar is a fixture or a fiction. By venturing neither on the water nor underground, I miss experiencing this time around the impressions rendered by Didier Daeninckx and Erica Wagner – but once you've walked along the canal de l'Ourcq and descended into the catacombs, you never quite forget the damp melancholy they share.

Some details are everywhere: the café in which Ismail Kadare's intellectuals discuss the book to end all books could be any one of a thousand. The mythical heroes – and villains – brought to life by Kim Newman stare out at you from a hundred shop windows. The beggars and the dispossessed and the charmingly naive expats in Adam Thorpe's 'Debauchery' have not changed much since 1956, except that now there are more of them.

Dusk finds me heading with sad inevitability up the rue St Denis, where the brash majesty of the area's prostitutes never fails to amaze. I'm led to wonder if up any of those narrow staircases, behind any of those closed doors, there's anything going on that's quite as unsavoury as in Toby Litt's 'Story to Be Translated…'

Finding Le Drouot on the rue de Richelieu unaccountably closed, I make instead for its sister restaurant, Chartier, on rue du Faubourg Montmartre, where a starter of *carottes râpées* followed by *entrecôte grillée frites* and *un quart de vin rouge* brings change from 100 francs. A quick dash along rue Richer, where an elderly lady driver is so close to running me over she catches my finger in the Mercedes Benz star on her bonnet, and up rue du Faubourg Poissonnière, and I'm Eurostarring my way out of Paris like the narrator's ex in Ron Butlin's 'The Convalescents', except I'm hoping I don't bump into a certain customs officer on my return to Waterloo.

Nicholas Royle
Paris, January 1999

Paris

Patricia Duncker

The car was a black Mercedes with a 75 registration. That means they come from Paris. We watched it coming down the steep curves towards the village. How many are there? Two people, both wearing dark glasses. They must have rented the Barthez house. He always does summer lets to Parisians. Bit early for the holidays, isn't it? Perhaps they don't have children. Does Monsieur Barthez advertise? Yes, in *Le Monde*, the holiday supplement. And he's got the house with an agency. Must cost a fortune. The agency takes a commission. Worth it, though. He charges more than Mimi does for her little place with the balcony. No comparison, is there? Emile Barthez has got that swimming pool. No water in it though? Or has he filled it up? Of course he's filled it up. His nephew was down there yesterday. Topping up the chlorine.

I prefer the sea myself, says Olivier.

Here's a point of contention. The Barthez family own the only swimming pool in the village and he has never offered us the use of it, even when the house is empty, not even for a moderate fee. The swimming pool is reserved for the Parisians. So we had better prefer the sea. We haven't any choice.

We stroll down to the bridge and lean picturesquely against the stone barriers. We are the reception committee. And we want to get a good look at the Parisians.

They drive into the village very slowly, taking the bend in front of Simone's bungalow with exaggerated care. Pause by the Mairie, now deserted, unused, the shutters grey as driftwood, banging against the walls in the high winds. Left turn into the main street, leaving the vegetable rows behind them. Beans, cabbages, peas, aubergines, chillis, peppers, courgettes, pumpkins. I've already dug up all the potatoes. One of the cats scuttles out of the path of the oncoming Mercedes. They sweep past. We peer in, stony-faced. Olivier nods his *bonjour.* Well? Hmmmm. What do we think?

They look as if they have already been on holiday. Both of them are nicely browned. A man and a woman. Young, unsmiling, no children. They pull up in front of the Barthez household, climb out of the Mercedes and begin fiddling with the lock on the storm door. We watch the woman leaving him to get on with it. She turns her attention to the geranium pots, which descend the steps. She snaps off the dead flowers with surgical accuracy. She is wearing rings and bracelets made of gold. They are rich, rich, rich. Just like every other holiday-maker who ever comes from Paris.

For most of us, the nearest we ever get to Paris is our ritual espionage upon the visiting *vacanciers*. Some of us have never been to Paris. Ever. The city remains a symbol in our school books, an image on the television, the source of news and evil things, VAT forms, tax increases and for me, the closest consulate.

Our village is very isolated. We are eight miles from the nearest post office, 30 miles from the nearest supermarket. The *boulanger* negotiates the tiny climbing roads every day. We can always see him coming. There is one road in and one road out. We are surrounded by mountains covered in scrub oak, the scented garrigue and an exploding population of wild boar. We can hear them scrabbling in the river at night. We wring our hands and shake our heads over the damage they do in the vineyards. Then, as soon as August comes round, we hunt them down and shoot them. Everyone, except me, lives for the hunt. My nearest neighbour is Papi, well into his eighties and still roaming the mountainsides, armed to the teeth. The women don't actually go out shooting of course. They stand on the bridge counting the mass of white vans that depart for the wilderness. Then they count the number of boar that come back and are laid out in the middle of the village square. They either consign the meat to freezer boxes or turn it into huge steaming pots of herbal deliciousness in a rich red wine sauce. We shoot to kill. We shoot for the pot. We are hunters. The real thing, undreamed of throughout all the effeminate streets of Paris.

Sébastien is telling me that you have to pay 570 francs to get there and back on the TGV, change at Montpellier. And you had better book weeks in advance. *Réservation obligatoire*.

But I don't want to go to Paris. I hate going to Paris. I spend too much money and smoke too many cigarettes. I buy too many books and I come home with a hangover.

Simone sits next to me on the green bench. She thinks that Paris was once a beautiful city full of *haute couture* and elegant *soirées*, but that it has now gone to the damnation bow-wows and is full of blacks *sans papiers*, living in churches or on hunger strike, chained to railings in public places. Once upon a time we earned fair wages if we worked hard, but now there are dozens of young people who don't want to work and evil bosses running sweat-shops, who pay two francs an hour. As if it wasn't hard enough to make ends meet down here, let alone trying to live in Paris.

Olivier, aged 18, just went to Paris with his mates for a dirty week-end and they had never been before. So they spent all their money in Crazy Horse on the Champs-Elysées and it was just like it was on TV with geometrically identical girls, bobbed wigs, oval bums and perfect boobs. They all weigh 55 kilos and no more. You daren't put on a sliver of fat. For if you do, you're sacked.

I reflect upon my oozing, lavish rolls of flesh. Then I tell Olivier that I weigh nearly 85 kilos.

You couldn't get a job at Crazy Horse, he nods sagely, with all the certainty of youth. But even if you lost weight you couldn't anyway. You're too old.

I have become one of my own worst nightmares, an aging expatriate with a red nose and a spreading waist who wastes time in bars and sits on a decrepit green bench in the village square, gossiping with whoever else happens to be there. All that I can say in my favour is that I left England because I hated it and that I live in the Midi because the consumptive English, who came here to fill the graveyards, many degenerate white Russians, also all dead, and even more Americans, sliding down the bottle, can testify, each and every one, that this is the closest to Paradise most of us will ever get. Mind you, I don't live on the Riviera. That's now full of hamburger bars, tacky film stars, the Aga Khan's yachts, drug freaks and the massed tramps, fluent at begging in several languages. No, I live in a little bit of France that has a bloody history of Catholic slaughter and a perpetual present of sunshine and vineyards: Cathar country.

There are 26 of us in my village. I'm the only foreigner. Everybody else owns their own land or works in the vineyards, or both. I have a job in the city, a much-envied, much-discussed job, which pays well. I am the English-language schools broadcaster for the entire region. I do three one-hour schools broadcasts every week in term and five specialised professional lessons, 18 minutes each, which go out at 11pm every night during the vacations. I research these carefully and we've taped them all beforehand. If you want to get the best out of these courses you have to buy the booklets I've produced. We make a packet out of the booklets.

The live broadcasts are alarmingly stressful. A good deal can go wrong and often does. I'm told by the teachers who either record them or use them directly in their classes that the live broadcasts make for electrifying listening. The most dreadful being one of our outside events, when I had the bright idea of interviewing English holidaymakers on the beach at Carnon. They had all come down from Luton in a coach and appeared to be taking time off before destroying a dozen bars in the evening. The first sunbathing cadaver looked very promising, huge pink hairy stomach, grimy white handkerchief knotted at the corners, protecting six blond hairs and a mass of red freckles.

Excuse me, sir, we are from Radio Cathar. Are you enjoying your holiday?

Fuck off, mate! he roared amiably, and I found myself rowing backwards into a sea of umbrellas.

Well, that's what I do for living. Needless to say, I have never worked in Paris.

Next morning we were all gathered round the *boulanger*'s van, gossiping. Nobody was prepared to admit the fact, but we are all waiting for the Parisians. Here they come, in tracksuits, ready to go jogging. In this heat? Goodness, she is very pretty, long black hair, tied back, and a light green sweat shirt, which glows against her olive skin. They are both still wearing their dark glasses, the sort that curve around your eyes, like ski-goggles. They are as elegant as successful gangsters.

Bonjour.

Bonjour.

Bonjour.

Quatre francs soixante.

Merci, madame.

She speaks.

He says nothing. They smile, but ever so slightly.

They jog away. She wields her baguette like a sten gun. She has a quite beautiful figure. We are all very impressed.

Well?

Pas grand chose.

We have failed to gather any concrete information. Let's go back and look at the Mercedes.

A black Mercedes now bears mythic meanings. We peer in, leaving breath marks on the darkened windows. We want to see the smooth upholstery, the central panel which will glow red at night, the mobile phone in a little leather holster, the carpeted floor, the lack of crisp packets or maps. What we see most clearly are our own faces, reflecting back our grimaces of curiosity.

It's like the one she died in. A year ago.

I was there, breathes Claudia and we all sit up straight, astounded. Yes, I was. A week later. I was in Paris for the day on a coach tour with my grandmother. When I was staying with my cousins in Auxerre and I'd never been to Paris. So we went. And the coach driver took us past the Pont de l'Alma where there were flowers on the grass by the golden flame and we even went through the tunnel. And the coach driver went really slowly and pointed out the pillar where the black Mercedes crashed and she died. Just at the moment when she had found love and true happiness.

You're making it up, snapped Olivier.

No. She did go up to Auxerre. Last September. One week. Don't you remember? Simone intervenes.

Simone is Claudia's aunt. This is a family quarrel. All the quarrels in the village are family quarrels. Apart from myself, we are all related. Claudia flounces off. Her veracity has been challenged. Olivier is not convinced.

I don't believe she ever went to Paris.

But now we are contemplating the events of a year ago and all the intimate geographies of Paris. Would they have crossed the river? Wouldn't have to if they were coming from the Ritz. Where is the Ritz? Isn't it in the place de la Concorde? No, that's the Hôtel Crillon. It's in the place des Vosges. Has anyone got a map of Paris?

We spy into the interior of the Mercedes. The glove compartment is clearly shut, probably locked. The red eye of their alarm winks back at us. The Parisians have no visible map of their city.

Next day I do the schools broadcast dictation. This is the last one before *les grandes vacances*.

There are holidaymakers visiting our village.
They have rented a house with a swimming pool.
They drive a big, black Mercedes.
They come from Paris.
They keep fit, cycling, swimming, jogging.
They don't like sunbathing and they eat very late at night.
They continue to behave as if they were in Paris.

The green bench in the square sags under the weight of our communal speculation. We hear, but cannot see them using the pool. There are no jolly shouts or sounds of sexy teasing. No giggles, denials, threats, such as usually rise up from holiday swimming pools. We hear an almost simultaneous crash as they hit the water, twice a day, with uncanny regularity, very early in the morning and just after six o'clock, when the sun begins to move down the mountain. Every morning and every evening they traverse the chlorinated blue water with steady strokes for half an hour before re-emerging in black tracksuits to vanish up the valley at a steady trot.

It is as if they are in training, not on holiday.

It must be very expensive to train at a gym in Paris. Maybe that's why they come here.

I went to Paris once, says Simone, just before Christmas. With my sister. The one who lives at Auxerre. We went Christmas shopping at the Samaritaine. And they were selling mistletoe for 13 francs a bunch, outside in the street.

All eyes swivel down the green bench towards her. Mistletoe is easy to procure from the cousin's orchard in Auxerre. We could go in my car. It may be decrepit, but it'll hold all five of us. We could spend a day doing up little bunches with red ribbons. We could sell them all at ten francs a shot, undercut the competition and spend the rest in Paris. We begin to plan our weekend in the glittering winter city, financed by poison kisses of mistletoe and red ribbons.

The Parisians hire two light-weight racing bikes in the first week of August and re-invent themselves as a Lycra-clad speed team. He has one of those watches that measure your heart rate and beep if you slow down. We watch them racing along the edges of the precipice. They continue to say *bonjour* once a day, when they collect their bread. No one has ever heard them say anything else. They have not been seen in St Chinian. Do they ever shop in St Pons? We ask casually in the Ecomarché whether anyone has ever seen the black Mercedes with the Paris registration. No one ever has.

I ring up Emile Barthez to borrow an electric pump and in the course of idle conversation enquire about the Parisians that are sleeping in his bed and churning up the chemicals in his swimming pool.

Oh, he says, surprised, what are they like? I don't even know their names. They came through the Holiday Houses agency in Paris.

You know, Simone remarks, there's something very odd about that couple from Paris. They never use the barbecue and they never eat outside.

We all agree. Yes. Odd. No barbecue. Sinister.

As the schools broadcasts are finished until *la rentrée* I am occupied with a new series of *Professional English for Professionals*. We have had a request from the head office of the Gendarmerie in Montpellier. Will we do a mini-series on English for the police? To run during *les vacances*? Of course, says my producer. Delighted. I cannot see why the French police need English. But my producer is adamant.

It is the only language offered by some international criminals, she insists. Here's our chance to provide a real public service. Not just Computer English, Hotel English, Café English, Tourist Office English, How to Book Your Flight English, Arriving in London English, Doing an Arms Deal in English, Eating Out English, Hire Car English.

OK, OK, I get your point.

I begin to imagine interrogations in translation. Techniques of subtle menace. It all comes out in Film English. Sign this confession, you slimy little bastard, or I'll spatter your intestines all over the table. Which no one ever actually says. What are the most common French crimes? Burglary, theft and doing drugs. Drugs English defeats me. It has never been researched, fashions change daily and there are no available booklets. I go for Car Theft English. Now this has actually happened to me in France and I know all the linguistic moves.

My black Mercedes has been stolen.

Are you quite certain that it has been stolen?

Please write down the immatriculation number.

Was it equipped with an alarm?

Did you leave the vehicle unlocked?

No, there is a central locking system.

Did it have an Identicar Security number?

Are you on holiday in the area?

Yes, we have rented a house in the mountains.

We are on holiday.

We live in Paris.

Their holidays are endless. By the second week in August we decide that they are in fact Olympic athletes, in early training for the millennium games. Nothing else explains their relentless, energetic pursuit of cycling, swimming, jogging, gymnastic aerobics and early nights. They go on saying *bonjour* once a day and nothing else. They never take off their dark glasses. They have perfect figures. They are ravishingly beautiful. We have never seen their eyes.

The weather suddenly changes gear, just before *l'ouverture de la chasse*. A white cowl of heat descends like a mask over the village. I go into work twice a week, cursing, and make scenes at my producer and the technicians. Otherwise I lie in darkened rooms, with the windows shut, breathing heavily. We meet on the green bench after eleven o'clock at night to exchange clichés about the *canicule*: worse than last year, quite unbearable, global warming, stream drying up, dogs can't bear it, when will it end? The Parisians set off for their daily run at dawn, before the white cowl drapes the mountains. The thermometer races past 38°C. We water our vegetables twice a day and welcome the Pompiers-Forestiers, who turn up in their yellow emergency trucks, gasping for cold water. They are fire-watching from the hilltops. They have nothing to report.

La chasse est ouverte! Open season. The men dress up in their paramilitary fatigues, topped off by their red caps, and set out for the garrigue in their white vans, the dogs howling for joy in the back. Madame Rubio tells me that she loathes the hunt. Her favourite dog was gored by a wounded boar and cost 750 francs in veterinary repairs. She snorts with irritation as the vans roll past. Yvette is terrified of meeting a wild boar while she is pruning her vines on the red slopes. She hopes that the men will kill them all. I hear the wild boar, snuffling among my blackberries. I lock all the doors.

And I see them, sometimes, at night, ponderous, hairy, unhurried, grey in my headlights, as I cruise slowly across the mountains, coming home.

The men only hunt in the early mornings. By eleven-thirty they are back in the village, sharing the kill, feeding the dogs, sharpening their long curved knives on the whirling stones. The heat is too fierce to go out in the afternoons. The dogs lose the scent and cannot track the boar through the scented bush. In the afternoons they lie flat, bored by flies, their bells clinking on the shaded gravel.

Papi collars me as I languish on the green bench.

It's about time that you came out hunting with me. You should see what it's all about.

Papi is 83. He has been threatening to take me out with him on one of these wildlife dawn raids for the past seven years. Suddenly, he insists. I understand why. Papi fears that his hunting days will soon be over. And alas, he wants to prove something. He has spent one month this year in the clinic down in Perpignan, dealing with his bronchitis. He's right. I should go. I agree. We stagger back to his house and Papi pours a deadly glass of 'eau de vie', 75 per cent pure alcohol. Men sell not such in any shop. Chin, chin, Papi. This is it. We smile at each other beneath the gloom of a 40 watt bulb, all that he will consent to install over his dining room table, and he takes his gun down from the wall above the fireplace.

We decide to move at dawn on Wednesday next.

But on Tuesday night the police stop me at the motorway exit. Béziers West. They are waving on the other cars. They are looking for someone. My God, they are looking for me. I've been caught in a radar trap. I sit panic-stricken and surrounded. Am I drunk? No, not yet. My tax disc and insurance are in order, but both back tyres are practically bald. And I should have put the thing through the government test over two months ago. I thought I wouldn't go until I had changed the tyres. If they throw the book at me this could mean nearly 5,000 francs' worth of fine. Far more than the tyres and the test put together would ever cost. Shit, shit, shit, shit, fuck, fuck, fuck, fuck, bugger, bugger, bugger, bugger.

Vos papiers, Monsieur. Pause. *Excusez-moi. Madame.*

Madame? Who cares. Go on. Fine me.

Où habitez-vous?

You've got the address in front of you, mate. Right there, on my *carte grise*.

He stands there, looking at my papers, *carte de séjour*, passport, credit cards, insurance documents.

C'est vous qui faites les émissions en anglais pour Radio Cathar?

Yes, yes, that's me. Fame at last! Do you listen regularly? To the police broadcasts? Really? And do you find them helpful? Ah yes, that's me. An essential public service. Delighted to be of assistance. *Vive l'Entente Cordiale*. Now let me off, Monsieur le Gendarme. I'll change my tyres at once, if not sooner. Only please, please, please, let me go.

Oh dear God, he wants to chat. And to practise his English.

We very much enjoy your broadcasts. Very interesting. And do you use your own experiences?

Always. All the time. Drawn from life. Every single sentence. Am I being let off this time? Just this once?

Do you often talk about people in your village?

Yes, of course. Not directly. But I like authenticity. All the details about the tramp who burgled Simone's bungalow and ate a tin of peas are just as they happened. It's more useful. More convincing. May I go?

And that story about the stolen black Mercedes?

Ah yes, good, wasn't it? The Parisians who are on holiday in our village have a black Mercedes. But, of course, it isn't stolen. I beg you. Let me go.

He waves me on.

By the time I get home my encounter with the police has become a Bruce Willis–style car chase with crashed barriers, screaming wheels, fast talking and bold lies. Everyone on the green bench is thrilled. We all love a good story.

Papi hauls me out of bed at dawn and I stumble after him and his straining dogs. It is beautiful out in the valley, waiting among the vines in the still blue light. We are not far from the village. I can just see the tiled roofs. The ground is hard and dry. We stumble over the rough white stones in the vineyards. I watch the day hardening, gaining ground. We can hear the bells on the dogs' collars, far away. Papi has an elderly pair of binoculars. Through the smeared lens I can see the red caps of our neighbours; they are perched on the edge of the steep road leading up to Vilanove. We wave from time to time. The breaking day is peaceful and quiet. Suddenly we hear the sound of the dogs, a deep howl, in chorus, lengthening. They have caught the scent. We strain forwards. Yes, I can hear it, far below in the river bottoms, something heavy, rising through the bush towards us. Papi scampers down the vine rows, heading for the road, wielding his gun, nimble and expectant. I watch the freckled hands, tightening on the buckles of his sack. You are not allowed to stand around with a loaded gun. If you are going to fire you must charge it up just beforehand. Papi is loading his gun. I stand well back, completely panicked, covering my ears. Oh no! The crashing, howling bush is coming upwards, closer and closer. We are on the road. Papi has levelled the gun, snug against his shoulder. His hands are steady and firm. He knows that the boar will cross the road.

The events of the next few moments pass so suddenly before me that I can make no sense of them. There is Papi, standing on the road, ready to shoot. I hear more than one car coming down the curving precipices behind me. And round the corner, surging upwards, heads down, thighs braced, moving at speed, come the Parisians, hurtling straight towards us on their racing bikes, their dark glasses clamped to their faces like black diving goggles, their mouths open. They see Papi pointing his gun directly at them. Shrieking with fear and fury they skid past us. I cannot understand a word they say, for as they clip me with their elbows the boar breaks cover with the dogs at his heels and flings himself across the road. Papi fires twice and we are both covered in a great fountain of warm blood as the boar falters, staggers, buckles, falls. We hear the Parisians screaming. They have almost turned the corner behind us.

I am overcome with horror. I have never been afraid of the wild boar roaming the hills. Now I see that I should have been. The thing is enormous, with giant yellow tusks. I will never go walking in the mountains, ever again. Papi is looking at the boar and at the blood pumping on to the road. He must have shot the monster through the heart. The dogs are swirling around him, slavering, yelping, sniffing at the blood.

Then the police are upon us, all around us, snatching Papi's rifle and raving. A pair of eyes in a face masked by a cagoule are glaring into my face and the muffled mouth is uttering a sequence of unintelligible yells.

I turn around.

There are police everywhere, dressed in dark blue with hoods across their faces, as if they were storming a hijacked plane. I find myself wondering if Papi and I are, in fact, on television. Then I see that there are bodies on the road behind us, all mixed up with racing bikes. And I am screaming,

Vous avez tué les Parisiens!

Shut up, snaps one of the hooded assassins.

Go home, Grandad, he roars at Papi. The old man retaliates and snatches back his rifle.

I'm not leaving that boar on the road. I've just shot it. I'm going home to get my van. My friend here will make sure that you don't touch it while I'm gone.

He stomps off, livid, his dogs trailing behind him. He ignores everything except the dead boar. I catch sight of my neighbours hurrying down the road from Vilanove, towards their vans. The situation is oddly inconclusive. I am not at all sure what has happened. I stare at the bodies, puzzled.

Why did you shoot the Parisians?

Listen to me, snaps the gendarme, and I realise that it is the same man who stopped me on the motorway, if you've got any sense you'll shut up and stop asking questions. We still have to check their real identities. But whoever they were, you're lucky that they didn't shoot you. And they certainly didn't come from Paris.

He shifts one of the bicycles with his foot. I see the woman's profile, revealed as if for the first time. Her face is unmarked, elegant, her sunburn even and attractive, a gentle spattering of freckles across her nose. The calm, dead face reproaches me with the vanishing charisma of distant cities.

Are you sure they didn't come from Paris? They told us that they did.

Une étrange aventure de Richard Blaine

Kim Newman

'Go, my darling, and God bless you, Ilsa.' It's like a hammer to the back of the head.

In an instant, everything good is gone.

The world is hell.

Ink running in the rain. A wet letter in my hands. Water pouring off the brim of my fedora. An insistent tug at the sleeve of my trench-coat. Clouds of steam. A train, about to leave.

'That's the last call, Mr Richard,' Sam says. 'Do you hear me? Come on, Mr Richard. Let's get out o' here.'

It's hard, but I can do it. My guts are lying on the rain-soaked platform, but I can walk without tripping in them. Sure, I can. It's easy.

Forget Ilsa.

Get out of Paris.

Now.

'En voiture,' the man shouts.

This is the last train out. The one we were supposed to take together. To freedom and safety.

Damn her. Damn her rotten silky hide. Damn.

'Come on, Mr Richard. Come on.'

Yeah. Let's go. Fade.

Clicking heels. A bark of gunfire. Men in grey uniform advance down the platform, pushing through panicky would-be passengers. The train lurches, wheels screaming. Sam is up in the carriage door, humping our cases.

I step up, resolved.

I can live without her. I can go on. Dead inside maybe, but moving.

A hand closes on my shoulder.

'Mr Richard Blaine?'

It's a harsh voice, rasping. German.

The train shifts, moving off. I see more than panic in Sam's eyes as he slides away.

This just puts the cherry on top of the day. The Germans are in Paris. And so am I.

'I'm an American citizen,' I tell the Nazi. 'Neutrality is my religion.'

'That was not how you conducted yourself in Spain or Ethiopia, my friend.'

I shrug, stomach plunging. My dossier is evidently extensive and annotated.

'SS Standartenführer Professor Doktor Franz Six,' says the officer. I believe him.

Six is a small man, almost totally bald but still young, blue eyes cold behind steel-rimmed spectacles, uniformed in black with silver lightning-flash highlights. His trenchcoat is the colour of midnight. His cap-peak is like the razor-bill of a predatory bird.

Field-grey goons close around me. The train has gone.

It doesn't really matter. The way I feel, summary execution would be a blessing.

Damn Ilsa.

'Your assistance is required by the Third Reich,' says Six.

'The Third Reich seems to be doing quite well on its own.'

The station is being occupied. German soldiers search through the unlucky crowds, looking for faces they've memorised, matching identity papers against names on a list. French railwaymen are standing down, their duties assumed by military policemen. All further trains are cancelled.

Someone makes a break for it. There are shots.

'Indeed, this is an encouraging day for the Reich, Mr Blaine. However, I'm charged with an especial mission for the Führer, one with which you can be of great help.'

'With which? Fine grammar.'

Six smiles, showing sharp little teeth. It would be a mistake to think him soft or stupid.

The station is emptying of civilians. Rain washes down over deserted platforms. Abandoned suitcases are soaked. Someone has left behind a double bass.

Filtering out the excess people reveals who it was that spotted me for Six. A wiry youth, with an impertinent forelock that stands up stiff as a wood-shaving. He has piggy little eyes and baggy plus-fours. With him is an annoying little white dog.

I recognise him vaguely, from around the cafés and cabarets. Though just a kid, he's some sort of a reporter. Though French, he's a fascist. Six nods, and he scurries over, dog at his heels.

'Our young friend has been of some help,' Six tells me, 'but he doesn't have the sensitivities for the job. Unlike you.'

The kid's eyes glitter. I don't have a friend here. He must have wanted to be Nazi Puppet Number One, and now he's just one of the gang.

We're all standing in the rain, which doesn't seem to bother Six. It's as if he has an invisible shield around him, a bubble of warmth and confidence. Hitler gives these monkeys something special.

'My friend, I'm responsible for the apprehension of certain individuals. Well, not so much individuals as types. Until they are in our hands, we cannot truly say we have taken Paris.'

'I should think that about now, you could say what you want and nobody will holler.'

Six giggles. It's like needles scraping your skull.

'You are on my list, Mr Blaine. Paris is important to you, and you to her.'

Her. Yes, the city is a woman. Ten minutes ago, she was a sweetheart. Now I know she's a whore.

The damned letter is a wet lump under my shoe.

'You're too late for that. I don't care about Paris. I don't care about anyone.'

'You only think that, Mr Blaine. Paris is a part of you. In your sentimental fugues, you might think it the better part of you, but it is your weakness. It is why you are, as it were, surrounded.'

'This is a waste of time,' the kid hisses, in French.

'I think not,' says Six. 'I think we have an understanding.'

Whatever. I'm not doing anything else. Any principles I had are washed away by the rain. Without Ilsa, I might just as well be a Nazi. I'll make a good one. I'll have just the right attitude.

I nod.

'Excellent,' the Nazi smiles. 'We three shall round them up, all the types on our list, all the creatures of the city. When we have them, we shall have taken Paris body and soul.'

The kid's dog barks. I kick it in the head.

Just like a Nazi.

The first individual on Six's little list isn't even a human being. That doesn't matter. Rick Blaine, dog-kicker extraordinaire, isn't afraid of anything that crawls or climbs, swims or slouches.

The ape is half-way up a building, waving a straight razor and jabbering in what sounds like Hungarian. Its gums are a scarlet wound. Its long limbs and round body are covered with a thick, bristly black pelt.

'Have Göring get into a biplane and shoot King Kong off his perch,' I suggest.

Six giggles again.

They want the ape alive. It figures.

I shrug, and walk into the empty street. An armoured car is parked at the kerb. The ape throws chunks of masonry at it. It could pitch for the Dodgers, hits the swastika on the hood every time.

I've got an automatic in my pocket. I could do better with a banana.

'Hey, Ingagi,' I yell, getting the monkey's attention.

Strictly, it's an orang-utan. It waves its razor.

I catch the ape's eye. It's not stupid. It doesn't recognise me, but it knows me, senses that we have something deep in common. We're both foreigners in this city, but we both have a connection with it that runs deep.

'Come down,' I shout, feeling dumb.

The ape tenses, and I think it's about to launch itself into space and crash down on me in a tumble of scrabbling hands and slicing blade. My strength is that I don't care. My guts have already been torn out, and they might as well be strewn in the gutter of the Rue Morgue as anywhere else.

Meekly, the orang-utan climbs down to the street. He folds his razor closed with a neat click and gives it up to me. Six's stormtroopers rush in with a net and wrap the ape up into a chattering ball.

Six and the kid reporter watch me. The Nazi applauds, slowly. I am being mocked but I don't care.

The ape is miserable, betrayed, chewing at the wires of the net, struggling with the six goons who are loading him into the armoured car. I don't care. Something tiny and hot and nasty is growing where my heart used to be.

If this is what the world (Ilsa) wants me to be, then fine. I'll be the best damn Nazi in Paris, Sieg heil and über alles.

'You've done well, my friend,' purrs the doctor.

Give me a medal, buddy.

Our expedition under Paris is a major adventure. In a motor-launch requisitioned from the river police, we whizz through the sewers, bowed low so as not to scrape our hats off on the tunnel roofs, leaving waves of disturbed shit in our wake. None of the maps the Germans have dug up are of much help: the city sits atop an uncharted labyrinth of interconnecting tunnels, sewers, caverns, catacombs, hide-outs and lost worlds that date back to the Romans and beyond. Down here, we're relying on my mysterious and new-found instincts.

I have talents I didn't know about. I've always lived half-in and half-out of the world. Dr Six has chosen me well. I can home in on the individuals on his list because I have a kinship with them but am estranged from them. I can thank Ilsa for that, at least.

I wonder if she's on the list too. Six has never let me see it, if indeed it is written down and not just in his head. She'd fit in with some of the others. We have rounded up a good many women: a barefoot gypsy dancer reputed to be a sorceress, with a goat for a familiar; an Irish singer with a blank face and a bell-pure voice, along with her terrified and terrifying Hebrew manager; a consumptive artists' model, spitting blood into her handkerchief; a beautiful commissar, seduced by silk undies. Sweethearts and whores, gamines and adventuresses, royal mistresses and gutter-waifs. All on the list, all in custody.

We chug through the tunnels, casting cones of light ahead and aft. Six, the reporter, the white dog, and a platoon of standard-issue stormtroopers. The soldiers don't like being down under the streets, in the dark, in the shit. They mutter together, heedless of their boss's enthusiasm for the chase.

Six tried to persuade the pipe-puffing policeman who surrendered so meekly to join us on this trip under the city. The inspector regretfully declined, saying that though he was forced to recognise the authority of the new masters of the city he could not lend himself to such an enterprise.

Damn the flic. He was elaborately almost sorry for me, and I didn't need his pity. No wonder the city had fallen. Everyone was so weak, so frail. Most of the creatures we were hunting were crippled by their desperate, illusionary loves. Paris is the city of the Insanely Romantic.

I sense a presence.

'There,' I say, pointing ahead.

Searchlights are directed. There is a man in the water, swimming.

'It's the ex-convict,' says the reporter. 'The fugitive thief.'

Six giggles.

Our boat gains on the man. Waves of sewage drag at him. He flails. Is he trying to drown himself rather than be recaptured? He's been on the run most of his life, in and out of the Château d'Yf and Ile du Diable.

He is hauled out of the water in a sorry state. He lies in the boat, breathing heavily, stinking.

We emerge into a cavernous space, an underground lake in a cathedral-arched chamber. The searchlights play upon a vaulted roof hundreds of feet above us. Six whistles in awe.

The lake is big enough to harbour an island. It is a long shape, like a sea-monster lying on the surface. We pass by, and I see it's not a true island but a man-made thing. Rows of rivets stand out on its metal hide. A serrated, horn-like protrusion juts out between eye-like green windows. It is abandoned, I sense. Left here to distract us. I wave us on.

'Keep going,' I say. 'It's just a lost toy.'

Music sounds out. Thin, reedy organ-tones.

I know this is one of the prizes of Paris, one of the types at the head of the list. Six smiles at me. The Opera Ghost is nearby, driven out of the extensive cellars of the Paris Opéra into the larger catacombs. I know something of this creature's story. His tragedy is an impossible love, too.

The boat crosses the lake, our lights playing on the far shore.

'Be careful,' I say. 'This guy is known for devilish trickiness. There'll be traps.'

One of Six's troopers, having conquered the world, begins to sneer and his head is sheered in two just below his eyes. Some sort of flying guillotine. The Nazi crumples and splashes into the water, leaving behind the top of his head, still in its helmet, rolling in the flat bottom of the boat.

I kill the searchlight. We all crouch in the dark.

The music swells in mocking triumph.

It occurs to me that the ex-convict has led us into a trap. It was only a matter of time before the names on our list caught on to what we were doing and began co-operating. How many others are out there?

We collide with the shore and pile out of the boat. A jagged ripping and a scream. Some new, clever device. There is a gleam of gloom up ahead, through a tunnel. I blink and get some sort of night vision. The organ chords pour at us. The musician has lost the tune, and is improvising in a frenzy.

I tap Six on the epaulette and nod ahead.

We are to proceed, with caution.

The journalist steps into the tunnel first, and is yanked off his feet. I hear him gurgling as he dangles. A noose is cinched around his throat.

His white dog leaps up around his kicking heels, yapping.

My arm up to protect me, I run into the tunnel. Six and his men are behind me.

I know there are enemies up ahead.

Not just the Opera Ghost, but the masked Master Thief, the Poet Swordsman, the Vengeful Count, the Pianist With the Knife-Thrower's Hands, the Tramp From the River, the Children of Paradise, the Queen's Musketeers. A full swoop of Six's types. With them apprehended, there would only be a few very small fish – boulevardiers and ex-patriots – to gather.

'Friends, friends,' I shout. 'I have led them to you. I'm one of you, not one of them. Vive la France! Liberté, égalité, frat–'

A cold hand closes on my mouth and yanks me from the tunnel. A nose pokes at my face. Cold steel lays across my Adam's apple.

The duellist wears a huge hat and a froth of lace around his throat. But it is impossible to look away from his prodigious nose, which sprouts out from his face like a swollen bulb. If I look at his eyes, the tip of his nose goes out of focus and seems even bigger.

'What are you staring at, American?' he asks.

I try to shrug, but am held firm.

'You have such lovely eyes,' I say.

He laughs, lustily.

'Take me to your leader,' I say.

'We've no leader,' he replies. 'We're too rowdy a lot for leaders.'

I understand.

'Take me to him, to the master of the machine in the lake.'

A smile curls in the shadow of the nose.

'He is dead. The spectre plays for his funeral.'

I am pulled through a secret door. Candelabra light up the space all around. I see the thin black back of the man at the organ. Bone-white hands play over the keys. He turns and I see his skull-face, enormous eyes active in a white mask of death.

Others are here.

A thief in immaculate evening dress, face half-masked. His companion, a sylph-like woman in a black body-stocking that shows only her eyes. A hollow-eyed aesthetic adventurer, delighted at last to have sunk as low as it is possible in Paris. A young girl, trained from infancy to be a courtesan. A lazy-eyed apache loafer, cigarette dangling from his snarl, a tight-skirted floozy at the end of his leash. The captain of the good ship Atalante and his child wife. A young man with the look of a philosopher who has discovered futility or has been nauseated by the wallpaper of the world. And the older ones, older even than my big-nosed friend. A couple of Englishmen, one dashing in disguises, the other ready to go to the tumbril for a friend. A woman cackling bloodily over her knitting. The swordsmen and the gallants, the ones whose legends have grown with the city. Shambling in the shadows is a form more twisted than the ape of the Rue Morgue, hiding behind pillars, face hidden in shame.

'We are Paris,' says my captor.

He is right. These people are the heart of the city. When you think about Paris, you have to think about one or two or all of them. You might not find them there when you arrive, but they are why you go there.

I'm one of them.

Yet not.

I can forget Paris. I want to, in fact. Ilsa saw to that.

When all these people are gathered up in the pens under the Théâtre du Grand-Guignol where Six has been assembling them, and are shipped out in cattle-trucks to some death camp of the spirit the Nazis have built in the East, then I'll be free of Paris. The city will mean nothing to me.

I'm not sorry.

'You are all under arrest,' I say.

My automatic is under the gallant's nose. A gun trumps a sword.

'Don't anybody move.'

The organ wheezes to silence.

'Six,' I shout. 'Through here!'

Eyes fix on me with hate. They expected me to side with them, I see. They misread my story. Or came in at the wrong reel.

'I stick my neck out for no one,' I explain.

The deformed boy pokes his head out of the shadows. His misaligned eyes look up at me, full of tears. If I had a heart left, his ugly lost face would reach it.

But...

Six and his surviving goons arrive.

'I believe we have a full house,' he says.

'I thought you'd want to be here my friend,' Six says. 'To see the job through.'

It is an overcast day. Three trucks are parked outside the Théâtre du Grand-Guignol. Soldiers stand around, waiting. Orders are posted everywhere. Passers-by don't want to know what is going on here.

The prisoners, shackled together, are herded into the trucks. Some are unused to showing their faces by day. The Opera Ghost, in drab prison pyjamas rather than evening clothes, is less fearsome in thin daylight; not a demon lover, just a hairless, noseless old man. Without his domino mask, the Master Thief is a dull bourgeois in handcuffs.

'Where will you execute them?' I ask, empty inside.

'We would not waste so valuable a resource, Mr Blaine. We shall keep our catch safe. Away from the city perhaps, but carefully unharmed.'

I wonder if they can live away from the city.

'Only now do we really have Paris, you understand. With these people in custody, we control this city's soul. All great cities have a collective soul, an über-mythic collective heart. The Führer understands this. What is London without the Demon Barber and the Consulting Detective and the Mayor's Cat? Or Prague without the Golem, the Alchemist, the student who sells his soul? These are our real enemies in Europe, Mr Blaine. Not armies and politicians and populations. These can be overcome, crushed, destroyed, absorbed. It is these individuals, who in some sense are not even real people, these creatures who stand against our Nazi dream. We understand and believe in über-myths too. But there is room for only one vast myth now, a German myth that has no time for the squabbling, petty, monstrous, feeble-hearts we see before us. With these people gone, our myth can truly occupy the city. Who knows, maybe some of them can come back. The reporter understood, was willing to let himself vanish into the larger story.'

'Like me,' I say, hollowly.

'No, Mr Blaine. Not you. You have helped us not out of conviction but out of spite. All very well. We understand spite too. You may go, because it is not important that you be here. You are a part of some other city's myth-pool. It is important that you have a memory of Paris, but be estranged from the city itself. That is why you were so perfect for our purposes.'

The reporter's dog is still hanging around, sullen and angry. Its white coat is muddied, almost the colour of a German uniform.

It's hard for the soldiers to get the weeping hunchback into the truck, which holds up the rest of the coffle. Chains clank. The orang-utan is already inside, drugged for travel. Last in the truck is the policeman, grumpy because he is not allowed his pipe.

I can walk away safely now. Join Sam, and get on with my life. My myth, as Six would have it.

One last prisoner is too delicate to be chained with the others. She is brought out on a stretcher, thin shoulders shivering, cold white hands crossed on her breast. She won't last the journey.

Six shrugs sadly.

'We Germans love her, too,' he says. 'This girl and her type and her city. But we have iron in our soul. New-forged. We have the strength to strip the city of her.'

One of the soldiers loses his grip, and the feet-end of the stretcher hits the pavement. The girl coughs blood, and her huge eyes catch mine.

She looks like Ilsa. Every damn woman in Paris looks like Ilsa, somehow.

I'm neutral. I've done a job, in exchange for freedom. These people mean nothing to me. Less than nothing. Paris is overrated anyway. Nothing but whores and pimps and murderers. All these people have blood on their hands.

The girl is close to death, always has been.

My heart starts beating again.

'Shall we see them off, Mr Blaine?'

I put my hands in my pockets, and bring one of them out again.

'That is an automatic pistol, Mr Blaine.'

'And a very fine one, Six.'

The Nazi is disappointed in me. He makes a tiny signal. I am to be shot.

Then that blasted dog darts in and nips at the heel of Six's jack-boot, sinking sharp teeth into the black leather. The SS man is surprised and looks down.

I plug him in the chest. Twice.

'Doktor Six has been shot,' I shout out, to the soldiers. 'I'll guard the prisoners. Search the theatre. I saw a man with a gun, up on the roof. A jackal, running.'

Six is on his knees, dying. He doesn't understand why. He never will.

The girl smiles, thinly, blood on her lips.

The soldiers stand around, looking dumb. They were distracted by the dog and didn't see my gun spit death.

'Up on the roof,' I insist, waving my gun. 'Mach schnell!'

It gets through. They clatter into the theatre, shouting.

I take the keys from Six's pocket, and roll his corpse into the gutter. I wonder if he realised how close he came himself to an archetype, the Sardonic Nazi Officer. Of course, he was different from us. He was a real person. You can look him up in the books.

I toss the keys to the Master Thief, who gets everyone off the chain in double-quick time. I had an idea he would have the fastest fingers in the group.

'Quick,' I say, 'into the sewers.'

The ex-convict groans 'not again', but his fellows hurry him along. A manhole cover is wrenched up, and the escapees plunge into the darkness. I watch the last of them – the Jewish singing master with the scraggle of beard and the neon-glowing eyes – disappear, and pick up the girl from the stretcher. She is frozen, but I carry her underground.

Inside, the submersible device is a riot of leather upholstery and polished brass. Its captain may be gone, but it has been maintained in perfect working order. There is even a pipe organ, and the Opera

Ghost plays a Bach fugue on it as we sink below the waters of the underground lagoon.

At the helm, the captain of the Atalante scratches his head and tries to understand the unfamiliar controls. He is the master of Paris's waterways, and will soon learn how to manoeuvre this marvellous contraption.

We are all cramped here, but there is a joy in freedom.

I don't want anyone's thanks. It's due to me that Six got as far as he did with his project. There have been casualties. The model girl died in the sewer, and is stowed somewhere. But she'll always be here, in Paris.

I'll leave now. Hook up with Sam, head for Marseilles, cross the sea. After all this French rain, I'd like to live in a desert for a while, have my own place. Six was right about me. I have a story to finish.

They are arguing, this leaderless crowd. The braggart with the nose and one of the Queen's Swordsmen butt heads over the charts, each certain of the course they should be plotting but neither with any experience of navigation. The captain smokes his pipe and carries on regardless.

The orang-utan is waking up. The apache has stabbed his mistress. The ex-convict is outside, in the filthy waters again. The Opera Ghost has criticised the Irish girl's voice, and enraged the Jewish manager. A whore and a dancer are competing for the affections of the white dog. Cigarette and pipe smoke makes a pestilential cloud in the enclosed space.

There is a din of life here.

Despite Ilsa, despite everything, it's in me. Paris, and all it means. I'll never escape it entirely.

I'll leave these people soon. There's a lazy-eyed thief here who dreams of Algiers and the Casbah; I shall follow his example, and light out for North Africa. They'll break up, return to their hiding-places, play catch 'em with the Gestapo. Their city will be underground for a while, but a secret victory has been gained.

The Germans won't always have Paris. But I will.

Rosebud

Maureen Freely

My first night at the Rosebud, there is this girl in the corner. She has her back to me but I can see her face in the mirror that runs along the walls. She has alabaster skin and short, shiny, honey-coloured hair and the hard, fixed look of a doll, a doll that has just about had it with her glass cabinet. She's wearing a jean suit, every Parisian under thirty has one this year, but there's something about the way she presses her fingers into her crucifix, something about the way she keeps pulling the chain across her chin, that tells you she's not French.

Her companion – he's another strange one, short blond hair, square build, skin of a twenty-five-year-old, but dressed in a middle-aged camel hair blazer, with the posture and manners of a retired general. He does not seem at all perturbed by the lack of conversation. He, too, seems far more interested in the mirrors and from time to time, he sees something in them that makes him chuckle. He chuckles, and then, without fail, he shakes his head and reaches for his cigarettes. Without fail, he offers one to the girl. She accepts with a certain disdain, then waits with eyes closed for him to offer her a flame. It's after they have both inhaled deeply, and exhaled neatly over each other's shoulders, that the man looks straight into the girl's eyes and says, 'Mais écoute, Sisi…'

All he gets in return is a shrug and a pout. At first he seems happy to leave it at that, but after a time, he decides to persevere. 'Mais écoute, Sisi,' lie says now. 'You are overestimating this man's importance. Give yourself a month, and you will hardly remember his name.' Even after the shrug and the pout, he perseveres. 'Mais écoute, Sisi. Why not go back to Madrid? You're sure to meet someone new there.' And so on, but never getting a word in response, until he sits back, and says, 'One thing you have failed to take into account, my dear Sisi, is that your friend is not his own man. He is in the grip of a perversity that has nothing to do with you, as it is of a purely psychological nature.'

And finally, he gets her attention. She sits up and in a gravelly Spanish accent, she says, 'Ah. A perversity. How charming! Sergei, this time you've outdone yourself.'

And Sergei says, 'Perhaps perversity is too strong a word. Perhaps it would be better to think of it as a tragedy.'

To which Sisi says, 'Ah. Now you are truly surpassing yourself.'

Sergei replies, 'Mais écoute, Sisi, this is the only way of understanding him. The tragedy of this man, my dear girl, is that he has never known the privilege of having a whorish wife.'

'Ah!' says Sisi once again.

'You know I'm right,' says Sergei.

'Ah, bon!' says Sisi. 'But this is detection of the highest order.' She sighs, takes a long drag from her cigarette, exhales into the mirror, stubs it out with another sigh, picks up her crucifix, fiddles with it, gazes over Sergei's shoulder as if to catch it glinting in the mirror. Then she sighs and says, 'So I take this to mean that you think I should give him back the egg as if nothing ever happened.'

Sergei sits back in his chair. 'Evidemment, ma petite. At the end of the day, what other path is open to you?' I can still hear the pleasure in his voice. I can still see that knowing smile. It still comes back at the strangest times, when I'm sitting in traffic or killing time in a dentist's waiting room, when I can't get to sleep because I've been working flat out on a case and I'm just too wired. Sometimes, if I'm on the other side of exhaustion, it even happens in court. The faces melt into the wood panelling and turn them into mirrors and I'm back at that table one table from the corner in the Rosebud, looking at him, looking at her, looking at him again, and asking myself, Why is it a tragedy for a man never to know the pleasure of a whorish wife? How would his life have been different if I'd been able to understand what they meant? Why was it important to give eggs to men who devoted their lives to women who were not whorish? Why did Sisi have no other choice? Why didn't I?

Other people from that same night who still come out of the wood-work at me, always in the same order: this dark, severe matron, could be forty, could be ten years older, wearing a man's suit with a gauzy, almost see-through blouse underneath. Hair pulled back, and held with a big velvet bow, pencilled eyebrows, blood-red lipstick, silver earrings, silver bangles, silver rings, two or three to a finger. Chain-smoker — who isn't in this place? She's sitting with these two blank-faced waifs dressed in jeans and skin-tight tee-shirts. One of them stays silent, while the other engages in a passionate argument about Louis Malle. At one point, the woman says, 'Finally, there's nothing unnatural about a woman making love to her son. What harm can it do, if they're made of the same flesh?'

The talkative waif gives a reasoned response to this that I can't quite hear. The woman says, 'But of course it happens in Lyons! Mais quelle bêtise!' She takes herself off to the ladies'. Talkative Boy turns to Mute Boy and says, 'You know, you could try harder, It's not fair to make me do the work.' This makes Mute Boy very angry. 'But really, Armand, this is the last straw,' he begins. Why it is the last straw I will never know. His explanation is drowned out by a roar of laughter, and then the protest, 'But it's true, I swear, it's true!'

The speaker is a portly man with a full head of white curls. His hands are streaked with yellow paint and he is dressed in a pressed business shirt, suspenders and beltless tweed trousers. The story he can't get anyone to believe is from his boyhood in Buenos Aires, when he caused a family crisis by giving his grandmother crabs. His set-piece, which he does several times, complete with scratching motions, and each time to louder and more raucous laughter, is the visit he and his grandmother pay to the family doctor. He plays all parts, always in French first, but then switching to English for the benefit of some of his listeners and then lapsing into Spanish to argue with the two men who are sitting opposite him, whose hands are also streaked with yellow paint, and who are continuing to insist that no one has ever caught crabs by letting her grandson borrow her linen sheets.

To prove that they are wrong, and perhaps to widen his audience, he does his next performance standing up – this to the visible annoyance of the lone rangers at the bar. As he goes through his scratching motions, they crane their necks the way you would if you were watching television and someone was trying to block your view. Finally a tense, tight-lipped woman in black turtleneck and suede trousers takes it upon herself to tell him to sit down. Her name is Marie-Rose, at least that is the name Mr Buenos Aires uses when he tells her not to act like his mother-in-law and invites her to join them. She does not grace him with an answer. Instead she puffs out her lips and lets out an impatient sigh, the same way shopgirls here do if you pick out a dress you ought to know is too small for you.

She looks at her watch, looks over in the direction of the door, looks at her watch again. Then she marches across the small, packed room to join the waifs, who greet her in the absent-minded but vaguely affectionate way you might a colleague. The conversation is at first gentle and inaudible, but then, as she rises abruptly from the table, she raises her voice to say, 'Jean-Baptiste, I'm warning you. *Not* like a dog. It's understood?'

Although she has her back to me, I can see her pinched, disdainful face in the mirror. She catches my eye, and stares straight at me as if to say, 'Who do you think you are?' When she heads in my direction, I think, oh no, what have I let myself in for? But this is what she says: 'Perhaps you can help me. I am trying to construct a set for a play and I need to know what colour you might have expected a gin bottle to be in South Dakota in the mid-fifties.'

'I'm not sure I *can* help you,' I tell her. 'I come from Kansas City, and I wasn't drinking gin yet in the mid-fifties, and I'm afraid my family were teetotallers.' I recite the dictionary definition word for word. I only looked it up yesterday, and here it is, already coming in handy. But Marie-Rose is not impressed. She says 'Oh là là!' and strides smartly back to to the door, where she seems to get the information she needs from these two long-haired bearded guys I know immediately are American because they're still in the clothes they wore to march on Washington. They read too much into her question. They put everything they have into their answers. But she reads their bright eyes and animated gestures perfectly, and so as soon as she has what she needs, she turns her back on them to speak to another man I decide must be Russian because he is dressed in shorts and a Hawaiian shirt even though it's still the middle of winter.

Our boys are devastated. One of them clenches his fists and says, 'Oh, man.' The other says, 'Can you believe it?' They stand there with drooped heads and stooped shoulders, but before long, a sad, elegant swan-necked black woman sidles alongside them, and they begin to look hopeful again, but snowball, hell, they must know that's what their chances are, because this woman is using the mirrors to go after the same guy Marie-Rose and just about every other woman in the Rosebud are after. It's this other American who's leaning on the bar right next to the door.

I can tell he's American because he's wearing work-boots and white chinos and a weatherbeaten suede jacket and has a pony-tail that goes down to his waist. He's talking to the bartender in halting, twangy, but confident French. I can only catch a phrase here and there: 'Our frame-work is too limited.' 'In reality it is not linear, because it bends.' 'If you travelled three light-years…,' The bartender keeps shaking his head and saying, 'But this is the stuff of myths, my friend.' At which the American says, 'Then let me try and put it like this.' He gets so caught up in his argument that he will light up a cigarette and then forget to smoke it. He goes for long stretches forgetting his drink, too, but then when he remembers, he'll down a whole glass at a time. He uses his forefinger a lot. He does not like to be interrupted, and when Marie-Rose taps impatiently on his shoulder, he says the same thing he later says to the morose Sisi, and to the swan-necked black woman, and to the hundred and one other women who follow. 'Honey?' he says in a deep, polite, measured voice that only a fellow Midwesterner would know was crackling with annoyance. 'Honey? I'm sorry. But it's just not a good time. As you can see, I'm talking to my friend Gilles here.' And he turns back to the bartender and says, 'So. Where were we? Yes, I remember. This is the gist of it. When the man returned, he would be eighty years younger than his twin brother.'

This is Earl.

This is Earl, but I don't meet him yet. My first night at the Rosebud, I'm not there alone. I'm with this superstraight guy from the language school, I can't remember his name now. He's doing his junior year abroad out of Cornell, his favourite book is *Beyond Freedom and Dignity*, but he's acquired a few Hemingwayesque affectations during his time here, and he spends most of his time at the Rosebud jotting thoughts into the notebook he takes everywhere. From time to time he reads them out to me. They have headings like 'What if Jung was right?', 'Can a feast be moveable?' or 'What would Clausewitz have had to say to us about Vietnam?' He notices nothing, nothing, about this secret society swirling around us, nothing, that is, except the smoke, which is his other topic of conversation. Every time he gets hit by really big cloud of it, he looks over his shoulders to see who did this to him, but of course he can't, because it could be anybody. So then he says, 'Hasn't anybody bothered to tell them that they're chopping two decades off their lives?' Until finally I tell myself, we're going to have to leave right now, either that or I'm going to chop five decades off his.

So we go back to the Residence. It's only ten minutes away, up this back street on the other side of boulevard Montparnasse. But it seems longer, because it's late, the streets are dark, the only people we see are the ones you change direction to avoid. My room is dark, too. There's only just enough light coming in from the streetlamp outside for me to see my roommate has her hair in rollers. I take off my clothes as quietly as I can. Then I look at my bed and this thought comes to me, that if I get into it now I'll have to lie in it for ever. I don't want this, I'm not ready for this, that's the thought that's in my head as I pick up my jeans off the floor. Minutes later, I'm back outside again, heading up to the boulevard Montparnasse, and there are these two Arabs trailing me. It's after two, all the cafés are dark, the cinemas and the pharmacies and the restaurants obscure behind their iron bars, as I head around the corner into the rue de l'Hambre, the two Arabs have almost caught up with me, they're beginning to talk to me, and now there's another group of men walking towards me. I begin to run, and then both the men behind me and the men in front begin to run, too. I just manage to get to the Rosebud before them. I hurl myself in. I slam the door shut behind me. I make my way through the smoke, the whiskey fumes, the competing reflections, the saxophone solo swirling out of the speakers, and the voices riding over it. I go right up to the bar this time, plant myself right next to Earl.

I can see his face now, his profile that is, and it's not what I expected. He has deepset eyes and high cheekbones that make me think he must have some Indian blood in him, and a wide, thin mouth. He's still talking to Gilles the bartender. He acts like I'm not there. He's drawn this graph on a napkin, and he's poking his pen through it, and trying to explain why, if you were a being that could only see in two dimensions, the pen coming through the napkin would look like a point that widens out to become a blot. Gilles has a hard time grasping this idea, but Earl has unlimited patience. He goes through it again and again, and it must be going on three in the morning when he reaches into his pocket and takes out his billfold and turns to me and says, 'So, how are you doing. Time for just one more?' He buys me a cognac and soda, and then he asks me, 'Which part of Kansas City are you from?' I tell him, and he nods, and says, 'I thought so.' Then he tells me the name of his home town, which I've never been to, but it can't be more than twenty minutes away. I ask him what high school he went to. He tells me and then I tell him which one I went to. Then he says, 'Well, that's enough of that.' He looks at his watch and says, 'So. What do you think? I'd say we should call it a day.'

He takes me back to his hotel, which is a few hundred yards down the street. It's one of those boxes-for-pillows, room-with-sink-and-bidet, you-have-to-share-a-bathroom-with-a-cast-of-thousands places. His room smells like socks. There are clothes all over the floor, paperbacks flung here, there and everywhere. On the bedside table there's a folded *Herald Tribune* sitting underneath two overflowing ashtrays. Both are plastic and bear the name of a crêperie.

On the table next to the window is a manual typewriter. There's a sheet of paper taped to the wall above. On it is one column of adjectives: throbbing, pulsating, glistening, heaving, pleading. And one column of verbs: ram, grab, suck, punish, conquer. On the top of the dresser are two manuscripts, one very thick, the other very thin. The thick one is his novel, he tells me, and the thin one is the fuckbook. As he takes off his clothes, he explains how he works it. He spends a week a month writing porn for this outfit that operates out of Monaco. And that's what buys him the three weeks a month he spends working on the novel.

I ask him what his novel is about. He says, 'Maybe one day I'll know.' I ask him how he manages to write a whole fuckbook in a week, and he says, 'It was hard the first few times. That sheet of paper you see on the wall there, those are the words that I have to mention once a page. I don't really like to talk about it. Take off your clothes, why don't you, and get down on that bed.'

The next day, I wake up to a burning cigarette and rapid typing. The bed is empty. I look across the room to see him at his desk. 'Which one are you working on today?' I ask. 'The fuckbook,' he says. 'What's it about?' I ask. And he says, 'That's for me to know and you to find out. Listen,' he says, without taking his eyes off the page. 'You can stick around for a while. It's fine with me so long as you keep the noise level down.' He goes back to his typing, and I just lie there, watching the clouds pass across that little patch of sky, watching the bursts of sunshine turn him into a shadow, watching his features return with the clouds and the white light. I think of all the times I've walked down this street since I got to Paris, maybe even looking up at this window, maybe even hearing him tapping away at his fuckbook, maybe even passing him in the street, and never once suspecting that one day, when

I was supposed to be sitting in a classroom less than ten minutes away, listening to a lecture about Baudelaire and Mallarmé, I would be lying naked in this bed, watching the real thing.

I think how amazing it is, that we come from almost the same place, but had to go halfway around the globe to meet. I think how amazing it is, how I seem to have known without knowing. Suddenly it is clear to me why I chose French is a major, why I chose Paris for my junior year and not Aix or Montpellier, and why, when I went back to the dormitory last night, I looked at my own bed and knew that I couldn't, wouldn't lie in it. I think how close I came to ignoring my intuition. How if I had refused to listen to that warning, I would have gone to bed as usual, and woken up as usual, and never known that I had thrown my only chance away. I think what a close call it was, how easily I could have not met Earl, how I could have gone through life knowing I had missed meeting my fate, but not even knowing what his name was. I think, how strange, I've always hated the name Earl, but in a strange way it suits him. And in a strange way, I'm glad he's ignoring me, I'm glad I can just lie here watching him type his fuck-book, because it gives me a chance to study his beautiful features without his knowing. But he does know. Because at five he breaks for coffee, and it's when we're sitting in the café that he sets me straight.

He tries to make it as easy as possible. He says, 'Listen, Lydia, I'm about to tell you something that I hope you don't take personally. You're a nice kid. I like spending time with you. I like fucking you, too. But you have to know now that it's never going to be more than that. I never have and never will let a woman take over my life.'

Woman, I think. I'm a woman! He carries on grimly, unaware that he has just paid me the ultimate compliment. 'I know what I want,' he says. 'If I didn't, do you think I'd even be here? Companionship is important to me, Lydia, but it's the ship more than the companion. I'm a creature of habit.

'I don't do mornings,' he continues. 'Not for anyone. I have one coffee and a roll between twelve and one. I break at five, for another coffee, and then I work till nine. I eat all my meals standing up. I haven't had a single sit-down meal since I walked out on my high school sweetheart. I get to the Select about ten. I'm usually at the Rosebud by one. And then, if I'm not fucking a woman by three am, I go over the OK Bar for a hot dog.

'Now I know this must sound pretty strange to you, because it's not like back home. That's why I'm taking the trouble to spell it out. I fuck lots of women, Lydia, and you'll meet them all if you stick around. So if you can't take the heat, get out of the kitchen. This is my life, and you can take it or leave it.' But then, because he can tell he's upset me, he takes me out for a crêpe.

If I hadn't known his rule about sit-down meals, this might have meant nothing to me. But because I know it, all I can think is – this man is bending his rules for me. Over the months that follow, he bends many more. When I turn up at the Rosebud, he always says hello to me. Even if he has other plans, he never tells me not to interrupt his conversation with Gilles, the way he does with the others. If he does have other plans, he makes sure to tell me himself. Then, if he can see he's upset me, he buys me a cognac and soda on condition that I go straight home. Once, when Marie-Rose throws a drink in my face, he comes to my defence and gets Gilles to eighty-six her. Another time, when he's already told me it's my turn, and Alphonsine, that's the beautiful black woman, tries to muscle in on me, he gives her what for. When Sisi the Spanish girl takes to following me down to the toilets, and blocking my way when I'm trying to come back up the stairs, he tells her that through her unacceptable behaviour, she's gone to the bottom of the waiting list, and is going to have to wait another four days now before he can give her what she deserves.

She says nothing. Like the others, she knows it's just a matter of time. The day before I'm due to go back to the States, they each make a point of coming up and saying goodbye. But I can see the smirks inside their smiles, and that night, when Earl is asleep next to me, their smirks come back to me. They come back to me the next morning, as I watch the taxi driver pile my suitcases into the trunk. As we wait for the light to change on the boulevard Montparnasse, I know I can't let them win. As I sit with my suitcases on that café on the rue de l'Hambre, and the hour hand on the clock moves past one without Earl appearing for his coffee, my nerve begins to fail me. But the moment I hear this voice behind me, saying, 'This isn't funny, Lydia, rules are rules,' I know it's just a matter of time before he sees that he has no choice but to let me move in with him.

I tell him that I'm not going to stop him seeing his other women, but he shakes his head and says, 'Things always tail off in the summer, anyway.' The happiest part of the summer is the month the Rosebud closes. By now we are subletting an apartment just around the corner from my old Residence. It has a fully equipped kitchen, and cookbooks in English. The happiest day is the day his crêperie closes, and I make a beef stew, and get him to sit down for it.

But it's not always good to get what you want, because when the crêperie opens again, we're the first customers through the door. It's the same with the Rosebud, and now that we have our own place, now that I've gotten him to sit down for a meal, it tries my patience to spend hour after hour standing next to him at the bar, while he dazzles Gilles with amazing facts from the world of science. All the things that once beguiled me about this place, are the same things that now bore me to tears. These paper dolls with their five and a half sexual innuendos. These stories we've all heard over and over and over. These women who just won't give up, who keep cruising in and out of the place like barracuda, sending special messages to Earl via the mirrors, waiting for me to let my guard down, Why can't this man guard himself? One day I ask him. I ask him if he's ever thought where this life of his is leading. What his goals are, if he ever worries that he is going to spend the rest of his life writing fuckbooks, if he really thinks that anyone who stays out until three o'clock every morning drinking beer with cognac mixers ever finished a novel. He tries to reason with me. 'Listen,' he says. 'This was never part of the bargain.' 'Listen,' he says. 'I'm just not ready for this.' But little by little, I make more headway. We start going home before three some nights. Some nights we don't go out at all.

And now that I seem to have won one battle, maybe success goes to my head. I begin to play with the idea that maybe Earl and I were brought together for a reason. This is a man who is all over the place. He doesn't know what's good for him. He's not a creature of habit, he's a slave to his habits. And unless I stop him and get him to straighten out, these habits are going to kill him. Then there's this novel to think about. It has only progressed eleven pages since we met and I'm beginning to wonder if the fuckwork is damaging his style. I share these thoughts with him. He listens with stooped shoulders and says, 'Maybe you're right.' As September turns into October, he becomes increasingly pensive. I tell myself it's only natural, he just needs some time to think things through.

Then one night I wake up and he's not in bed. I try and tell myself he's just gone out for some fresh air. To clear his head. To think. But deep down I know where he's gone. I know what he's up to. I wait for an hour, I throw on my clothes and go to the Rosebud.

He's not there. I ask Gilles if he's seen him. He says, 'I think you should go home.' But then I see the Alphonsine coming up the stairs from the toilet. I see Marie-Rose in the corner, and I see the two women exchange nods. When Marie-Rose heads down the stairs, I'm behind her. The sign on the toilet says occupied. Inside it there's a woman crying. 'Please,' she says. 'Please.' I hear Earl say, 'For God's sake, Sisi, what is it with you? The answer is no. If you don't put that fucking thing away right now, and I mean *right now*, I'm leaving.'

But it's me who leaves, and I don't hear that voice again for fifteen years.

By now I'm a solid citizen, married, and dividing my time between my family, my law work and my gym. I can go for months without even going near a bar, but one Friday after winning a long shot, I take the boys to this place around the corner from our offices. It's not a business haunt, I should add, it's pretty funky, there's blues in the evenings most nights and a murder or two a year, and when I'm at the bar, getting the drinks, I hear this halting, twangy monologue, punctuated with a terrible cough, about why, to anyone who saw in only two dimensions, a pencil going through a graph would look like a point widening out into an inkblot. I look over my shoulder and it's him, it's Earl.

He's looking a little shopworn, that's putting it kindly. I'm on the verge of walking off without saying anything but then I hear, 'Lydia? Is that really you?' He tells me he's been in Kansas City almost three years now. He came back for his father's funeral, and he's been wrangling with his brother over the will ever since. As soon as he gets it wrapped up, he's heading back to Montparnasse. He can't understand how I can hack it here. In his absence, he tells me, the country has sold its soul. 'How's the fuckbook business going?' I ask him. He looks at me and says, 'Do you think I'd even be here if it was good?'

It's strange when you see an old flame who's fallen on hard times. Who's become his own caricature. Who has lived unwisely and wasted all his talents. Who maybe never had any talents to start with. Who lived unwisely, maybe, to cover that up. You think, what was I thinking? What did I see in him? Why did I lose so many years of my life trying to see into his shadows, asking myself why I wasn't enough for him? What a fool I must have been. Did I make it all up? It does me good, it does me good to drop by that bar from time to time and see how little there is to him. It's always the same conversation, it's like putting on a record, except he doesn't know it's a record, and I don't push it, I'll give myself that much. It's clear some of his brain has gone, and even I have a little heart. He's always just one step away from resolving the legal wrangle with his brother that will allow him to go back to Montparnasse, or about to drop the whole thing and damn his brother to hell and help this great new friend of his take his sailboat to the Mediterranean via the Canaries. I don't believe any of it for a minute, but one day I drop by, and he's gone.

It's almost exactly a year later when I get a call from his brother, who tells me Earl's back in Kansas City and in the hospital and has been asking to see me. The story, as far as his brother has been able to piece it together, is that he was en route to Paris via the Canaries when he got into some sort of trouble in a bar in Barcelona, where he was either drugged or beaten up and abducted. At some point, he lost his memory, the brother tells me, and it hasn't come back. But when I go in to see him, he knows who I am. He stretches out his emaciated arms, makes me sit on the bed with him. I can hardly bring myself to look at him. His skin is so tight and taut you can almost see his skull. His gums are black and he smells like sour beer. He says one thing over and over. 'The next time you see Gilles, make sure and tell him that I saw not one, not two, but three bearded ladies in Lisbon.'

And I promise. Even though I don't mean it. I haven't been back to Montparnasse in twenty years, and I'm not about to go back now. But it's strange how things happen. Less than a week later, the firm has to send someone to Paris to see an important client, and without missing a beat I volunteer. But I'm still not sure I'll have time to visit my old haunts. Honouring an ex-boyfriend's insane last wishes is still at the bottom of my list. I go straight to work the moment I hit the city. We're at it till after midnight, and when I get to the hotel on the rue de Rennes, I'm ready to drop. Then, when I've taken off my clothes, there's the moment when I look at my bed and tell myself that

Earl deserves better. Even though, to tell you the truth, I actually don't believe it.

But never mind. Ten minutes later. I'm getting out of a taxi and walking back into the Rosebud. And I have to laugh. Because nothing has changed. It's as packed as I left it, with the same sort of people playing the same games with the mirrors as they chop two decades off their lives with as many affectations as they can muster. The same saxophone solo is weaving its way though the same tangle of arguments that suggest so much more than they reveal. 'He's a parasite, pure and simple,' says a gelled young man in leather, as I push my way past him to the bar. His woman friend, who is also gelled and also dressed in leather, looks right through me as she purses her lips and says, 'Then perhaps we should rejoice, that he's in the pay of a phallocrat.'

Gilles, too, looks right through me when I address him. He does not recognise me, and I ask myself now if this is because I have changed so much, or because he never liked me. I ask him for a cognac and soda. This gives him pause, but then he measures it out without emotion. 'We have a friend in common,' I say as I pay. 'But I have many friends,' he says with sarcasm. 'The friend is Earl,' I say. And Gilles makes a grimace and says, 'I have many friends, but Earl, that's something else.'

'Have you heard the news?' I ask.

'What a question!' Gilles lets out an ironic laugh. 'Let me tell you what I know. He went away five years ago, just for a month, he said. But then he never came back. Never even sent a card. We know nothing of him since then. I am sorry, but in my opinion, this is not the conduct of a friend. A friend would have sent a card,' Gilles says. 'At the very least.'

'He sent me instead,' I say.

'And now I shall return the compliment,' says Gilles as he heads down the bar. 'If he wants to send me a message, he can put it in writing.'

And so I tell him, it's too late, Earl is dead.

I shout, because he's a way down the bar now, and I have to speak over talking heads, but when they hear what I'm saying they fall silent. The gelled woman puts her hand on my arm. 'What name did you say?' I tell her. She claps her hand over her mouth. The man who is with her turns around and shouts over to a friend at a table. 'It's Earl!

He's dead!' The friend gasps. At the next table, a woman screams. And now, in front of me, is Gilles. looking over my head, hands clasped as if in prayer, sobbing. 'My son! My son! My son, do not think I have forsaken you!'

'Tell me how it happened,' he asks when he has pulled himself together. When I explain, not just to him, but to the crowd of anguished faces that now surrounds us, he breathes in deeply and says, 'I should have known. I should have never doubted him. He was on his way to see us, he was coming back to us, he was struck down by brigands on the way.' Then he looks at me and says, 'But why did he never think to call his friends, his truest friends, who would have helped him?'

'We don't know why,' I say. 'By the time he was returned to his family, he had lost his memory.'

But they had not lost theirs, and they devote the rest of the night to sharing stories about their lost friend. There are moments when I think there must be two Earls, because I cannot connect the things they say about their Earl with the things I know about mine. One woman talks about how Earl had saved her from death by correctly diagnosing a malignant melanoma on her lower spinal cord. Another talks of the way he could take any car of any age and somehow spirit it back to life. 'He was like a guardian angel,' says one man. Another says, 'If it weren't for him, I would still be a drug addict and a thief.'

'He had a mind like an encyclopedia,' says Gilles. 'There was nothing this man didn't know.' 'But he didn't exploit it for personal gain,' says another. 'He employed it for the common good.'

'He gave us his life,' chants a woman over and over. Every time she says it, she looks me straight in the eye, but not accusingly, as she should do. To my shame, she addresses me as a fellow mourner: if she were less upset herself, she would see this is the one thing I am not. But it is not clear to me how sane she is. She has pale, watery eyes, and the limp, spineless look of a rag doll. Whenever Gilles pours her another free cognac, she crosses herself in a way that makes me think I must know her. When dawn comes and we gather up our things, she says, in an accent that is suddenly slightly foreign, 'Gilles, will you let me? This once? Just for old times' sake?'

Gilles says, 'You don't need to give me anything. Especially on such a night.'

'But you know how much it means to me,' she protests.

Gilles thinks about it, and then, with some reluctance, he says, 'All right, just this once.'

'Think of it as an act of atonement,' she says as she reaches into her handbag. She gives him an egg.

The barge

Didier Daeninckx

The canal de l'Ourcq, I realised as soon as I set eyes on it, is my idea of paradise. However far back I go in my library of happy memories, I find images of water, foliage, birdsong. The smell of happiness is the scent of damp earth, leaves tossed in the wake of a barge, the tender flesh of young grass stalks sliding between my teeth. It's the oval reflection of a stone bridge disturbed by the wake from a teal or a mallard. At home, my parents had nothing to say to each other but they couldn't find the words to say it, only shouts and screams. When it got so bad that I could no longer hear the television, I left, slamming the door behind me, and took the shortcut through the little municipal wood to come out right by the pont du Vert-Galant. You only had to go a little way along the dirt track for the insistent murmur of road and rail traffic to fade and gradually yield to chirping, lapping, rustling. Weighed down by my problems, numbed by anger, I walked with my head down, unaware of this new world surrounding me. Then, as I approached the locks, the tranquillity began to get to me, to work its magic on me. I had just sat down on the embankment, a supple young hazel branch in my hand, and I was whipping the grass while waiting for a barge to appear either above or below the lock gates. I would read the names and the ports of registry on the hulls and I would dream of the northern lands represented by two or three colours on the flags beating in the wind. The boats, plunged into the murky depths right up to the waterline, were bringing grain to the mills at Pantin, sand and gravel for the concrete tower blocks on the quai de la Gare or at Aubervilliers, sugar to the sweet factory at Bobigny. Children sometimes ran around on the bulging corrugated-iron covers stretched over the cargo. They would interrupt their games, as the lock gates drew near, to guide father into the channel and assist mother in gathering up the ropes. There would be no laughter, just clipped orders, calculated gestures, but while their craft rose, with the great, swirling movement of water and growling of the locks, I envied them. One day, one of the lock gates got stuck half-way and they had to send for the frogmen of Villeneuve-la-Garenne, who removed the carcass of an old gas stove from the canal bed. The incident brought me into contact with an old roach fisherman. He confided that he was retired from the inland waterways himself, then he explained that the two frogmen were the descendants of an impressive line of deep-sea divers. He told me they lived in a wooden barge that they had towed into a cutting in the river bank opposite the Ile-St-Denis. Their ancestor's equipment, genuine Denayrouze gear dating from 1907, occupied pride of place at the entrance to their refuge. The brass helmet with porthole, the rubber cape, the lead-soled shoes, the oxygen tubes and the bronze buckle complete with double-edged sword with a Bakelite handle were topped by a wooden board on which had been engraved these simple words: 'Take pride in your family. Try to be like them.'

He didn't understand why my reaction to this was a mere shrug of the shoulders.

We saw each other again, less than a week later. He was yelling at a boat that had just sped past. His trousers were soaked, the waves created by the boat's wake having broken on the bank, also causing his lines to get fouled up. With the fisherman's shouts of protest drowned out by the noise of the engine, the sailor maintained his course, his nose in the air. I was sitting on a post marking the start of a path through the parc de la Poudrerie. Idle chit-chat led to the exchange of various confidences and by midday the fisherman knew all there was to know about me. He told me about the bargemen who greeted him as they sailed past, about the cereal ports of Jouarre and the Ferté-Milon, about the blast furnaces of Trith-Saint-Léger, about Denain, riverside inns, friendly lady lockkeepers. I ended up confiding in him that I had never set foot on a barge, not even one of those gaudy Canauxrama affairs that ferry tourists between the bassin de la Villette and the cathedral at Meaux. He got to his feet, leaving his tackle where it was, took me by the hand and forced me to follow him to the locks, determined to organise there and then my baptism as a sailor. The second barge to come past heading for Paris, *La Wazemmes*, was skippered by one of his former captains, Milou, who agreed to let me come on board for the rest of his journey, which would terminate in the heart of Paris. Once past the locks, he let his wife, Marlène, take the tiller while he went down below to check on the progress of the grilled meat in the galley, which was tucked away beneath the cockpit. I followed the barge rail to go and position myself directly above the propeller. I tried to identify the stretches of countryside that drifted slowly past in front of my eyes like a never-ending tracking shot, countryside that I usually saw from the misted-up windows of a suburban train. The heavy trees and the dense summer vegetation transformed the factories, the waste ground and the housing estates, and I had the impression that I was seeing for the first time places such as Freinville station, Bondy bridge and Picasso terminus. We ate beef in a dark sauce with fat oven-cooked chips while passing through the parc de la Villette. Later I joined Marlène in the cabin and she explained a few basic rules of navigation, even letting me take the tiller for a hundred metres or so in the basin where the canal de l'Ourcq and the canal Saint Denis meet. After the Hôtel du Nord, Milou invited me to go down with him into the hold so he could show me the mysterious cargo that *La Wazemmes* was carrying. The portholes admitted a diffuse light over the hundreds of wooden boxes piled up either side of a central gangway. We approached one of the boxes, its side, measuring one metre by two, stencilled with a series of letters and figures. He used a crowbar to raise the lid and I stood on tiptoes to see what treasure might lie within. Incredulous, I opened my eyes wide to be sure of what I was seeing. I turned to Milou.

'I don't understand. It's just books. What's in the other cases?'

'The same. What did you expect? These are collections of rare works that have been sitting in warehouses in the north of France for decades. Once a month I ferry a full load of them to the great library by the Seine, on the quai de la Gare...'

He took out several gilt-edged, bound volumes and laid them flat on the lid. I read a few titles – *La Route des Indes et ses navires* by J Poujade, *Histoire de la marine française* by CG Bourel de La Roncière, *Collection des Lois maritimes* by JM Pardessus – and skimmed through a little volume, whose author was not named, entitled *Rivières et Canaux de Paris et des environs*. Milou leaned over my shoulder.

'I learned plenty about the canal de l'Ourcq in there, even though I'd lived and breathed it for more than thirty years. I knew that the digging was authorised by Napoléon, to supply Paris with water, but I didn't know, for example, that the first workmen were Austrian soldiers made prisoners-of-war at the battle of Wertinger.'

He went back up, summoned by Marlène, but not before asking me to be kind enough to close the case when I'd finished reading. I don't know what possessed me, but I slipped the book under my shirt into my waistband. I climbed back up after him and insisted on disembarking when we drew level with the hôpital Saint-Louis. From the lock I watched *La Wazemmes* move away and disappear into the dark tunnel leading to the Seine, beyond the Bastille.

At home I hid the book right at the bottom of my chest of drawers, under a pile of socks. I read it and reread it that evening after the shouting had died down and a semblance of peace had settled over the house. I ended up seeing the canal as a series of lines of print: I no longer dared to take refuge on its barges for fear of bumping into the fisherman or coming across *La Wazemmes* and being branded a thief. The holidays were almost at an end when I decided to cross Paris as far as the great library. I climbed the windswept flight of steps, entered the first glass tower and deposited the book on the counter at reception before running off at full pelt.

Since then, I return every morning to the canal de l'Ourcq. I stare at the fishermen, I scrutinise the names on the hulls of the barges. In vain.

Before me, the lock gates release their waters, like an open book lets loose its words.

Translated from the French by Nicholas Royle

Story to be translated from English into French and then translated back (without reference to the original)

Toby Litt

The Polaroid was still a pale and sickly yellow-white, even as I hurried down the spiral staircase and out of my apartment building. As I strode towards the Métro station, the image of what I had left behind me was slowly developing. At the moment I stepped off the empty platform and into the crowded carriage, the image was ghostly but unmistakable. By the time I took the Polaroid once more out of my greatcoat pocket, it had darkened into a full existence.

Never before had a relationship of mine, an erotic relationship, reached such unbearable intensity. Never, throughout the entirety of my sexual life, had I found myself running, in horror and outrage, away from my own bedchamber. Horror and outrage at the possibility of the outrageously horrid extent of my own possible pleasure.

I felt as though I had committed a soon-to-be-notorious murder – and that, if I hadn't quite yet, perhaps I still might.

Careless of the people around me in the crowded carriage, I examined the Polaroid.

There Edith lay – as she was still lying, as she couldn't help but still be lying – strapped by the slenderness of her wrists and ankles to the sturdiness of the iron-construction four-poster bed. There was the blindfold, the blindfold that we'd laughingly bought together only an hour or so ago. There was the gag that she herself had decided was the best, the most efficient, the most gagging, in the entire extensive shop. It was Edith, too, who had asked the matter-of-fact assistant which were the most restrictive, most painful, hand- and

45

ankle-cuffs. All I had done, it seemed, was smile, inspect, agree, pay.

A gasp from over my shoulder startled me from my reverie. I turned and saw a beautiful young woman, ice-blonde, sculpted, her mouth open and glistening. She had seen the Polaroid.

'Sir,' she said, lowering her eyes. 'I am very sorry… I couldn't help –'

'What do you think?' I asked.

She looked into my face but completely avoided eye-contact.

'You are making pornography.'

She might, I noticed, have invested the word *pornography* with a far greater disgust than she had. There was fascination in this young woman – and fascination fascinates.

'I'm not busy at the moment,' I said. 'Why don't you allow me to buy you coffee? We can discuss it. Perhaps you might even be able to assist me.'

She looked down and hunched her shoulders, as if about to walk into a very strong and gusting wind.

There was defiance even in her acceptance.

'I choose the place. I leave when I say. You do not follow me when I leave. If I so choose, we never meet again.'

'Agreed,' I said.

We did not speak again until we reached her chosen stop.

As I stood there, beside the young ice-blonde, I closed my eyes and tried to imagine what Edith must be feeling.

Antoine has been gone for a long time now, perhaps an hour, perhaps more. I am getting thirsty. This gag is starting to hurt. I wish he would come back and release me. But perhaps this is part of his game. That's interesting: I didn't know he had a game. When we were in the shop, it was I who had to make all the suggestions. If I had left it up to Antoine, we would have come out of there with a too-lacy basque and some cheap black stockings. Not quite what I had in mind. O, he is such a bashful young man. I practically had to beg him to hit me the first time. Since when does a woman have to beg a man to give her pain? Since when was a man reluctant to force a woman's legs apart, to bind her hand and foot, to gag her, silence her, not to have to endure her incessant female language? Antoine was almost as disappointing as my husband. I wonder how long he will leave me here. Perhaps he has gone back to the shop to buy some more equipment – some of the more exciting pieces he baulked at before. Such a bourgeois little prude. You could tell he'd never done anything

*like this – never even tied a scarf over one of his little bourgeois girlfriend's eyes.
But he soon got a taste for it. All men do. All men, that is, apart from my
husband. 'O, my darling,' he will say, 'How could you ask me to piss on you?'
Boys from good families! You couldn't imagine that from a ghetto-child. Hmm.
That must be blood at the corner of my mouth – it tastes like blood. Yes. A
taste I should know well enough by now, even in the dark. My ribs hurt quite
a lot. I think he may have cracked one. If he doesn't come back in five minutes, I will piss all over his lovely four-poster bed. That will serve him right for
being so boring as to leave me. Then, perhaps, he'll teach me a real lesson.*

'May I see the photograph again?' asked the young woman, once we
were seated at a table outside a cafe I'd never before visited.

'Tell me your name,' I said.

'Marguerite,' she said, holding out her perfectly manicured hand.
'True or false.'

I dropped the Polaroid on to the tabletop and slid it towards her,
face up.

She winced a little, then said: 'What a lot of blood there is. I assume
that it's real?'

A gendarme walked past not three feet away, his right hand on his
sub-machine gun. He smiled briefly at Marguerite and at the thought
of Marguerite.

'What do you think?' I asked.

She said nothing for a moment, then: 'I can see that she is smiling
– almost sneering. Who is she?'

I took a sip of my double espresso.

'Guess,' I said.

'If she were just some model, I don't think she would sneer – not
unless you asked her to. And this doesn't look like a sneer that has been
asked for. It is too enjoyable. So, she is either your wife or your mistress. And as you are not married…' She dipped her head towards my
ring-finger. 'I am guessing she is your mistress.'

'Very good,' I said. 'Now tell me why you think I was looking at
this photograph on the Métro?'

'Perhaps because you are a pervert. You like to look at this kind of
thing in public. Maybe you want other people to glimpse them as well.
That may be part of the fantasy. Women – women you find attractive.
They must see, too. Did you choose me particularly?'

'What do you think?' I asked.

Our gazes met properly for the first time. Her eyes were a pitiless, viewless snow-blue.

'I think perhaps I was wrong – you are not a pervert. You were look-ing at this photo because you wanted to see it, because you *needed* to see it.'

'But why would I so *need* to see it?'

'You mean right then?'

'Yes.'

'And there?'

'Yes.'

'Because you were looking for something new in it… or…'

I could see the thought forming, the smile rippling out across her full lips.

'… or you were looking at it for the first time.'

'You are a real detective,' I said. 'Now, Ms Marguerite Maigret, take your deduction one stage further.'

Under the table one of her feet kicked out unthinkingly as she looked back once again at the image. Her toe knocked my ankle, very gently and pleasantly.

'I'm sorry,' she said, in an absent voice. She tried to lift her eyes to accompany this apology, but they wouldn't pull themselves away from the sight of Edith's damaged body.

'You were looking at this photograph for the first time. It is a Polaroid, so it might have been taken some time ago and then thrust into a pocket, forgotten. You put on your coat today for the first time in months. It is cold, the start of winter – you reach your hand into your pocket…'

Finally, she looked into my face for confirmation – but saw some-thing entirely different.

'Your lips,' she said. 'You have blood on your lips.'

'Do I?' I asked.

'Oh my God,' she said.

I reached over and took the white-framed square of crumpled sheets and injured flesh out of Marguerite's hands.

'Exactly,' I said.

We gazed into each other's eyes for a full minute: she, into my impas-siveness; I, into her expanding horror.

'Where is she?' Marguerite finally said. 'Where have you left her?'

'She is in my apartment, on my bed, lying there, exactly as you see her.'

'You must go back and release her,' said Marguerite.

'Actually,' I said, 'I was thinking of visiting my parents – just getting on a train and going down there and surprising them. I really don't see them often enough.'

Her horror expanded still further.

'Where do they live?' she asked.

'A little village about an hour from Toulouse. Perhaps I could stay over the weekend. My mother is such a delightful cook. I've nothing better to do.'

'The woman will die.'

'Quite possibly.'

'In your apartment.'

'That is not in doubt.'

Marguerite stood up, magnificently calm.

'You are mad!'

'Listen,' I said. 'Unless you do *exactly* as I say, I will leave Paris and visit somebody, not my parents, they are dead, but, wherever I go, I won't be back for five or six days at least.'

'You wouldn't,' she said.

'Come with me,' I said.

'Where are we going?'

'The train station.'

Again, as the taxi took us to the Gare d'Austerlitz, we sat in silence.

I'm dying. It must be three hours – four. I was never any good at that silly children's game of guessing the time in the dark. He can't have gone back to the shop to buy more equipment. He'd've been home by now. Perhaps he's gone to see another woman – perhaps that is his game. Not a game I want to play. I think this will be the last time I see Antoine. An hour, I would accept. But this… God, I'm thirsty. Even the blood has stopped flowing into my mouth. When I get to see my husband, the bruises will be old. He won't believe that I was just that moment mugged. He'll know I was hanging around for a while. I'll have to tell him I was beaten unconscious, driven to the suburbs, left for dead on a piece of waste ground. I'll have to pretend they robbed me. I won't be able to use my credit cards until I get new ones. He'll insist even more forcibly that I go to the hospital, to the police. I'll have to tell him that I was raped.

O God, it will be so tedious. Really, Antoine is terrible. He has no sense of timing. This is so boring. I expect there will be terrible bruises on my wrists and ankles – which means I'll have to wear trouser suits for the next decade. How tedious. How boring.

Marguerite watched me as I bought my train ticket. She watched me as I found my seat and sat down. She watched as the clock ticked towards departure time... ten minutes... five... three... two... She watched my face, still impassive, as the guard blew his whistle. And then, as the last of the train doors slammed shut, she cracked...

'All right,' she said. 'I believe you. You would leave. You would go. Now, let's get off this train.'

I could feel the engines starting up.

'You'll do what I ask?' I said.

'Everything,' said Marguerite.

'Exactly?' I said.

'Exactly,' she replied. 'Come on!'

The engines engaged and the train started to glide forwards. We dashed along the aisle, opened the door and leapt down on to the very end of the platform.

Another taxi, another silence.

O, my dry aching throat. O, my sore ankles. O, my rubbed-raw wrists. I hate Antoine, but he is a stronger man than I thought he was. He is more of a true sadist – taking no account of his victim's pleasure. I hadn't found this being left at all pleasurable – not until I thought how truly sadistic Antoine was being. He knows my husband will find out, but he is not afraid of involving our real lives in this. I've started to get really wet at the thought of his unflinching cruelty, his unwavering pursuit of only his own pleasure. If only some of that wetness were in my throat. And now I've pissed in his bed. I can't wait for him to come back. I will offer myself to him. I will be his slave for ever. I will say, 'Do what you want to with me. Take me wherever you want.'

As we drove towards the shop, I saw a pharmacy and told the driver to stop. When I returned to the taxi I was carrying a brand-new Polaroid camera and several packets of film.

'Load it up,' I said, and handed it to Marguerite.

In the shop I asked for another set of everything. I could tell that

even the matter-of-fact assistant was impressed by my reappearance
(only a couple of hours after my first visit) with a completely different but equally beautiful woman. How my manner had changed in the
meantime. How confident I was.

Marguerite had become sullen and unresponsive. Her eyes were dull.

I'd told the taxi to wait for us outside.

*Antoine is a god. I am a worm. Antoine is splendid. I am worthless. All I
ask is the chance to be at his merciless mercy. Let him express his contempt for
me in any way he sees fit. I will not question his wisdom. He will be my
master. Let this pain be my tribute to him. Let every ache cry my devotion.
Let each drop of blood weep him out of pity. O let my abasement be total and
his domination ultimate. If he would only come back. If he would only release
me into my greater servitude.*

For a few moments, as the taxi drove away, we stood facing each other
on the leaf-strewn pavement.

'When you come inside,' I said, 'you may behave as you wish.'

'I do not know how I will wish to behave.'

'That is fine,' I said.

'This driver has seen us together,' she said. 'You are not safe. If you
kill me, you will be caught.'

I looked at the departing Mercedes.

'He has seen me with you as well as you with me.'

Marguerite seemed puzzled.

'You will understand soon enough,' I said. 'Come on.'

I took her by the arm and led her past the concierge.

*What's this? I hear the lift being called, the lift descending and rising, voices,
footsteps, a male voice and a female voice, the key in the front door, Antoine's
voice and the voice of a woman I've never met, footsteps down the hall and into
the bedroom, a conversation, a conversation about me –*

'What's her name?'

'Edith.'

'And is she your mistress?'

'Yes, she was – but maybe she won't want to be any longer. What
do you think?'

'Ask her.'

'Edith, nod your head if you're still my mistress.'

O, how my neck aches as I nod and I nod and I nod. Yes, Antoine, I am yours. I am yours for ever. You have brought another woman back to see me like this. Perhaps to do other things altogether. I am in such pain: it is exquisite.

'No, she really isn't my mistress any longer – whatever she thinks. I'm going to get rid of her. I will release her. She can go. This won't happen again.'

'Thank you,' said Marguerite.

'I'm not doing this for you.'

His voice in my ear, saying: 'Listen, Edith. You have to do exactly what I say. I am going to release you. After I release you, you are going to get up, get dressed and get out. I never want to see you or hear from you again. This is finished. Do you understand? Nod if you understand.' And my neck and my heart and my soul wrenching with agony as I nod. His voice again, saying: 'Do you agree never to see me again?' I do nothing. Antoine's voice, saying: 'If you don't agree, I will leave you here until you die.' A small nod. I feel the buckles at my left ankle being undone, my right hand, my left ankle, hand. The gag being unbuckled behind my head. The blindfold being ripped away. I try to look at him, but the light – O, the terrible light.

Marguerite was waiting in my study when I came through, after I'd helped Edith – crying, begging, calling me a god, clutching the soiled equipment – into the lift.

'Let's go,' I said.

Marguerite let the manuscript page she'd been reading fall back on to my desk.

'But you are – ' she said.

'Let's *go*,' I said.

'This is – '

'Yes, I am.'

'Go where?' Marguerite asked, blandly, as if she didn't know.

I held up the bag full of new equipment – the new gag, the new blindfold, the new hand- and ankle-cuffs, the new Polaroid camera.

'Wherever you want,' I said. *Wherever you want.*

Fluency

Michèle Roberts

It is odd, now that I think about it, that I have never considered Paris
as a possible home. Yet I'm sure it could have been perfectly feasible.
As a photographer I could have worked anywhere. My French is
not as fluent as I'd like, but I speak well enough to get by. My French
always improves, anyway, when I'm actually in France, surrounded by
French sounds; soaked in them; saturated. Perhaps I've simply hung
on to cliché, a wornout dream of romance, wanted to keep Paris as
my special Somewhere Else, my paradise, the golden city in which
I experience life as intensively and ecstatically as though I were on
acid. Perhaps this visionary bliss could not survive daily reality. Perhaps
if I lived in Paris then I'd have to become a tourist to somewhere
else instead. London, probably. I've carefully kept Paris as my place
of pilgrimage by associating it exclusively with the moments of
heightened awareness it's offered me, with epiphanies of various sorts
– those four small Vuillards I discovered in the Musée d'Orsay last
year, for example, on that June day smelling of hot dust, lime blossom
and vanilla, that day when I wandered into the little gallery in the
rue de Seine and met Pierre for the first time – with the pursuit of
particular beloved artist or writer ghosts – their flats and studios and
favourite cafés – and with love affairs. I've gone there with all my lovers,
for doomed or magical or awkward weekends. Each different lover
provided a different view of Paris, different museums and art galleries
for us to frequent, dawdling hand in hand or arm in arm, different
cafés and bars for us to lounge in while we talked for hours over a
single *express*, a single glass of wine. And because I haven't always had
the courage of my convictions and desires, and so haven't had all that
many lovers, I cannot claim to know Paris very well. I need a map, a
bus guide, a plan of the Métro, to get me around. A few Métro stations
shine for ever with my lovers' names superimposed on them, written
up above the entrances to those labyrinthine underworlds in loops
of stars.

I had assumed I was finished with Paris as a site of assignation. That

I could return to it as an ordinary place and get to know it properly. No more secret passions. No more love affairs. I certainly never intended to fall in love again. All that was over and gone. The pain and suffering and loss – all finished. Now I would learn to love Paris as I loved London, with a modicum of calm. Now I'd visit Paris simply as a reasonable adult, as a professional photographer happily trawling the galleries.

London is the city in which I grew up, got married and reared four children, the city in which I have become a widow and grown old. I know London and how its districts fit together as well as I know how to spell my own name. I don't depend in London on the company of other people to make discoveries. I go by myself. And I never put a foot or a letter wrong. I have learned London so well simply by walking around it, combing and re-combing its tangled patterns of streets, ever since I first left my parents' house over forty years ago. When I was young I moved about a lot. I lived in bedsits, communal houses and squats in several different districts: Pimlico, Finsbury Park, Holloway, Clapham Junction, Stepney, Stoke Newington, Notting Hill, Bayswater, Holland Park. For twenty years, with John, I lived in Bethnal Green. Now I am sixty and I live alone in a tiny flat in Stew Lane in the City, near St Paul's, within the sound of Bow Bells. Until last month I could see St Paul's out of my bedroom window, if I leaned out far enough, but now the derelict warehouses next door, on the other side of Stew Lane, are being renovated to make a block of luxury flats, and the surging concrete-pillared six-floor-high building cuts off my view. I don't mind. There's a better view from the communal roof terrace, anyway, across the river to the Globe and Bankside. As a girl of eighteen up from the suburbs, exploring London at weekends, I prowled around the City on Sundays. I loved its emptiness, its grand buildings, and the names of its streets. In the suburb where I lived the roads and cul de sacs and crescents had absurd, meaningless names presuming to evoke a bucolic and pastoral idyll of the past, the vanished farmland of Middlesex that had been paved over to make way for these meek estates of mock-Tudor, names like Fairmead and Bullscroft which seemed to me merely sentimental. Whereas the City names were signposts that pointed to images from poetry, a trading past that remained vibrantly real. Milk Street, Bread Street, Paternoster Lane, Godliman Lane, Saffron Hill, Garlick Hill. I recited the words to myself as though I strung beads on a rosary, I sang litanies of free-dom. I discovered Sir Christopher Wren's house, opposite St Paul's on the far bank of the river, whence he would emerge every morning to be rowed across the busy tide to superintend the building of his great work, and I climbed over the back wall to explore the tiny garden. I wandered the deserted quays, scrambling past Keep Out signs and under fences of barbed wire, diving in and out of crumbling alleys. I remembered Lucy Snowe, in *Villette*, coming to London for the first time, arriving in darkness, falling asleep in her small and ancient hotel and suddenly realising, as she hears the great bells ring out, that she lies in the shadow of St Paul's.

A lot of those streets and alleys got bombed to smithereens in the war. A lot of other places got pulled down in the postwar rush to mod-ernise, the love affair with concrete. Now the City has been restored, re-built, reinvented. It's an image, refurbished and re-painted, of its former self. Now I myself live in the City, which I never dreamed, all those years ago, could ever be possible, bang opposite Sir Christopher Wren's house, which is still standing in the tiny terrace that squeezes in alongside the spanking-new pretend-old Globe, and I stand on the roof, leaning on the parapet, to stare across, and I remember that opti-mistic girl I was, with her flared loons and strings of beads and wild hair. Going wherever she fancied. Trespassing. Breaking and entering. Falling easily in love. Nowadays you can walk along the river all the way from Westminster through into Blackfriars, past our little block at Queenhythe, and down through gleaming new malls and cobbled narrow streets as clean as film sets into shiny amazing Wapping. At dusk the strings of silvery lights switch on, and the cafés serving cappuccino and smart fashionable food sparkle enticingly. All stage-managed. A brilliant spectacle, a newness that is both pleasing and disturbing. For the millennium celebrations the City traffic halted, all the bridges were garishly lit and turned into theatres, fireworks broke up the sky, the crowds of people jammed together on the new steel arch slung between St Paul's and Bankside cast strange elongated shadows into the dark dazzling waters of the river. I watched from our rooftop, sipping champagne with my neighbours whom I scarcely know.

Loving to walk through London, by night or day, taught me to look at things. That was what made me a photographer, my fascination with the material of streets, with street furniture, with the fabric of which the city is made. Strolling eye to eye with windows whose cracked stone sills sprouted feathery weeds, with old brick walls streaked with astonishing and subtle colours, blue and yellow on pink and brown, spotting the ghosts of old stencilled ads on the sides of Victorian shops, the decorative details of iron railings, the bits of debris caught by the sturdy grilles over kerbside drains where the water swirled black and shiny in the gutters. People warned of rapists and muggers but I refused to fear my fellow-citizens. I strode aggressively when necessary, glaring and growling if I had to, clad in a huge old coat and big boots. I did not look vulnerable. I knew the street codes. Even as a naive girl too wide-eyed for her own good, I escaped all harm.

Aged sixty, I still go for long walks around London, and of course continue to discover parts of it I haven't known before. Walking home from the West End along the Strand and Fleet Street, for example, I slip in and out of the alleys lacing together the riverside and the law courts and the gardens of the Temple and the secret pubs hidden at the back of slits between shops, and I think of Virginia Woolf walking there and thinking of Defoe and Dr Johnson doing exactly the same thing. Or I explore north through the backstreets of Smithfield, Clerkenwell, Finsbury, Angel. A magical incantation, every time, sings in my head, of names and places. Blake went for long walks like these, weaving north and south, Hampstead to Westminster to Peckham Rye. Keats, while he studied at Guy's, had lodgings in Borough, just a stone's throw away from me. Mrs Gaskell thought nothing of walking up to Highgate and back in a single afternoon.

I like wandering aimlessly, with no fixed goal, unsure exactly where I will end up, letting my feet choose their own route, as the whim takes them. Mapping the City I once knew on to the City that I live in now, so clean, so full of swooping marble façades that are designed to seem old but were built only yesterday. I've hardly begun to understand this extraordinary palimpsest. You can lift up a corner of pavement and peer at a Mithraic temple. Shards and coins surface from Thames mud at low tide. Builders excavating rubble to dig foundations of new office blocks unwittingly become archaeologists, discovering the traces of old trading posts or burial grounds. The City heaves and contorts and gives birth to its past.

When you go for long walks through cities anything can happen. When you fall in love it's the same. You're not in control. When you walk around on your own you have adventures and meet strangers. Fear of going out is linked to fear of love. You might meet a stranger and fall in love. You might feel afraid that love is dangerous.

I'm sitting here in the bar feeling puzzled, a little light-headed perhaps. Light gleams on the brown wooden table top, dances on the surface of my glass of Côtes du Rhône, sparkles on the long curve of zinc to my right across which the barman is sliding glasses of pastis for the waiter to load on to his round silver tray. I'm thinking of Pierre and I know I'm smiling. I'm not dreaming. But I don't understand what has happened.

I left the flat at three o'clock or so. I needed to get out and stretch my legs, and a walk seemed a better idea than a swim or a visit to the pub. I strolled north for a couple of blocks, turning right into Cheapside and then veering left up towards Liverpool Street. I had a vague idea of reaching Spitalfields Market and buying some flowers and bread. Fool. I'd managed to forget it was Saturday and the market only opens on Sundays. So I retraced my steps, meaning to return home by some pleasantly roundabout route. To wander down to London Bridge, perhaps, and back along the river towards Blackfriars.

I was thinking about love, how it creeps up on you and grabs you and knocks you out before you're aware of what's happening. Love the stalker. Love the mugger, the boxer, the bruiser. Love the poacher, setting you traps, throwing a net over your head and capturing you in a fierce grip. Love like a force of nature that cannot be checked, an avalanche, a mudslide, breaching your carefully built defences, flooding through you and possessing you. Love like a disease too: an infection, an obsession, a kind of madness, a wound, keeping you sleepless by night and restless by day.

Or – love like language, flowing out and surrounding the other, looping the loved one together with the self, cocooning you in shared stories and jokes. Love like a conversation that is endlessly renewed and renewing, a strong web that holds you up like a hammock. Love as the urge to talk, to tell the beloved everything that happens, to make life more real by drawing pictures of it for the other, your face turned endlessly towards his, wanting to give him all your words and receive all of his, wanting to create the world anew, pile his hands with gifts, wanting to give him yourself, it's that simple.

I'd stopped really noticing where I was going. My feet pulled me along as though they knew exactly my destination. I'd crossed the river, on to the south side, I'd gone past Sir Christopher Wren's house and was pursuing the path westward. I was vaguely aware of the grey December sky darkening and yet it was only mid-afternoon. A part of me remembered: yes, it's the day of the winter solstice, the shortest day. With my fur collar turned up and my hands thrust deep into my coat pockets, I strolled on.

I was thinking how women of my age were not supposed to fall in love. I had been a widow for ten years, very well, but now I was a grandmother, I had put away childish things, my four children, scattered across London, needed my services as a regular babysitter, counsellor and good samaritan, I was fortunate enough to be able to continue working as a photographer, I had several close men and women friends and many acquaintances and colleagues, I made enough to live on, could afford to travel a bit if I budgeted carefully. My life was organised, busy and full, with no room in it for wildness or extravagance. Besides, as I knew very well from what the culture shouted at me from every angle, every advertising hoarding, every TV programme, every cinema screen, old women were invisible and should stay that way. Worse, they were obscene and disgusting if they entertained thoughts of love and sex. Women past the menopause should cut their hair and retire from the field. They should not want physical pleasures, they should not have desires. Their ageing, sagging, unspeakably ugly flesh should remain hidden. They should not be occasions of shame and disgust to the young. And so on and so on. Perhaps that was why my latest project had been to make portraits of people over fifty, some women and some men. I photographed some of them naked and some clothed, according to the sitter's self-image on the day of shooting, according to our joint fantasy. I thought they were dignified, beautiful, angry, tender pictures but my children were not so sure. Pierre had liked the pictures I had pulled out of my bag and shown him, that first time I met him, when we had decided to have a coffee together in the Bar du Marché; he had written to say he liked the pictures I had sent him afterwards from London. And of course I warmed to him. A man taking the time and trouble to look at what I had seen, to try to see things through my eyes, to gaze at my gaze, this pleased me. This was not vanity so much as gratitude. I don't usually expect men to see things my way, and am surprised and pleased when they do. No gallery had yet offered me a show, partly because other women photographers were perceived as already doing the same thing. My work was not original enough. Pierre liked my work, though. I could make something beautiful. That made me feel beautiful; that I had something to give. All of us need this validation from time to time, I think, not only children. Pierre was a painter. He was funny and clever and kind. He was fifteen years younger than I was. I fell in love with him in a matter of days. He didn't know anything about it. I'd had the sense to keep it to myself.

But love is a blessing, whether or not it's reciprocated, whether or not it's consummated, whether or not it can even simply be declared. Love had woken me up and made me want to work harder than ever, and make something more beautiful than I had ever made before. Love makes you feel you're being born all over again, catching you, then swinging you by the heels in the air, that midwife love, laughing as you roar. And love also makes you humble as well as hopeful, realistic as well as mad. Men of Pierre's age don't fall in love with women of sixty. What would he see in me ? I didn't think he'd laugh at me, he's too kind for that, at least he wouldn't laugh to my face, but he would be embarrassed, I was sure. He didn't need me to love him. He had plenty of love already, a young and beautiful lover. He'd shown me her photograph. Happiness and liking women generally made him charming to all the women he met, and I had fallen for his charm. It was a fantasy. That was all. On to his handsome surface I had projected unconsciously the movie of my loneliness, my desire, my sexual need. I was using him. It was unreal. This was what I told myself fifty times a day. It will pass, Pauline, I told myself sternly: it will dissolve, and go away eventually, and all you have to do in the meantime is keep a firm grip on yourself and not behave like too much of a ridiculous fool. I thought I sounded just like Charlotte Brontë berating her plain heroines for daring to fall in love with Mr Rochester, with Dr Bretton. But at least Jane Eyre and Lucy Snowe were young. They did have youth on their side, at least.

I leaned on the parapet and looked at the Thames. The tide was high and flowing fast. While I had been walking, the grey afternoon had been turning into *l'heure bleue*, into glittering dusk. Now the city swam in full darkness. Across on the other side of the river, the edge between water and land was marked by loops of pearl lights, long curving ropes of gleaming bulbs that swung a little, to and fro, in the night breeze. Two barges were stationary in midstream, providing a solidity and shape of blackness and mirroring shadow beneath that contrasted with the light gleaming and dancing in long wavering stripes on the surface of the water. The far reach of the river was black and purple rippled with dark green, and the nearer stretch was indigo shot through with silver, streaked with gold-pink. The barges rocked up and down on the tide, and their reflections rocked too, shading out to triangles of black, and the lights poured down on to the river in stripes of pearl and silver and gold and red. More light glimmered in the dark sky, as the enormous moon slowly emerged from enveloping clouds, strongly developing itself like a photograph, warming to gold. This play and dance of light and water was prodigal, dazzling, an enchantment, it drew you into itself, dissolved you into long ripples of black river water streaming fast, into moonlight and lamplight circling and glossy on the racing tide. I had no camera. All I could do was stand and look.

I don't know how long I stood there. My face felt cold, and my feet too, but I wasn't yet ready to return home. I was supposed to be baby-sitting for one of my sons tonight, I remembered, and I didn't want to. I thought I'd go and have a drink, and perhaps be brave enough to phone my son and be thoroughly selfish and cancel babysitting. First of all, though, I had to find a pub. So I turned left, leaving the exquisite vision of darkness and light, the calm and emptiness of the riverside walk, and plunged down the first side street I saw.

I walked rapidly, in order to keep warm, turning corner after corner at speed, skipping out of the way of passersby. I was impatient, now, to be inside, somewhere warm. But I could see no pub ahead of me. When I turned, to retrace my steps, I hesitated, unsure which way to go. These little streets all looked the same, gay and enticing, hung with Christmas lights in the shape of snowflakes. One long, narrow tunnel of brightly illuminated shops led into another. For some strange reason, despite my familiarity with this bit of Southwark just east of Waterloo, I could no longer recognise where I was. I was lost. I had apparently strayed into some new development, some project of re-building and restoration that had happened seemingly overnight without my knowing anything about it. The stone façades of buildings were grey, cream, pale pink. Blue enamel signs, indicating house numbers, were nailed up alongside enormous wooden doors with smaller doors cut into them. Glass frontages displayed paintings and prints, new books, piled pots of pâté de foie gras, swathes of silk and velvet scarves. Everything looked delectable and expensive. Cars hooted as they tore past, taking little notice of pedestrians crossing the street, and poodles in gilt collars lifted their furry legs against the pillared entrances to boutiques while their ferociously chic owners tugged indulgently on their leads. There were a great many tourists around all chatting to each other in French.

I turned a corner and found myself walking past a bar, whose wicker tables and chairs spilled out on to the pavement, and into a street market. I remembered the flowers and bread I had set out earlier to buy, and I slowed down. Here was a treasure trove. The vegetable stalls were heaped with chestnuts, pumpkins and various kinds of wild mushrooms, while further along a butcher displayed fluffy white rabbits hung up by their heels, brightly feathered ducks and pheasants, legs of wild boar. A delicatessen offered tiny spinach quiches, so fresh you could see the nutmegged egg custard wobbling, the lightest of cheese pastry puffs, ham-stuffed mille-feuilles and sausage rolls, a mouthwatering array of buckets of olives and pepper strips and artichokes in oil. I couldn't see a pub so I decided to settle for a bar. I turned and went back towards the one at the other end of the street, the Bar du Marché that I had passed earlier.

A discreet oblong sign, neat art deco lettering on a faded mauve background, stopped me short. Hôtel Louisiane. There it was, exactly as I remembered it from all those years ago when I'd first started to visit Paris. A friend had recommended the Louisiane because it was cheap and also, more importantly, because Simone de Beauvoir had lived there once. I had stayed always on the fourth floor, in an austere little room high up under the eaves. The room contained a single bed covered with an orange chenille spread, a hard chair, a small formica table under the high shuttered window. In the tiny adjoining bath-room was a threadbare towel and a minuscule bar of Palmolive soap. Across the street when you stood on tiptoe and peeped out was the *oeil-de-boeuf* window of the attic floor of the facing building. I would lie on the hard bed, daydreaming after my shower, waiting for my hair to dry, waiting for the next rendezvous with whoever it was.

If I was standing outside the Hôtel Louisiane then I was in the rue de Seine which meant I was in Paris.

I have come into the Bar du Marché and sat down near the zinc and ordered a glass of Côtes du Rhône. I am not asleep and I am not dreaming and I am not mad. I am in Paris. I am scratching this down, these black marks on this white paper. This is real.

The door opens and someone comes in from the street. He looks like Pierre. When he sees me he smiles.

The Events

Edward Fox

In the second week of the Events, I went to see my professor in hospital, the mad philosopher. He was sitting up in bed, reading a newspaper, and wearing an undignified white gown that didn't cover his body properly, but that rather suited him because it made him look like an angel. His uncombed white hair formed a dandruffy nimbus around his lunatic head. The drugs had made his skin look sallow and translucent to complete his ethereal appearance.

His gaze fixed on to me as soon as I entered the ward. The hospital, on the outskirts of Paris, was a monument to the stony charity of France's last empire and had long corridors and immense open wards where patients were tended in a regime of military rigidity.

'You know what they're doing now, don't you?' he said, without greeting (he maintained the Socratic rigour of the teacher–student relationship even when he was in hospital, which was understandable since he spent so much time there), as soon as I was close enough to him that he could speak to me without raising his voice.

I had no idea what he meant, of course, so I prompted him to tell me once I had sat down at his bedside.

'The French authorities have introduced a secret weapon for use against the students. It is to be deployed in street battles. The weapon consists of an electronic oscillator, mounted inside a van, which generates a sine wave at an ultra-low frequency, but with terrific magnitude. The wave is below the threshold of human audibility, but it causes intense nausea in anyone within one hundred metres of the source, temporarily but totally disabling them. A subsonic tear gas.'

A little rocket of amusement went off in my head. I had to concentrate hard to prevent myself from smiling at this wonderfully absurd idea. I prized the professor's flights of imagination during his periodic mental crises – the exquisite fruit of mania.

'I see you have been reading the newspaper,' I said. 'I came to tell you what has been happening, because I thought you wouldn't have had any news in here.'

This irritated him. 'I have been reading the newspapers daily. I know what you *delinquents* are up to,' he said with a faint smile, pronouncing with ironic emphasis the word that the *Figaro*'s editorial writer had used to describe us a few days earlier. Then he noticed the scuffed bruise on my cheekbone. 'Were you hit with a police truncheon?' he asked.

'No, not exactly,' I said, and told him what had happened.

The night before, I had found myself caught up in a march, mostly of students from the University of Nanterre, who were on their way to the Sorbonne, which had been occupied by the police three days earlier. It was not my original intention to take part in a battle with the police. A girl from the Sorbonne whom I had chatted with after a seminar on Mao Tse Tung thought told me that she was going. She was really cute, even if I found her politics a bit naive, and I wanted to see her again. We may have been in the vanguard of liberation, but it was still hard to meet girls.

So we met outside the Sorbonne just as the crowd was entering the Latin Quarter, and we joined it, and took up the chant, *'No to repression! Free our comrades!'* – referring to the hundreds of students who were arrested when the police invaded the university. As the procession turned into the rue St Jacques, we found ourselves almost in the front rank, facing a double line of riot police who were blocking the street.

We were forced to stop in front of them. But the majority of the crowd, who were behind us, hadn't yet turned into the rue St Jacques and couldn't see the line of cops barring our way, so they continued to pour into the street behind us, pushing us right up against the police line, and while all this was going on we kept chanting the slogan, *'Free the Sorbonne! Free the Sorbonne!'*, and pointing our fingers at the police to taunt them, because it was they who had invaded the university.

I don't know what happened next, except that the police very suddenly started hitting anyone in sight with their truncheons. One of them chose me for a target, and came towards me with his weapon held high. I ran on to the pavement to escape him, but I tripped on something and crashed head-first into the metal tables and chairs outside a café. I sat there for a moment with my eyes closed and my arms over my head as the battle raged around me. When I looked up, the girl was nowhere to be seen, but the battle was still going on, so I pulled myself up and rejoined the students. It was an amazing feeling, there in the street. The sensations of fear and excitement combined in my guts and I felt a momentary flash of a kind of ecstasy. We were fighting the police and winning! I saw some people pulling up cobble-stones with their hands and hurling them at the police. I joined them, and flung a cobble-stone in a high arc into the swarm of blue uniforms. I don't know if it hit one of them.

I looked towards the professor like a proud son seeking approval for a good deed. I was setting this description before him, and indeed the whole student movement, everything that had happened since the Events began, as a great gift in tribute to the teacher who had instructed us in his seminars at the École about the inevitable revolution and the renewed science of Marxism. We were now carrying out that revolution. The state was quaking at the knees before us and would soon fall. This kindly and gentle man was the father of our movement, despite his occasional bouts of infirmity, and I was the first and only one of his students to come to him to acknowledge his role. I thought it would boost his morale, and hasten the healing of his shattered faculties. Instead, it seemed to have the opposite effect.

'The situation is not revolutionary,' he said, in a weary voice, a little slurred. He looked feeble and sad.

'What?'

'Your movement is an ideological revolt, not a political revolution,' he said. He paused, summoning up from a mind fogged with medication the terms he was seeking. 'It is only subjectively revolutionary. It is libertarian, or neo-Luxemburgist, but not revolutionary. You are living in a dream.'

'But that's precisely the point. We are liberating desire. Our slogan is, Be realistic: demand the impossible. We pull up the cobble-stones in the street and find the beach underneath.'

'It is utopianism. You know what Lenin said about utopianism, don't you?'

'No.'

'"Utopianism is an infantile disorder which can be cured if it is properly treated."'

When I looked at him again, his eyes were closed, so I got up quietly and left.

That night at dinner I sat with two friends, Georges and Alain, fellow students at the École. We were a bit mad ourselves those days, though we considered ourselves superior to the rowdies of the Sorbonne. As students of the celebrated professor, we were by right the ideological commissars of the movement. Georges had been carrying out this serious duty in the course of the past week by writing particularly obscure and erudite graffiti on the walls of the narrow streets of the Latin Quarter. He spent whole days composing them in his room and then would steal out from the hall of residence at night with a can of spray paint. The authorship of these masterpieces was unmistakable: Georges always used very straight, regular block capitals and was careful about grammar and punctuation. They also tended to be the longest graffiti around. This had two consequences: they lacked the epigrammatic brevity of the best examples, and they took longer to write, which increased Georges's risk of being caught. As each night approached, he worked himself up into a knot of anxiety as he faced the dangerous task that lay before him.

'I wrote a new one last night,' he said gravely. 'It's on the wall beside the Étoile bakery. It says, *The image of death: the sleeper's real self: Return, the repressed!*'

'What does it mean?'

'It's an adapted quotation from Lacan.'

'Bourgeois nonsense,' Alain huffed.

I said, 'It's too cryptic! I can't understand that and I have no idea who would. Would you please go back tonight and add an explanatory footnote, and perhaps a bibliography?'

Georges winced. 'I'm afraid of the police.'

Then I told them about my visit to the professor in hospital, and how confused and disappointed I had been by what he had said.

'I don't understand why you take him so seriously,' Alain said. 'He's just crazy, nothing more. Half the time he's doped up to his eyeballs and doesn't know what day of the week it is, or even what country it is. You say he's an important theorist, but he's hardly published anything. There is a rumour about him, you know, that he hasn't read the whole of *Das Kapital*, that he has never got past the first chapter, because he doesn't understand it, and he's terrified that people will find out. Besides, what good is he now – to us – here – with the police shooting rubber bullets and tear gas every night, and breaking our skulls, while he lies in bed in hospital, supine and helpless?'

'That is just the point. To be crazy is the only logically possible response, the only course for a person who is rational.'

'Response to what?'

'You know: what we're all opposed to. To the fascist monolith of France and its armed police. To De Gaulle. To the war in Vietnam. To the church, to the family, to what he calls the "ideological apparatus of the state", including the École itself. His withdrawal is both logical and correct. It is a potent and effective act of rejection of a state of affairs that is itself in the last stages of a fatal disease. Faced with an obscene situation, the self has no choice but to go on a psychic general strike, to enter an inner state of revolutionary turmoil.'

'That too is bourgeois nonsense,' Alain said.

Over the next few days, the situation in the street intensified and moved towards a climax. The government was still refusing to release the students who had been arrested in the siege of the Sorbonne, and the university was still closed, despite an announcement that it would re-open for lectures. A big confrontation with the authorities seemed inevitable. By that Friday the streets of the Latin Quarter had been turned into a revolutionary carnival, with open-air lectures and black and red banners hanging from the windows. I saw the surrealist poet Aragon, a member of the French Communist Party, and as such a symbol of the old order, booed off the platform he was sharing with the leader of our movement, Daniel Cohn-Bendit.

The showdown came that night. A march had been planned for that day, which was intended to go through the boulevards of the Right Bank, but the police had sealed off all the bridges across the Seine. So a spontaneous decision was made to occupy the Latin Quarter. I was with a large crowd that had gathered in the rue Gay Lussac. I could feel the tingling of fear and anticipation building up inside me. At one point, the word swept through the crowd that we should build barricades. A group of us discovered a building site, which we plundered for materials, and we piled the stuff up in the street until it was a metre high, and others were doing the same all around us, when at about 2am, the storm broke, and the police descended on us. This time they seemed to be using grenades, in addition to the usual tear gas and truncheons, because I heard a number of explosions mingling with the menacing double note of sirens. The blue revolving lights of their trucks streaked across the fronts of the surrounding buildings.

I felt a sudden, overwhelming nausea. My head spun on three axes; I buckled at the knees and fell to the pavement. The last thing I remember seeing before I passed out was a strange van with its side open and inside it a monstrous black cone.

A week later, *Libération* reported that an estimated two hundred people were struck with the same unexplainable symptom, which was nothing like the symptoms of tear-gas inhalation. A new secret weapon had been introduced, the paper said, although some dismissed the reports as paranoiac delusion.

The convalescents

Ron Butlin

Having stuck it out for an extra three months caretaking at *Les Montagnes Blanches* I was pretty flush – ten months' money and only the Alps and fresh air to spend it on. Free flat, free booze, green fields, green trees, flowers and blossoms of every colour. Finally, one evening, Anna said she'd had it with the majestic scenery, the jacuzzi picnics, the 36-channel TV and the limitless hot water – she wanted a home, a real home with me, or without. She'd done her three months extra as well – which had felt like three years added to my sentence – but that was it, she said. Not a day more.

We had just sat down to the traditional cut and thrust of Sunday dinner together: a haunch of defrosted venison, three veg, two bottles and one carving knife. A romantic candlelit interrogation where she grabbed my hand and did a Van Gogh, holding it over the candle flame. Marriage? Children? The future? I shook myself free and we pretended she had been joking. She had. Then she hadn't. Then she had. The Van Gogh motif would have been developed further had I not seen the carving knife coming and moved out the road to safety, taking my right ear with me. She'd been joking again, of course. Yes, she had. No, she hadn't. Yes, she had. Because, what she'd really meant to do was –

This time I wasn't quick enough.

A flash of sharpened silver by candlelight, and she'd turned the blade against herself, falling forward with a crash of her head on to the table. Her glass was knocked over; her hair and her face lay in a pool of '85 Margaux. She didn't move.

'Anna! Anna!' I grabbed her shoulder to pull her up. 'Anna! For Christ's sake!'

There was no response. The knife was somewhere under her. What the hell was I to do?

The right answer was: get up, walk out, drive down to Sancerre, find a doctor, give him the address and directions, then keep on driving. Levites always get a second chance, these days there's no shortage of people needing help. But I was still too much the Good Samaritan; and so, no right answer from me. I stayed.

Very, very carefully I lifted her head: the blondeness of her hair was soaked blood-red, her eyes were closed.

'Anna!'

Not a sound, not a flicker of life.

I was kneeling at her side, about to try raising her a little more to see how badly hurt she was, when I felt her hand grip my arm.

'Gave you a fright, did I?'

Gripping me tighter she hauled herself up straight. The carving knife clattered back on to the table as bright and shiny as before. She'd been pretending. Or rather, as she explained it, she'd been showing me how devastated I would feel to lose her – and, therefore, by implication illus-trating the deeper truth of how closely bound together we were. It was time for a change of scene, she added. We were ready to move on, weren't we? Then she smiled, righted her glass and poured out refills.

Naturally I was relieved to learn she was perfectly all right. Within seconds she had recovered from post-traumatic stress and, across the candlelit table, began to detail our future together. Back to Britain, to Edinburgh; get a flat and a real job; get married and start a family; begin to live in the real world. The venison was cooked to a treat; I ate it and tried to enjoy it.

Notice given the following day, the final pay cheque cashed a week later, a farewell liberation from the cellars, and we were ready. We loaded up the rustbox, and left.

We nearly didn't make it. The hairpin descent to Sancerre was easy enough – our troubles started once we had to switch on the engine. We shuddered, stalled and panted all the way to Paris, where we sold what was left over to a hard-nosed auto-pirate for the price of two train tickets to London. A few days in Gay Paree first? Not her. Douce Edinburgh – she couldn't wait. Even phoned my mum, asked her to stop work for an hour and fax us the latest property pages – reading material for the journey home.

So, picture us at the Gare du Nord: the noise, the dirt, the suitcases and overnight bags, the loudspeakers, the crowds – and us like a couple of marmots down from the mountains. We find the Chunnel train. We get on. She's chattering and laughing in an almost human way. Not that she'd let past my casual jest about travelling in the Tunnel being a bit Freudian. At once, the Big A crops up. Next comes the suggestion that when we're back I should think of signing up for three analytical evenings a week as well – we could go out together afterwards and talk through our respective sessions over a drink. Was that what finally tipped the scales: the threat of self-improvement as far as the eye could see? Or was it just her? Whatever, a paying passenger in a high-speed train I might very well have been at that moment, but I knew I was at a crossroads – and all around me life's traffic lights were turning red. I had only a few seconds' amber left, it seemed. Meanwhile she's laying out a mid-morning snack and I've got my hands on one of the bottles of Lafite, a parting gift from the cave of our mega-rich employer, that innocent philanthropist.

The train's about to go. I'm still holding my overnight bag when the departure warning sounds.

'Look who's come to see us off!' I point towards the platform.

She turns round, peers out of the window. 'Who? Who? Where?' She's straining to see.

'I'll get them at the door,' I call out as I rush off down the carriage.

I just made it. Behind me, the train was picking up speed. Orpheus may have made a right hash of things when he left the Underworld, but I was damn sure I wasn't going to: if Anna banged on the window or called out after me there was going to be no backward glance. Not that I intended hanging round to give her the chance: overnight bag in one hand, Lafite in the other, I went hoppity-skippity-jump up the platform towards the main station. Behind me, Anna and all her problems began Eurostarring out of my life at 150mph with no stop until the other side of the Channel. My share of the rustbox blown in a couple of seconds, but worth every centime.

Straight to the Café du Nord for a celebratory *demi* and an ear-to-ear grin after every well-deserved sip. Not the most creditable act of my existence so far, but probably the most necessary. It was either that or death by analysis, day and night. If I fancied it I could feel guilty later on, but for the moment there was the certainty of no more talking things through, no more screaming and raging, no more biting, scratching and stabbing: I had survived.

The traffic lights were green again. Two *demis* later I went and phoned Thérèse, our friend of last summer.

★

Her flat was only 15 minutes away at the edge of the Arab quarter near Barbès, at the end of a cheerless cul-de-sac that seemed to be mostly blank walls, uncollected garbage and lack of sun.

She didn't seem surprised to see me; and she didn't ask why Anna had returned alone to Scotland. There was a clutch of nearly empty mugs on a very smeary glass coffee table; the curtains were still closed. The speakers at either end of the mantelpiece were unplugged. Having sat down on an armchair that sagged over by the window she smiled at me; in jeans, a particularly off-white T-shirt and bare feet she looked as if she'd just got out of bed.

'And you, Ian, what are you planning to do now?'

The full extent of my planning so far had been to get myself, my toilet stuff, a change of clothes, a couple of paperbacks, passport and money off the train and into Thérèse's flat. As for the next stage, well, that was surely obvious enough.

On the wall above the mantelpiece was a large mirror, real Hollywood Louis-Quatorze. The gilt beading curved painfully and much of it was chipped and flaking off; the surface was clouded with grease, spotted with dirt and slightly cracked in one corner; here and there, pieces had gone missing as if they'd lost heart reflecting the dismal scene they'd been stuck with. If I'd had the strength of character just then to look into it – a hand on the glass to steady the image – what would I have seen? No red nose, no bells on the hat, no painted face – but for all that ('deep down', as Anna would have said) a perfect clown, moving from the old circus ring to the new one in search of a few laughs. Mind you, there was a lot to be said for the change of management: Thérèse was younger, nicer, and hadn't yet seen my handful of tricks a hundred times over.

So, I was pretty clear about what I wanted to do, but what I felt (Anna again) – as I sat there less than a yard from this very attractive young woman – was longing. Deep, deep longing. My mistake was thinking it was her I was longing for. Thérèse, poor girl, just happened to be the only person I knew in Paris. Since getting shot of Anna an hour previously and finding Thérèse on her own, I at once developed the most convincing feelings of tenderness, heartfelt caring and affection for her.

What was I planning to do now? she'd asked.

As there was no socially acceptable answer, I became diplomatic.

'I'm not sure yet.' I tried to look thoughtful: 'I wanted to come and see you.'

She fingered a silver chain around her neck, a crescent-moon pendant. She smiled: 'You're seeing me.'

I managed to say, 'Yes, so I am.' The need to be tender, caring and affectionate towards her was becoming overwhelming. 'And I'm very pleased to be here.'

A pause. She touched the silver pendant, looked down as if surprised to discover she was the person wearing it, then, reassured, glanced up but didn't speak.

Another pause. I leaned forward: 'That's a lovely necklace you have.'

'My father gave it to me.'

Not that I could have understood at the time, but these words of hers marked a desperate, last-ditch defence against everything she had ever known. I wasn't listening, of course; she could have told me the house was burning down and I wouldn't have paid the slightest attention. I could hardly see the moon for lust. My hand had reached forward to examine the silver arc and the rest of me followed. I moved in for the kiss.

From the first, living with Thérèse was like heaven after hell: she didn't want to make me a better person; she didn't want me to get in touch with my inner feelings/my childhood/my masculinity/my femininity/my real self. She didn't finish my sentences, explain my jokes or interpret my dreams. We'd make love and then, without having to note what had been learned from the experience, we'd fall asleep. There were the odd landmines here and there, but nothing that seemed serious – and with Thérèse they didn't keep moving around, but stayed put and could be avoided. These days she looked her real age – 18. She'd lied to Anna or, as she put it, not corrected Anna's mistaken assumption: 'She wanted a little girl, so I made her happy.' What, then, had she been thinking I wanted?

The small flat was dark and seemed to be all corridor. Clothes were everywhere, drawers hung half open, books lay face-down, broken-spined, like so many shot-down birds. I doubt she ever read one to the end in the whole of her short life. The tiny bedroom was all bed, a mattress on the floor: a nest where we spent most of our time. The flat was too dingy to be tidied up in one go, so we didn't even try. The carpets crunched underfoot, some parts were less sticky than others. Paths to the kitchen, the toilet and the front door were kept reasonably clear; the rest was a no-man's land of old newspapers, unwashed crockery, unwashed clothes, unmatched shoes and bruised furniture. The curtains were thick and usually left closed so we didn't have to see too much of the place.

We had enough money. No rent as Thérèse had inherited the flat from her father. Most mornings we stayed in bed, afternoons we walked. Summer was turning into autumn: dry, warm days that would be suddenly shot through with a rush of cold wind sending us into the nearest café. We must have covered the whole of Paris walking: the Bois de Boulogne, the Tuileries, Montmartre. Evenings we ate in cheap restaurants – a grease-trough off Pigalle or, if we wanted to be tourists, somewhere near St Michel. Another day, another dinner. Then back home, up the stairs, close the front door and along the path back to the nest.

It was a period of convalescence for us both: I was recovering from the year's sentence with Anna; Thérèse was resting, period. She was very calm, alarmingly so sometimes. Often she'd lie for a whole morning doing nothing. I'd have read 50 pages of sci-fi, been to Alpha Centauri and back a couple of times, and she'd not have moved a muscle from staring up at the ceiling, her hands clenched at her sides. Only when I put down my book and leant over to kiss her did she again seem aware of where she was.

The phone rang a few times at the beginning, she bothered answering it only once: when she returned to bed she said it had been a friend who was leaving Paris and had wanted to say goodbye. There were no further calls and it was several days before I realised she'd pulled out the connection. Sometimes she wasn't there when I woke. Then around lunchtime she'd come back with 'surprises' as she called them: a new shirt for me, cooked duck breast in aspic, a portable CD player that turned out to need batteries and never got any. Once, I came across a bundle of 500-franc notes down the side of the couch, another time a roll of hundreds fell out of her coat: 'Pocket money,' she joked and peeled off a couple to squander on the afternoon walk. A woman of mystery all right, but I never asked and she never explained. Things were going well between us so why go looking for problems? I'd had more than enough questions and answers with Anna. And whatever

Thérèse said would have been lies anyway. Of that I am certain.

A month to the day after I had moved in we decided to celebrate by going into society, into the noise and bustle of a large restaurant: we'd wash, get dressed up and make a night of it. Two minutes after Thérèse had kissed me goodbye and set off down the long corridor towards the bathroom there was a knock at the door – the first since I'd knocked on it myself with the overnight bag and the Lafite. I answered it. A man in his fifties was blocking up the doorway with a dark suit, a rust-red hairpiece and an eager-looking smile; he was clutching a bottle of champagne. When he saw me he stopped smiling, gabbled something too fast for me to understand, handed over the bottle and hopped it down the stairs.

'A bit long in the tooth for an admirer,' I remarked in as casually pointed a manner as I could manage while climbing into my end of the bath.

'Jealous?'

'Only subconsciously.' I opened the champagne and passed it over: 'You can lick the froth off, little girl.'

'Thank you, daddy.' We laughed and she splashed some water in my face, took a swallow and almost choked. Drinking champagne straight from the bottle is an acquired art.

Hairpiece was one of her lecturers at the university, she explained later. Ton-ton Pascal, he was called by the students, and he'd always had a particular soft spot for her.

'Seemed more like a hard spot to me.'

She shrugged. 'Perhaps. But he is always the perfect gentleman.'

'Meaning?'

'Uses the butter-knife even when dining in private.' She stuck out her tongue.

We had come to Chartier's: garlic snails and oeuf au cheval for me, a plate of langoustines for Thérèse. The restaurant is a barn of a place, a Toulouse-Lautrec poster of waistcoated waiters with turn-of-the-century moustaches, white aprons, armfuls of plates, art-deco wood and stained glass; like a Victorian railway station minus the trains.

I became serious. Seriously middle-aged. 'What do you mean, "perhaps"? Are you saying he did have a hard spot for you?'

She was already on to her second langoustine: rip off the head, rip off the tail, and a fingernail up the belly to push back the feelers. Strip off the shell. 'You're the one doing all the saying.' She bit into the white flesh. 'Mmm. Very, very tasty. Fancy one?'

I wasn't going to be put off. Not me. Not Mr Midlife-crisis Morality. I gave her a midlife stare: 'So, Hairpiece?'

'You don't want one? Don't know what you're missing.' She ripped off another tail. 'Some people eat the heads. The soft gooey bits. Yeuch!' Little-girl disgust, then a little-girl smile as she picked up the next one and pretended she was going to toss it into the air: 'Heads or tails?'

'Has he always had this particular spot for you?'

For a few seconds she didn't reply. She laid down her langoustine and took a sip of wine. There was a smudge of red on the rim of her glass after she replaced it on the table. For a moment that smudge was the only thing in the world I was aware of. I might have lifted the glass and flirtatiously placed my lips against where hers had touched, but it was not romance I was feeling – it was terror. A sudden, overwhelming terror: I felt quite certain that when I looked back to her there would be no one sitting opposite, and never had been; that I had come into the restaurant by myself, and the glass with the lipstick smudge on its rim – left by a previous diner, perhaps, and not yet cleared away – was something I had latched on to as desperate proof I wasn't alone.

A moment later the feeling passed. I looked over to Thérèse. She was obviously expecting me to respond to something she'd said.

To my surprise I heard myself declaring, 'I think I've fallen in love with you.'

Next thing, I was aware only that she had taken my hand and lifted it to her mouth. She was kissing it.

'Yes,' she said as if she were a child, uncertain about what was happening, 'This is love, isn't it?'

We were in bed.

'Well, Ian, a month ago you said you liked my silver necklace, and now…' she laughed. 'That was the first compliment you paid me. It was a present from my real father, not my stepfather, did I tell you? Anyway, he's dead.'

Was she about to cry? No, she turned her face up to be kissed, then continued: 'Sometimes at night, when I was very little, if I was having a bad dream he would come and hold me. Maybe my mother did that too, but it's him I remember.'

All lies, of course, but I think Thérèse believed them, at any rate she'd believe them while she was telling me. From that night on she would sometimes ask me to hold her and promise, 'Promise,' she'd repeat in her most serious voice, not to let her go until she was asleep. The worst I could do was fail her in this.

We spent over three months in Paris, then, one morning near the end of October, I was woken by the slam of the front door echoing back to me along the length of the corridor. One-zero-two-five was red-numbered in the darkness. Near enough the middle of the night. No Thérèse, she must have gone on one of her 'surprise' errands. Someone was kicking their way down the living-room path towards our bedroom.

The door was thrown open, the curtains wrenched back and there stood Thérèse: washed, dressed, teeth cleaned, and hair brushed in the morning sunlight.

'Happy Birthday!'

Was I dreaming? 'Eh?'

'One for you, one for me.' She was waving two white envelopes in the air, 'Catch!'

It landed on the pillow, but before I could pick it up she'd rushed over and was kneeling on the bed, her hand covering the packet. Like in the kids' game I put a hand on hers, then she on mine and lastly I pressed down to hold the pillar of hands steady.

'It's not my birthday till –'

'Ssh!' She leant forward, her hair falling like a screen behind which she kissed my hand. When she sat up again she looked very serious. Not little-girl serious either, but very, very grown-up. 'If you don't want it, you're free to cash it in.' She paused, bit her lip, took a deep breath: 'And that will be that, I suppose.'

Breaking up the game we lifted back our hands one at a time. Without saying anything else she gave me the envelope and watched me open it.

For the rest of the day she told me about her life in Australia. Because of immigration bureaucracy she had to go back there to renew her papers – her time was up in two months.

We were walking up to Montmartre. It was a chill day, a grey sky patched with watery-looking clouds and the sun spattering colour almost at random. The last of the year's 'Scènes de Paris' hung from the railings, a rather dog-eared, windblown-looking collection. Tourists rushed across the *place*, pursued by artists in their official berets, moustaches and black corduroy, clutching clipboards for ten-second portraits in charcoal and rain.

She'd already told me a little about her mother, Claudine, who, she now added, was nice-looking, considering her age. 'You'll probably fancy her!' she laughed as we turned towards the Sacré-Coeur. Her stepfather had taken her and Claudine away from France to start a new life in Australia. 'I was only seven and hated, hated, hated it.' There was real venom in her voice, then she grinned: 'I didn't speak for two years – only French. I refused.' A grin of little-girl triumph.

We had sat down on the steps outside the church. A view over the whole of Paris, almost deserted of tourists in the late afternoon apart from a murmur of Japanese posing and clicking their way down to a waiting bus. Below us, an unreal smoggy mist covered the city, making the stone buildings, the patchy blue sky and the Seine in the distance look like another 'Scène' that hadn't been sold. It was starting to turn even chillier so I put my arm around her. She shivered:

'We'll be there in time for summer. Real summer, not this northern apology.'

Then she told me about Currawinya. 'In Aborigine it means "where the two rivers meet".' It was a place in the wilderness where she had friends who lived back to nature.

'Old hippies?'

'No, this is the real thing. They build their own houses, grow their own food, trap and fish. A bit like paradise.'

Despite everything that has happened since that moment of hope and togetherness on the steps of the Sacré-Coeur, I can still remember Thérèse's voice just inches away, snuggled into my coat out of the cold, telling me what it would be like here. The wild horses, the clear water, the parrots, wild budgerigars. Yes, it's even more beautiful than she described, and far crueller than either of us could have imagined.

I love Paris

Marie Darrieussecq

I love Paris. It's the only city where I could possibly live. Because one of the great things about France is the centralisation: everything is in Paris. My husband is in Paris. My editor is in Paris. My thesis director is in Paris. My best friend is in Paris. My friends are in Paris. My house is in Paris. My cat is in Paris. My goldfish is in Paris. My bakery is in Paris. My computer is in Paris. My post office is in Paris. My email is in Paris. My shrink is in Paris. And even my address is in Paris. In short, in Paris everything is to hand. It's marvellously well organised.

In the beginning it was much more complicated: indeed, I was born a long way away from Paris, at the point where the frontier meets the ocean, tucked away in a corner. I had to study for a long time and take lots of trains, I even had to wait for the TGV Atlantique to be constructed, in short I had to wait until it occurred to someone to release me, before I could come to Paris. You can imagine how tired I was, how torn; I couldn't live, not without Paris. My house had been standing since the nineteenth century, my husband had been born twenty years previously, my cat's great-great-grandmother was already quivering with desire for the aforesaid's great-great-grandfather, my baker was vigorously kneading dough for baguettes I wouldn't be eating, and my shrink hadn't yet met me, which he greatly regretted. As for my best friend, constantly by my side, she was impatient to get on: she had the same problem as me. We were born in the same place, in that little corner a long way from Paris. Our lives were becoming increasingly complex.

Fortunately, everything fell into place and turned out for the best. I live in the only city where I could possibly live. There are magnificent parks and gardens, as many cinemas as you could want, museums, shops, smart avenues, colourful neighbourhoods, and Parisians everywhere. I often walk around underneath the Tour Eiffel, between its four great arms. I head right for the middle, I look up and fall into the big hole that is the centre of the world. There are Japanese who come here for this reason alone; but afterwards they have to go and get on a plane and go an awful long way away. When I think that all of this has been put there for me, provincial girl that I was, abandoned and huddled up in my corner, I tell myself that life is beautiful, that the world is extremely well put together and that everything in it functions to perfection.

Translated from the French by Nicholas Royle

Debauchery

Adam Thorpe

When I first came to Paris, in 1956, I felt like a refugee. My family were rich and stifling, part of a great Boston clan, something out of Henry James with the addition of electric gadgets and tupperware bowls, television and Saran Wrap. These things didn't sit well with their cut-glass accents, but I didn't like the accent either. I didn't even like the Oldsmobile Ninety-Eights in the garage. I wanted something else, but I wasn't sure what that was. I stood there on the Pont du Carrouse and looked down into the still grey water that first morning in Paris and thought to myself: I want to be wicked, *poetically* wicked. Only I didn't know how.

My coat was all wrong. It was smart and wool with a wide collar, it looked expensive because it *was* expensive. There was a cold wind blowing with some light rain but I took the coat off and dangled it for a moment over the edge. It was a Sunday, there were very few people around. In those days there was so little traffic you could wash a car on the lower *quais*, stroll among the pigeons, savour the low hum that was almost a silence, hear the bells coming from far away. Now the sides of the river are like freeways apparently. There's no room for anyone.

I left the coat on the parapet, rolled up neatly. I was too decent a guy to drop it into the river. Hemingway would have done that. But the rain was dampening my hair and darkening my suit – it was a beginning. I wanted to go downhill a little, unbutton myself and look disarrayed, but honest to God – don't laugh – I didn't even know where the damn hill was, let alone how to go down it. I'd always been high up on this kind of plateau. My birthright. I was intelligent, I tested well, I was smothered in Ivy League values like a young sapling planted in the wrong place. I had a year free in front of me before I took the legal track, straight towards the heavy oak doors of the family law firm. Once they'd shut behind me, there'd be no going back. My parents were paying for this year. I don't know now whether they knew what Paris stood for, what might happen to a callow youth let loose there.

The best way to improve your French, my uncle told me on my departure, was to translate Racine. But I could translate Racine in Boston, I replied. A flicker of some subdued panic passed behind his eyes. He'd been in the last war, in Normandy. He'd seen France after the Liberation. Perhaps he'd gotten unbuttoned too, for a time.

I made it to the end of the bridge and then I glanced back at my coat. It looked so neat and well-behaved there, I felt disgusted at myself. I ran back and swept it with a pitcher's toss down into the river, where it kind of curled up slowly and sank with its arms spread out. There were two lovers in their Sunday best standing on the path below but they never looked up.

I made straight for the Latin Quarter. The tug-boats were hooting and the cobbles were wet and slippery, the light mist made everything almost industrial. It was a weird moment. There were ragged humps with bottles lying in the lee of the *quai*, mumbling or snorting, and a few guys fishing off the bank down below. There was someone getting their poodle to swim, but it didn't like it. The first leaves were dropping. Smart women walked by with their dogs, both species with their noses in the air. The women were muffled in furs but still elegant on high heels, clicking past me one after the other as I advanced with a beating heart toward what I could only think of as my destiny.

The cold and wet of Paris was soaking in. I mussed my hair, but it was too short to muss properly. As I crossed the place Saint Michel I vowed to grow it long. Then I had to consult my tourist map. It was given to me at the hotel, where I was staying until I found suitable lodgings. My hotel was on the quai d'Orsay. In those days suitable rooms could be rented cheap even on the quai d'Orsay. As I struggled with my map in the wind off the river, trying to figure out exactly where the Latin Quarter started in case I missed it, I pictured this garret and me inside it, painting or writing poetry. I was stained with oil paints, ink, the juices of the streets and boulevards, you name it. I was *living*.

Not clean-living but *dirty*-living. Europe was old and dirty, we all knew that. That's why my fellow Americans were such notorious tenants: they left their apartments looking dirty and broken because that's what they thought Europe expected. No one else could figure this out, but I could. A cream-and-blue bus, open at the back, flicked its tyres over the wet cobbles, *flicker-flacker-flicker-flacker-flicker-flacker-flick* – one of those crazy Parisian mating calls of the old days. I responded. The map crumpled in my hands. I knew where the Latin Quarter was: it was in my heart.

I was feeling really mushy by now, so I stopped at the first café I came across, near Saint Severin, and ordered a coffee and a pastry. The place was almost empty, but it was warm. I was so green that I tipped the waiter. We Americans still think that money buys smiles, but all it does is spoil the fruit of the soul. Then I explored, looking around for this hill, the garret, some tight buttons to fumble at inside my head. I liked the little dead-end alleys most of all. Paris was darker in those days, blacker, it had a deep smell of drains, there was undifferentiated poverty, a shabby-genteel joy that had drawn itself out like a greasy greatcoat's thread all the way from the nineteenth century. Everyone old back then in the fifties was not of our world, they were born elsewhere, in some other time, before technology and American ease and the glide of cars. This guy with the white hair, he might have passed Mallarmé or Baudelaire. That old dame with the moustache, she might have slept with Auguste Rodin. Rimbaud or Verlaine or both at once might have heard this legless guy blowing his flute through his nose.

I remember that legless guy, he was there most days that year, I got used to him like I've got used to wealthy nuts in a thousand divorce cases since. But he'd jerk his head like a maniac and I couldn't stand the sound that first time, the guy looked like a grub, he was completely bald, all you could see was the top of his glistening head. They were washing the street and the soapy water sailed past his stumps, making a stream between us. There was the damp, soapy smell of a Sunday morning in Paris, with grey-black buildings and somebody singing high up and this jerky head with a flute stuck in one nostril, wailing and whistling over alien shouts down the street. There was me, fumbling for foreign coins, feeling so young and American and excited and lonely and disgusted all at the same time. Frightened, even. Frightened by the prospect of so much life in front of me, this strange land I would have to negotiate in strange tongues. Shivering without my coat.

I scurried back to the hotel and ordered up my first pernod ever. To go.

Then I fell asleep in that heavy, linen-scented room, on that big double bed, and tipped my drink over. A lonely American from Boston, still suffering *décalage d'heure* or maybe just too much champagne and turbulence in the downstairs bar of the Pan American Stratocruiser, President class. Paris rumbled and snored outside through the afternoon, dropping fall leaves into the sweet mush. I dreamed I was a plane tree along a flicketty-flacketty boulevard, growing up through my ironwork doily, its spokes trapping cigarette-ends and gum and torn pages of newspapers. I had one last leaf and I wasn't letting it go, not even when my father and mother hugged my trunk and shook it. The leaf turned into a bird and flew off over the grey shining roofs and towers. I tried to join it, but the metal doily wouldn't budge. Then I changed into a curvy *pissoir* and nearly wet myself. When I woke up properly I felt like death. I would go do it with a prostitute, I decided. In one fell swoop I would gut my moral well-being.

A small excursion into the Mouffetard that night yielded no more than a fellow American, drinking a secretive absinthe through a sugar lump. It was outlawed, absinthe, but he knew the right places, the under-the-counter places. I tried it (it was not to my taste) while enduring the guy's drone. He came from Missouri, was here as a clerk in the war, had never gone back. He and the *patron* talked about the war, about power cuts and painted stockings, how the rich got by and the poor got cold and hungry, how even tobacco was so short the *patrons* would collect up the butt-ends at the evening's end. I started to feel good, heady with the absinthe; the place smelt of musky baskets, like the pantry at home. My fellow countryman, who was about sixty and bald with wet eyes from his cheroot, started checking out my knee. I looked down and there was this hand sliding on to my crotch. I fled, stumbling on the step. Laughter in my wake. I didn't even recognise the hill when I was standing on it, I was so green.

I explored some more, after a day or two hiking through the galleries and museums. I checked out the Folies Bergères; these slim beauties with glitter on their nipples dangled on floats in front of me, but I felt like a kid. There were deeper places of pleasure with steep steps but I was too chicken, and I didn't even figure for a while that the women on the sidewalk with tight skirts and cardigans and black gloves were whores. I hadn't pictured cardigans. Mom wore woollen cardigans, but these cardigans were kind of sharp and thrusting. The bright-red mouths did not look easy to kiss, they had this sardonic curve and kept opening up to yawn. Sometimes they whistled at me, jeered in some language I couldn't identify. Then I realised they were calling out to me in English. They were as awesome as the giant cut-out of Marilyn Monroe in her flowery underthings, the height of three storeys. It towered over this sober queue of men and women in hats waiting for the evening movie, all looking over at me as if I was to blame for something. STRIP-TEASE STRIP-TEASE flashed in neon down the next street, straight off some lousy dive back home. Then a student sitting next to me in a jazz concert told me that Paris had been raped not by Germans but by Americans. He was a Red with thick spectacles and I hated myself for feeling hurt.

I found a room to rent in a side-street off the place Maubert. Too bad that a greasy slate roof hid the view of Notre Dame's spire. It wasn't a real garret, more a dirty top-floor hole out of Dostoevsky, but it was cheap. I was reading *Crime and Punishment* and Raskolnikov's student cupboard was my model. It meant I had plenty of extra money: I wanted to slide in style. What I liked about Raskolnikov was his total existentialism. I had already studied Sartre and Camus back home and had now bought myself a black polo-neck sweater and black trousers and black brothel-creepers. My new coat was what the English call a 'duffel'. My hair was growing out and I wasn't washing it every day. I had the uniform, but I lacked the confidence to volunteer. Debauchery meant tearing buttons off your best shirt. Buttons sewn on by your Mom. I liked my shirt too much, if not my Mom.

The room was not free until the end of the month. Every day I received a letter from my folks, with news of everything I wanted to forget back home and a reminder to write and to bathe daily. I should have torn them up but even Raskolnikov read his Mom's letters. Then one arrived telling me about Cousin Ingeborg's apartment. Cousin Ingeborg was extremely rich and a bit nuts, and had shacked up with some Count in this palace near Seville. She had an apartment on the rue Bonaparte in St-Germain-des-Prés. She wanted me to 'sit it' for her until the end of the summer – around when I was going back home. This apartment was unbelievable, stacked with Louis XV furniture and even older tapestries and works by the School of Fragonard and a Boucher sketch and all that stuff. It smelt of floorwax and expensive scent. There were two maids and a cook on tap. It was all mine in return for keeping it warm and watering her ferns.

This was terrible. It was a terrible decision to have to make. I balanced the Raskolnikov hole with its bad drains and the swell suite with its marble sweep of stairs and came down on the swell one day and the hole the next. But the most debauched guy in *Crime and Punishment* is the one who shoots himself at the gates of St Petersburg. He had land, an estate, horses. I could be Byronic about my debauchery. Raskolnikov was a miserable, murderous runt, anyway. I could be lavish in my slide, I could be existential with gold-plated taps and rebellious with silk pillows. I mean, I could become *notorious*. I was standing under a copper-green cherub on the Pont Alexander and I felt myself smile evilly.

It was right at that moment that I saw him.

He was walking very slowly and kind of dazedly toward me over the bridge. He was a tramp. There were thousands of them in those days, they had their own little empires along the river. He had a beard and a cap and this stick which he didn't use to walk, and a long coat I knew very well. It was my coat. It was like watching myself walking toward me – myself in twenty, thirty, fifty years' time. It was my own phantom come to haunt me out of the future. I was frightened again, I wanted to run. Then he stopped and stabbed the ground with his stick and lifted it and took something off the end. It reminded me of the park attendants back home, harpooning fallen leaves off the lawns. He opened his – my – coat and put away whatever his stick had picked up. There was great deliberation in his actions. I know that deliberation. A lawyer has it, a business executive, an engineer, a surgeon. It's the mark of a professional engaged in his life's task. I didn't have that yet, not then. I was still one hundred per cent amateur.

I let him pass. There was a big bottle in his pocket. He had fished my coat from the water or maybe it had snagged on a fisherman's rod – whichever, he had salvaged my coat and taken it over, including the pockets. I'd worn this coat right through Yale, it was a birthday gift from my grandparents. Now there was a bottle stopped up with paper bulging out its pocket. Had I emptied the coat completely before dumping it in the river? Maybe there'd been some old loose change in there, a few cents or a dime, a dirty handkerchief, sticks of gum, a ticket-stub for a game. I caught the smell of spirits and body odour as he passed – and something else, something muskier, almost sweet. Off of his back hung one of those little accordions they call a *musette*.

I followed him. It wasn't easy, he kept stopping and stabbing at the ground with his stick. I remember the glistening fish-scale cobbles, the slabs, the uneven stones, and this stick with a long pin tied on the end, harpooning butt-ends. He only picked up butt-ends. He picked one up off an Eiffel Tower chalked in yellow on the sidewalk and the artist thanked him. He did it all with such deliberation that I became hypnotised, Paris fell away around me into something else, something totally outside of us both. He was wearing my coat. I had this strange, unpleasant sensation of familiarity with him, and also a kind of resentment, as if my coat had been stolen. Each time he came to a bench he would crouch and do some more stabbing underneath. Women would shift their legs, as if they knew him, as if this was an ancient custom. Old men would growl but shift their legs too. He was filling a bag of patched cloth underneath the coat. The sweet smell he'd had was of tobacco. His stick kind of flickered – so deft, so tried and tested was this action. But the closer I got, the more I saw how old he was. He shuffled and was dazed more with age than drink. Nobody drunk could have been so deft.

The only time he showed interest in anything other than his pickings was when he stopped by a movie poster near the Odéon. The poster showed a grinning and big-mouthed variety dancer with long curly locks baring her thigh under her flounced skirts. *Les Nuits de Montmartre*, it said, showing in Eastmancolor. In the background was this mean-looking fellow in a raincoat, wielding a pistol. I blushed with shame as I loitered in a doorway on the other side of the street, waiting for the old man to move. I thought of myself as the mean-looking fellow, desperate for action, for some Paris thigh. I'd been dreaming these dreams and this ugly movie poster mocked them, showed them for what they were. *Eastmancolor. Cinepanoramic.* And the old tramp in my coat was telling me this. Why otherwise had he stopped? I thought: this guy has been sent, like an angel or a devil, to teach me about myself.

The door behind me opened and a fat woman in a flowery skirt emptied her suds on the step as if she hadn't seen me. I hopped off and she laughed and the laughter echoed off the stone buildings. This woke the old tramp out of his dream. He shot a glance at me and then he carried on walking. It was evening by now, my feet were tired, but this guy took me along the café terraces of all the main streets and boulevards of the Latin Quarter. The night was warm for early October, warm enough to sit outside. He threaded his way between the tables like a shadow, stooping, stabbing from side to side, while I hovered like the shadow of a shadow out of the lights. Now and again a mean-eyed *garçon* would shoo him away or give him a squirt out of a soda syphon. Most of the time he was tolerated, greeted with a name – even an occasional bite to eat, which he instantly pocketed. I only realised it was his name because it was repeated so many times. It was le Père la Pêche. Or maybe it was one word and didn't mean anything. Just the name he was born with.

I stumbled through that night like a madman in a stupor. I had this idea, this *idée fixe*, that if I lost sight of him I would lose my soul. I was hungry, but I didn't eat. At about three o'clock we were in the slums of Les Halles. He squatted on a pile of rubble and rubbish and worked his way through the morsels given to him by the cafés and restaurants. His bag lolled, fat as a pregnant woman's belly, through my coat. No – *his* coat! Occasionally he'd glance up but his face was in shadow and I was huddled in my duffel further along the alley, by an overflowing dustbin that attracted cats and stank of piss and rotten vegetables. Cries came from nowhere, echoing and dying on the night air. Metal shutters slammed shut and there were high-pitched rows, or maybe they weren't rows. A woman, probably a whore, clapped by briskly on high heels. Her black bag was like our doctor's medical bag back home, only much smaller. She kept her head down and clapped by us like she didn't want to know, like she was afraid. She'd have reckoned I was a tramp, a *clochard*, a *pochard*. I ran these French words through my head as we ran through other words in the first classes I'd attended that week in the language school. If Mom could see me now! I didn't smoke, it hurt my throat, but I was wishing I'd gotten into the habit. Cousin Ingeborg's apartment was burning in my head, the swell pictures and furniture were engulfed in flames, the tapestries were charring and falling off the walls, the whole damn place was blazing. I was cold, but the fire was burning in my head. Meanwhile my familiar was chewing slowly, scrabbling about in his pockets. Then his sack became his bed and he slept right there, snoring and mumbling and coughing.

I was very angry about this. It wasn't safe for me to sleep here. It was a slum. I couldn't sleep. I could work my way back to the hotel, it wasn't very far, I could wake up the hotel porter and sink into my bed, my cotton sheets. I could be warm (the night had turned chill, now we'd stopped). But if I did this, I would lose him. It was a test, sticking it out, sticking to him. For once I had an aim, a challenge. If this beat me, then my whole life would beat me. My father and my uncle had been in the war, I remembered them being away and Mom crying quietly a lot of the time. They had both been lightly injured but they could have been killed, hundreds and thousands of Americans had been killed. There was a Red in our town, he ran the hardware store; before he was arrested he told me that very few Americans had been killed compared to the millions of our comrades in the Soviet Union and elsewhere. We had not been bombed, he said, we had not been bombed out of our sleep or lined up against a wall and shot, our women had not been raped and our kids had not been slaughtered in front of our eyes, our villages and towns had not been put to the torch. All this had happened in Europe. Sitting there in the slum alley, where there were gaps like the bombsites I'd seen in my stopover in London, I was suddenly afraid of Europe. Afraid of its hot women and cold nights, its strange tongues, its old dazed knowingness. I wanted the clean reliability of home. The fixtures that held me in a groove. And as soon as I wanted it, I knew I'd lost it. Because this man had led me to a place where I could want it as if it was outside of me.

When dawn came we both woke up. There was a trickling sound everywhere, as if it was raining. It was dry and clear. He shuffled off without looking at me and I followed him. He made straight for the river. The trickling sound was the streets being washed, the water sluiced along the gutters like the beginnings of a flood. Every day in this city started clean, I realised. It was a forgiving city. My limbs were half-frozen but movement warmed them, the fresh peeks of light through the mist excited me. I had never known the strange pleasure of a night passed outside without shelter, the triumph of passing it through your body and surviving, as if your skin has soaked up the juices of being alive as it's soaked up the juices of the city; the raw exhilaration of survival, of not ceding to the night's throat. The intense little victory that another day drums inside you – you who have previously taken the days as given, barely noting them as they meld into weeks and months and years until you're old and grey and it's too late.

He stopped by the river, near the Pont Neuf, down on the quai de l'Horloge where in those days you could hear the ticking of a bicycle or the plop of fishbait even when the rest of Paris was bustling and tooting. I leaned against the stone column of the bridge and watched from just a few yards away. It was only then, as he was cutting open his harvest, his catch, gutting them like tiny fish, husking them like barley, that he addressed me.

'*Je sais ce que tu veux,*' he said. 'You've heard about me.'

He wasn't looking up but it had to be me he was talking to, there was no one else. I came over and squatted on my heels and denied having heard anything about him. My voice came out like a little boy's. A name-tab was peeking out from under his lapel, above the inside pocket. It was mine. Mom had stitched it in. *James Sherman King, Jr.*

'English?'

'American.'

He grunted. He was reaching into the bag and pulling out each butt-end, cigar or cigarette, and slicing it open with the smallest Opinel in the range. The *musette* lay next to him. Its keys were like old yellow teeth, grinning at me. Some of the cigars were huge, slices of best American cured tobacco. The mist was rising off the river, the light was pearl. For some time we said nothing. I just watched him. It was very fine watching him. I felt I knew him better than anyone else in the world. It was the dawn of my new life, I thought to myself. But what exactly did he know I wanted? What *did* I want? Not my coat, certainly not that. I didn't even want to tell him about the coat: he would think I'd want it back, which I sure as hell did not. I wanted something deep and different and here it was, it was happening. He was making two piles on some sheets of newspaper. He pulled out small lumps of pipe tobacco like my father's dottle – they must have been dottle, knocked out against shoes as the smokers chatted and laughed on the terraces. This and the cigars' innards made one pile. The cigarette tobacco lay by itself in the second pile. There was care and industry in what he was doing.

'Americans, I know the Americans,' he said. His voice was so hoarse and deep everything emerged on a growl, I wasn't certain of his tone. His fingers were busy. The piles grew. A breeze lifted the edges of the newspaper around the stones that were holding them in place, the tobacco stirring like the fur of something alive. 'They always want things easy. But you are all lost. You are like *le Fou.*'

'Le Fou?'

He looked at me. He smiled for the first time. He had about five teeth.

'Le Fou,' he said again. 'How could you not know him?'

'I don't know anyone in Paris, not in the whole city.'

This was amazing to him. It was especially amazing to him that I didn't know le Fou, the nut, the most famous nut of the Latin Quarter. He had rat skins and mole skins stitched on his rags, his wand was topped with dead mice, he had hens' feet for feathers on his cap and a little tortoise shell bouncing on his belly. It was just as amazing I didn't know Sidi, Sidi with his obscene tattoos, mostly of his mistresses. Or Eugène le Foetus stinking of alcohol, selling his decaying foetuses out of a sack to painters and scribblers who liked the bones. Or Sapeck the practical joker with his ape's face and tiny dog or the poet Georges Caubel de la Ville-Hingat treating the ladies for venereal disorders or Coulet with his crazy monologues and dirty prints. It's amazing I could be alive and not know these people. Not know le Marquis de Soudin hawking his pencil portraits around the tables for 50 centimes or the blind seller of paper windmills in the Jardins du Luxembourg or the anarchist cobbler le Père la Purge or the would-be poets shuffling around like ghosts smelling of hashish and ether or Pharaoh with his glistening black locks selling his miraculous hair restorer or Amédée Cloux the pasticheur or Victor Sainbault hawking his verse in the crowds under the electric lights or the huge nymphomaniac at the Château-Rouge shouting, *Qu'est-ce que vous voulez, moi, quand j'tronche pas j'suis malade!*

'I haven't seen any of these people,' I said.

Amazed that I'd never heard Fifi l'Absinthe and Gaston Trois-Pattes singing and strumming in the Père Lunette with its crazy murals or had never picked my way through the rag-and-bone market of the rue Saint Médard between the chipped vases, the deformed corsets, the risqué novels and the rusty tools, brushing with my shoulder the firmness of laughing girls in their tight calico. Never never never. Amazing. I roamed the Latin Quarter looking for these people in the morning and listened to him in the afternoon. For about a week I did this. I saw only drunks and sidewalk artists and beggars and shabby street musicians. I didn't want to tell him that I hadn't seen them. I began to feel personally afflicted, I started to feel screwed up. Then he happened to mention the whores in their long skirts. Long skirts? Not cardigans?

In their loose frilly blouses. Frilly blouses? Their corsets with pink ribbons. Corsets? Had he seen *The Nights of Montmartre* after all?

No, this was not a movie.

Maybe it was a litany, maybe he gave the spiel to everyone like a guide does to a coach party, but I didn't care and I still don't. It was taken up again whenever I visited, which was nearly every day that first month. He growled it out like a tune on an accordion, a tune from sixty years before, from the last century, from the golden age. I didn't mind that all these people were long gone, long dead. Their echoes stayed. One time, walking back to the hotel through the place Saint Michel, I passed a blind man standing by a table on which a small gramophone player was playing a scratchy tune. Progress! But the old man's growl was like that record; it just needed me around to place the needle. The tobacco was damp with saliva and the night: I'd watch the piles of it grow, I'd watch him spread it out to dry in the sun when it was sunny, I'd watch him crouch on the steps and ease his boots off and wash his socks and shirt in the river, I'd watch him eat the cakes I'd bought – I'd watch him do all these things as if I was waiting for something beyond the lost world he was summoning back. It was like he was working toward something. Three weeks in, I sensed a change of tone, an alertness, an urgency. This was that something.

First of all, he became aggressive. Then he became personal. He included himself. I already knew, watching him and listening, how things had faded in his life, that when he said that once there had been thirty or forty in his line, how his *métier* had once been a proud one, he wasn't boasting. It was the truth. I even believed him when he said that he was the last *ramasseur de mégots* in Paris, that the *clochards* who picked up butt-ends and smoked them didn't count. He told me how the tobacco market had hung on in the place Maubert until the last war, when even butt-ends became scarce (and I remembered what that guy had told me over his absinthe, about the *patrons* gleaning the butt-ends for themselves, and felt the pieces come together and knowledge grow). Now the old man's stall was a couple of upturned crates on the quai de l'Horloge, and his buyers clutched their fiddles or their perambulators full of old clothes and bargained him down.

I guess he was legendary, and I was privileged. He would set out his stall at four o'clock in the afternoon and play his *musette* behind it. Tourists took snapshots, but tourists were fewer in those days. Some of them were American. I kept my mouth shut in case they'd realise I wasn't a guy born in the juices of Paris, with its bitumen and dust in my veins. I'd sit against the wire fence where the trees were and watch the boats go by, the tug-boats and barges and the *bateaux mouches* winking their glass in the sunlight. It was a fine autumn. Or maybe I'm just remembering it that way. I'd buy us coffee and croissants. I'd buy enough tobacco from him for a couple of cigarettes and roll my own, trying not to think about the spittle dried on the shag's threads, wondering how polio and syphilis were caught and then coughing and laughing at myself – loving this, loving le Père la Pêche, loving Paris, loving our lost world from the last century I could wander through with just a word, a nudge, a question.

I was a couple of days away from the final decision on the room. That's when his tone changed. It was after breakfast and a sunny morning, the water flickering and the leaves ablaze. I had a letter from Mom in my pocket. It wondered why I hadn't written, fretting about Cousin Ingeborg in Spain, who needed to know. I was pulling on a cigarette plump with cigar tobacco. A pretty girl passed and smiled at me. Le Père la Pêche had drunk too much of his sour liquor the previous night and his old eyes were very red, his movements were slow. I'd been working out how old he was: eighty, he must be eighty, because he remembered the brothels in the 1880s like he wasn't a kid then, he remembered the pungent powdered whores and their fixed-rate kisses like he'd actually picked their *fleurs du mal*! I was smiling after the pretty girl and feeling good and grown up and quoting Baudelaire to myself when le Père la Pêche came over from shredding his wares and held my elbow in a mittened grip that was almost painful. My reverie was broken. I choked, inhaling too swiftly. There was madness in his eyes.

'*Mon p'tit Indien* –' (that's what he called me, I liked it) 'I cannot stand it any longer. You are breaking me. You are here to steal.'

I was so taken aback, I couldn't find the French.

'You are watching me all the time, I know why you are watching me all the time. Don't you think I know these tricks? You've heard in your country of le Père la Pêche, of what he – '

Here the old man looked about him, let go my arm. But his eyes were still wild under his matted fringe. Then he brought his face very close to mine. The liquor was still hot on his breath. He never smoked.

This was the first time I realised that he never smoked, because there was nothing on his breath but liquor. His voice was a hiss.

'– of what he has for the *right man!*'

My look of total perplexity, a hint of tears even (the aggression was that sudden), must have persuaded him of my ignorance. He was old and knew how faces work. As I stammered some kind of reply, his suspicion relaxed into a distant smile.

'What *do* you have?' I asked finally, like a kid.

He took out a small tin from the inner pocket of the coat. (Not ever mentioning the coat gave me a secret feeling of intimacy with him.)

'This,' he said.

His hand was trembling. It had never trembled before, despite his age and drinking habit. Now it trembled so much he nearly dropped the tin. It was dented and pocked with rust, and the style of the smoker's clothes on the faded label dated it to the era he had opened up for me. And now he was opening the tin.

'*Voilà*,' he whispered, like a magician.

Inside was a cigar, three-quarter smoked. Something about it made me think that it had not been picked up yesterday, despite the musty aroma of tobacco. It looked almost fossilised, had the blank dead look of something in a museum case. I made to pick it out but he snapped the lid shut, almost on my fingers.

'Bibi la Purée,' he said, sitting on the slabs next to me. 'I must begin with Bibi.'

We watched the river. He told me that Bibi was the weirdest, the king of the weirdos. High gleaming forehead, piles of hair, no beard, a cadaverous face that should have been seen over footlights. He dressed like an old rake, a dandy – except when he was playing at being a blind beggar in front of Saint-Sulpice, when he'd don a frock. You'd see him sitting at a café table under his top hat, winking at everybody – then he'd suddenly leap up with a shoecare set in his hand and start waxing a lady customer's boots, planting a kiss on her stockinged ankle as a preliminary, her big skirts falling around his ears. *Ah, cher Bibi!* No one knew where he slept, but for eight days in the year he would pour all his savings into a hired suite of rooms, keeping open house, girl students drifting in and out like concubines.

Le Père la Pêche gave a great sigh. Amazing that I didn't know Bibi! Then he gripped the tin tighter in his stained hands. It was some kind of talisman, drawing him closer to whatever had lain beyond everything we had shared these last weeks.

He explained how Bibi would hang around some of the big guys of the *quartier*, the important poets and painters and thinkers, doing odd jobs and running messages. One of these big guys was Paul Verlaine. (I nodded: Verlaine's poems lost me but I knew he was extremely renowned.) The week after Verlaine's death in the winter of '96, Bibi set up a stall selling some articles belonging to the great man: his silk handkerchief, his calling card, his tin of shoe wax, a curl of his beard off the barber-shop floor, and the cane he wobbled around on towards the end, wracked by syphilis. Bibi did good business, and each day there were more of these treasures. But when the sixth tin of Verlaine's shoe wax appeared, fervour snapped to suspicion and Bibi packed up for want of custom. Le Père la Pêche raised the tin in his hand. The morning sun gleamed on its dull grey metal.

'I never told him, not then,' he said. 'His prices were too low.'

'What did you not tell him?'

'I told him afterwards, when the whole charade was long finished. But he didn't believe me. He laughed, *mon p'tit Indien!* Laughed in my face! He was guarding bicycles outside some café or other on the boul' San' Mich', I forget which one. Got up in a bolero, tartan stockings, spurs on his heels, chauffeur's cap on his head. Ridiculous!'

'No one dresses like that any more,' I said. I felt the weight of seriousness in my dark, existentialist clothes like I was in water and needed to struggle free.

'Laughed in my face! The d'Harcourt, that was it, always full of women, it was a women's café and the men were there to oblige them. With *sous*, my friend! I told him what I had seen.'

There was a pause. He was looking older and tireder than he was when I first knew him, and that was only three weeks ago. He was kind of bundled up on the slabs next to me, staring down.

'What did you see?' I said, gently.

'Verlaine was staggering up rue Racine smoking his cigar. I knew his face, this strange face with its Chinese eyes and bulging forehead and sharp whiskers – a bit like Comrade Lenin, now I think of it. I knew all their faces, of course, *mon p'tit agneau américain*, all the great scribblers and daubers. But he was alone. He took a last puff and dropped his cigar, coughing like a sick child. He disappeared around the corner, tap-tap-tap with his cane, shivering all over. He was a sick man, sick with the clap, like most of them. Dead within the week. The whole *quartier* mourned. Never read a word of him, mind. But I fished his butt-end like any other, that evening in the rue Racine, just like any other. It was only when I came to gutting my catch that I thought to myself: here, this is Verlaine's smoke, I'll hang on to that, there are strange folk about who like souvenirs of great men. So I found a little tin for it and then he was dead and then there was Bibi doing a roaring trade in fakes. This American soldier – the first cock-up I'm talking about, back in '18 – he loved poetry, he offered me a hundred francs for this if I could prove it was Monsieur Verlaine's. Prove it – I ask you! Who did he think I was? Bibi la Purée?'

He spat and growled an obscenity I hadn't covered in class. He stroked the tin with his dirty hand. The sweet cud of his body-smell enveloped me. I told him that I would buy it from him without proof because I knew him and trusted him. He looked at me with a suspicious grin, his teeth as yellow as his little accordion's. Perhaps he had engineered this whole moment, but I didn't care. In an instant I had decided what I must do, the one time in my life that true inspiration has ever come to me, whole, like a heavy gem. He gave me a price that was very high – I blush to quote it now. OK, it was a month's expenditure. I realised immediately that he wanted to keep it, that he expected me to balk, to back off. But I think now he was working in an old tradition: the rag-and-bone men of the rue Saint Médard would always sell at a third of the asking price, in the old times.

I didn't even beat him down. I came with the cash the next day, a fat bundle of notes. He was dealing with a shabby customer who had nothing but an old Vichy franc on him. I asked to see it, and bounced the thing in my hand – it was as light as play money. Dated 1942, when I was still a little kid. *Travail, Famille, Patrie*, and a sprig of oak-leaves. Exactly the values my own folks expounded. They didn't seem tall any more. Le Père la Pêche took the coin from me and spat on it and threw it over his shoulder. Tainted, I guess. The shabby customer plodded off without a word. I produced the notes and he stared at them in astonishment.

'For Verlaine's *mégot*,' I said. Verlaine's butt, in the version I make people laugh with.

'*C'est pas possible, mon p'tit –*'

'*B'en ouai, c'est possible.*'

He looked at me and laughed. Then he coughed. Blood dribbled out on to his beard. He wiped it off as if it was spittle. The last one of his kind. The last dodo. Where would he die? Right here. By the great river where he stretches out on the warm stone on nice afternoons and dreams with his beard pointing towards the sky, still, in my own dreams. He's done it now for over a century, and will do so until the parapet crumbles under him along with the rest, into rubble and weeds.

We did the deal. He didn't count the notes, just stuffed them into the coat. I took the tin, checked its contents, and said I would be back after the weekend. He clapped my hand as they used to do in the markets, carried on laughing and waving on the *quai* until I lost him to sight.

I walked out to the rue Racine and waited there until dark, sipping a big milk coffee and then a few pernods in a corner café where this black guy was playing some doleful sax. I walked up and down a bit, tipsy, thinking of everything le Père la Pêche had told me. At some point a gaggle of students bumped me as they were running past and the tin was knocked into the gutter, but it didn't open.

It was after midnight. The sax had stopped. A whore stood at the corner, scowling out of her heavy mascara. She was smoking. As I came up to her she kind of wiggled, with the usual stupid little bag in her hand. She was clothed too light, in a one-piece woollen dress buckled high with a thick black belt; her high heels clicked on the cobbles and she even smelt high above the scent. The wiggling was like some terrible dance, which had been spectacular once and was now faded to something so small it was grotesque. I asked her for a light, prising the tin open. I held Verlaine's cigar up to her silver lighter and drew on the butt. The flavour of the Latin Quarter of all those years ago, the whole *belle époque* of it, sank down my throat and filled my mouth and nose. Every drag drew me closer. It was Verlaine's breath in mine. I was more intimate than anyone could ever be with the past. Time was my whore.

I walked away from the woman as she began to talk dirty and sat on a stoop at the far end of the street, pulling on the butt with my eyes closed. The sweetness of all those lost names and places smoked in my head: true debauchery destroys as it pleasures and the butt was crackling down to plain nothing. I saw Verlaine and this young guy with a stick a little way behind him, they passed me and I was so very scared, crouching into my dark doorway. I thought: I will not tell le Père la Pêche what I've done. I smoked it down so far there wasn't anything to toss away, nothing to pick up. I burnt my fingers on the last breath.

I went to the quai de l'Horloge after the weekend but he wasn't there. I asked around and the sidewalk artist told me that he'd fallen into the river, Saturday night, and been fished out with a hook, Sunday. He'd drunk too much. The sidewalk artist was chalking out the spires of Notre Dame. The old man had gotten rich somehow and blown it all in every café on the San' Mich', then toppled into the drink. Nice way to go, the guy added, but we should be so lucky, *hein*?

I threw the tin into the water and watched it float. His old newspapers blew away and the stones were kicked and the crates were sat on by fishermen flicking butts that stayed there. I'd like to go back one day, to that place, smell him on the wind, catch him out of the corner of my eye, standing like a shadow in my coat. I've been all over, on legal business, but never back to Paris.

You'll be wanting to know which room I took: Cousin Ingeborg's or the bohemian one. Does that really matter, now? Does anything matter, in the end, but what you dare yourself to do just once in your life? Just once? As if that's enough?

Seven stations in
the Paris whirlwind

Michel Butor

1. Wanderings at Night

Those were the days of shadows across the pavements, neon lights flash-
ing on and off, gigantic signs above the gutters, the last leaves of autumn
clinging to streetlamps and phoneboxes, searchlights turning in the
sky, the throb of aeroplanes, the crackling of loudspeakers above the
screeching buses, taxis with daffodil-yellow headlights and ruby at the
rear, braking on red and starting up again on green.

Days of picture-houses with their ticket offices and coins changing
hands, stills from the film, forthcoming attractions, conversations
about the weather, the family, newspaper headlines, the queue, the
shuffling and tapping of feet, the ashtrays to throw away the cigarette
you had scarcely begun, the tearing of the tickets, the soft padded
doors, the usherettes, the steps, the seats you could pull up or down
then sink and wedge yourself into, and in between the shoulders
and ears of the rows in front, the rocks of the Wild West, the foam of
the sea, the perils of the jungle, the murky depths of Chicago, the
rooftops of Paris, flights into space, Scottish castles, medieval towns,
pharaohs, long-drawn-out kisses, Chinese emperors and bad guys with
hearts of gold.

They were the days of cyclostyled menus on restaurant doors,
delicious steamy smells coming out and the clatter of knives and
forks in the throng of people eating, the steamed-up glass wiped clear
by serviettes or bare hands – some wearing rings – to make a spyhole
into the darkness through which we could see the uncorked bottles,
the half-empty glasses, the plates waiting to be filled.

Days of the glass-fronted cafés, like encaged braziers, hot-chestnut
vendors with their newspaper cones, furs piled up on hatstands, beers
spilling over on to cardboard mats, infusions of tea, croque-monsieurs,
card games, chess or billiards, discussions about the next government,

town-planning, the future of the world. Stolen kisses, confidences and vanishings in the night.

Days of dodging between vehicles on the pavements in dark alleys, the iron shutters coming down like closing lids, and along the hoardings, brushing against someone, your scarf flying in the wind: the apologies, the questions, the looks, the hesitations. Days of sudden passions and disappointments, tiredness creeping up the legs, aching feet, pain in the back, dry throat, hands in pockets and nose icy-cold.

They were the days of florists' shop windows, chrysanthemums for All Saints, poinsettias for Christmas with garlands of holly and mistletoe, white fir trees ribboned and garlanded, the old market halls with their piles of cauliflower, plumes of pheasants, the silky coats of wild boar, scaly sea-bream, the last flower-sellers with roses done up in cellophane or bouquets of violets from the southern hemisphere, moving from table to table or from one crossroads to the next. Diamonds, real or fake, glittered on trays protected behind grilles by the last word in alarm systems and suddenly lashed by icy downpours. In squalls of sleet or snow old papers blew and the tramp snoring on the Métro grid turned over with a shiver and clutched his bottle to him.

Those were the days when, back in the cramped and scarcely heated little room up under the caves, you seized hold of your book as if to draw from it every compensation and the key to everything, but before you reached the end of the page your frozen fingers let it fall and you sank into sleep at the gloomy light of dawn, forgetting to draw the curtains and turn out the lamp. We were students then, on the threshold of everything. Malnourished, tormented, we walked the streets of this town, our savannah, without respite, trying to rid ourselves of innocence as if it were a toothache, supposing that our youth would last for ever and almost regretting that it might.

2. Diary

Monday May 1st, go to the flower-seller's, rue de la Rosée, and buy a few sprigs of lily-of-the-valley which she'll have dyed pink that very morning with her own blood. Kiss her hand to bring the colour back.

Tuesday 2nd, meet up with the physiotherapist, impasse des Caresses, and go for a run with her in the Parc des Antilopes. Feed them bread and strawberries, then dive into the pool with the transparent walls just opened at the top of the Tour de Vincennes. Snack at the Chinese place in the galerie Marco Polo.

Wednesday 3rd, early afternoon, phone my secretary-translator to fix the dates for our trip this autumn, courtesy of the International University of Numea, to finalise plans for our multilingual collection entitled *Classics of the Hidden Face*. Then to the travel agent's, place du Capitaine Cook.

Thursday 4th, without fail return the neo-Irish illuminations to the librarian-archivist in her pretty hanging garden in the escaliers des Palmes. She lent me them for the publicity for our book. Then, together, to the photographer's at the junction of ruelles Nadar and Alget, then all of us in a taxi to the model-maker/printer's, carrefour William Morris.

Friday 5th, remember to go and record a few stories in the child educationist's studio, allée Antoine Galland. Go armed, of course, with suitable books, drawings and sketches, but also with the numerous ingredients necessary for the select little drinks party at the illustrator's, cour Gustave Doré.

Saturday 6th, make the most of the last hours of daylight in the atelier of the weaver/dress-designer, square de Tihuanaco, to choose the shade and pattern of the piece of wild silk she has in mind for the Marie-Jo Michel dungaree-style evening outfit adapted for the launch of her exhibition in the Musée Lima, discuss the cut and the accessories (she is inexhaustibly inventive), then write a few words in felt-tip on the scarves of her collection. At twilight an elegant cocktail, with seafood.

Sunday 7th, dinner at the computer specialist's in the stalactite cave she's found and furnished under the Claude Lorrain Métro station, which children adore because of its diorama of glimmering lights, where she's placed not only the hundreds of inscribed bricks that her archaeologist sister has brought back from her last dig in Fayoum – bricks on which hieroglyphs are used to transcribe a foreign language into ancient Egyptian, hieroglyphs which specialists have not yet identified for certain and which they are trying to put in order, to work out what they are – but also scale-models of the playing fountains so enjoyed by Sunday strollers in the clearings of the forests of candle cactus in the splendid glasshouses of Aubervilliers.

Monday 8th, clavichord concert at the Scarlatti Hall, cité Guarnerius, the first half dedicated to the Spanish eighteenth century and, after the interval, even better, the world première of the quintet for plucked strings and added harp, lute and guitar with various electronic modulations and the play of mirrors, which she has been working at half-secretly for so many years and snatches of which I have already been privileged to hear.

Tuesday 9th, a lecture by the astronomer in the Copernicus room, Quartier Ptolemy, on the puzzling images and especially the recordings transmitted by the tracking station orbiting Titan (you really would think this time... but I shall refrain from comment until I have heard it). If we ever manage to get him away from his crowd of admirers we'll go back with him to his hotel on the corner of boulevard des Astéroïdes and quai Halley, right next to ours, carrefour Nicolas Cochin, and there enjoy a few hours' very necessary rest before catching the helicopter, silent at last, which will carry us to our private hideaway.

3. The Street's Skin

At the bend in the hoarding a poster goes up in flames; in the torn hole a letter rises again like a phoenix out of the ashes and glue on the broken walls.

These scraps of paper are feathers for Daedalus patiently making wings for his younger sons who will one day, as it is promised, take flight and avoid the snares of the sun. We have to start from scratch with the ancient legends. So, they will escape the network of pipes where waste and gases circulate, the tangled jumble of wires that transmit disinformation and lying talk, the underground swarming with rats and exhausted workers going home to their frumpy wives, whining kids, adulterated wine, mindless programmes on the box.

The eye, scalpel-like, scrapes away the layers from the crumbling space on the abandoned walls. You slide in through the cracks like an Australian mi-mi into the cliffs, till you reach the dreamtime with its organ music and dancing. This abandoned factory is Fingal's cave or the mosque of Omar or Ibn Touloun. The piles of earth on this waste ground devoured by bulldozers are the archaeological testimony of the last twenty years less known about than the famous finds of antiquity. As Christopher Columbus modestly disembarks from a rusty old *Santa*

Maria in plastic and galvanized, I push aside the Sargasso to take out idols and inscriptions.

Between the scaffolding and the demolitions, streaming with tatters of cloth like banners on a march, ladders are erected that we in multi-coloured rags, paint-spattered and dusty, can climb like guardian angels to the walkways of the clouds and follow the escapades of young adventurers in search of the Mountains of the Moon and the sources of the Nile, with stops at Cyprus, Aden, Harare and Warambot, after a wild time in the Ardennes, Paris, Brussels, London, Stuttgart, and on to Java, in the season of illuminations and bad blood, from one town to the next, new towns, new texts, new letters, the alchemy of the precise meeting point of city and wilderness, sphere and pyramid, science and silence, the depths and the surfaces, the goodbyes and the returnings.

The curtains of the theatre of the city rise all around the seeker, more and more curtains, even those of the night sky, even the chains of eternity. You pull away stupidity like a great lump of plaster to the sound of clapping, clouds of dust and a great flock of birds.

4. Circus in Winter

Snow falling on the boulevard. Brilliance of brass, the beat of drums, the unfurling of tunes and banners. Legs and biceps, *tricots* and feathers, bells and snakes. With a roll of drums, loudspeaker proclamations sweep through the crowds wrapped up against the cold. Cars slow down and join in the clamour with their horns, and little white-faced children drag their mothers towards the stalls of boiled sweets and sugared almonds.

Sting of the whip on the sawdust; the horse whinnies and bounds; shiver and shimmer of pleasure on his coat, and up he goes!

So unlike the virtuosity of the hang-gliders, spiralling and soaring sweetly along the cliffs, making their dreams of turning into birds come true. Here they do not fly, they dive. And they don't have fins. It's as though there were no longer an element to support them. They tame the void, playing with gravity like comets or satellites in twisting trajectories; curl around the abyss, hollow themselves out at a dizzy height; and are seized by a firm hand, moored to the trapeze like a ship at the very limits of its moorings on the quay.

There is a certain melancholy in the yawn, a deadly tedium in the slowly lifted paw, and yet a certain tenderness for the persecutor, for why should you not be attached to him when the whole world has let you down?

Outside the magic circle behind the scenes, in the stink and scent, smoke and smells, electric fires or braziers, a kind of silence, thick and lumpy, as different as can be from the crisp silence which precedes the clapping of hands, the cheering under the big top or the glass dome. Dressing-gowns; make-up, putting it on, taking it off; getting changed; a quick sip of coffee; a snatched kiss; constant cleaning, polishing, mending, darning, ironing, rehearsing; exercises, a breather, a sly cigarette, talk about the kids, their education, exploits, what they hope to do: will they be able to escape from this escapade, journey on out of this journey, opt out of this opt-out? And then the next venues, the ones they know already, the ones yet to be discovered; new faces, and, amongst the old ones, those who must change their act or even retire altogether.

But now come the whistles, the signals. We're on. A last glance to check your buttons, your mascara. Deep breath, over the nerve barrier, and you're in the eye of the storm where you juggle with the minutes opening out like the blooms of the far-off Easter festival.

The sadness of royalty demeaned, strength all for nothing, exile and no end, all that grandeur reduced to a heavy clumsiness in ridiculous imitations of the dominant species, sometimes it makes its most thoughtful members feel ashamed.

His walk is hesitant yet light; his shoes shuffle and gape, his accent is a mixture of all suburbia, every region, everywhere foreign, elsewhere. His mouth is full of mistakes, his pockets full of surprises: a tiny violin, a tie that goes on and on, a bowl with a real live goldfish. Hats that fall off and jump up and finally land like swallows on the cross of his arms; all the humiliation of urban poverty in the turn-ups of his huge baggy trousers, the need for a whole new life in the orange nasturtiums or loud check of his shirt with the tails hanging out; and the inevitable somersault at the end of the hazardous and miraculous journey along the boards.

All those sequins, spangles and jewels make his whole body sparkle like a mirror reflecting and deflecting the rays of light as the batons, plates and glasses go flying past. And now the chairs get mixed up in it as well, as do the tables, as does the furniture of caravan or house and even some sharpened knives and flaming torches, so that the ranked rows tremble in one long wave of light, and nobody is excluded.

Then out again into the snowy night.

5. Back from Tokyo

There I was the classmate of children with very black hair and buttercup-yellow hats who after the hard hours of calligraphy would wipe their brushes and stoically open up their little umbrellas. In my eyes I still have the teeming murmur of a forest of ideograms into which I had barely begun to advance. It amazes me that here I can read all the signs, and not just the letters but my own language as well.

How familiar the Paris Métro is! No need to memorise characters with 14 or 15 brushstrokes to find out how much money to put in the slot for the right ticket, nor what colour the line is to get to the right platform. And how short the trains are here! How sparse the crowd, even at the height of the rush hour, quite the opposite of what I thought! But my eyes are on the same level as other people's; I sink in this crowd, whereas over there I stood head and shoulders above it. And I miss the incessant clicking of the expert ticket punchers.

A sudden clash of colours, like a pachinko hall. Even the blinking, sparkling and crackling. Could their mafia come over here? Have we already been infiltrated? No, it's an illusion. True, I'm passing through a so-called amusement area and up one of these small streets with the leprous plaster I might find the pinball dens which are, so to speak, the illuminations of our modern myths, and their fauna, the nervous, wild-eyed priests in charge. But I shall look in vain for what I liked about those lights over there: cyclists carrying meal trays above their heads, balancing them like scaffolding with a steady hand, bowls of soup kept nice and warm under their lids; or, a stone's throw from the café, in between two grey wooden houses, a slender young girl in raptures over a bijou garden.

I come back to the lay-out of the big department stores, scarcely changed since my childhood, to their way of folding the wrapping paper. I have no trouble at all finding the counter or the thing I'm looking for, or at least ascertaining that they don't have it. And how comfortable it is in the restaurants. In the West even if you can't always get a table you can always be certain of finding somewhere to sit once they've let you in, with enough elbow room and the little set of cutlery for piercing or cutting and the basket of bread. But were the aroma of grilling eels to be wafted in front of my nostrils then, like a rat from Hamelin town after the Pied Piper, heedless of all present temptations, how happily I would scurry along, to nibble at one on the street corner or perch with my chopsticks and bowl of rice on the soft ground.

You may say there are plenty of Japanese restaurants in Paris or Geneva, and that some are excellent, but in them you won't hear people sucking up their buckwheat noodles, and certainly in the corridors and passageways there won't be that squash and variety of little stalls all wanting your custom. What you enjoy most is the nostalgia, just as you do in the French restaurants over there; but the Japanese touch in presenting the dishes gives them a charm you wouldn't want to forgo. For me now there's something vulgar about all these restaurants, however many stars the guides may have given them.

I even used to hear chiming from an episcopalian church among the birdsong and children's voices in my quiet little corner away from the noise of horns, bells and sirens. So that now in the ringing of even the most catholic bells I listen for the intrusion of a buddhist gong or a shinto mallet beaten at intervals. As for the noise of aeroplanes, it always carries me off over mountains and sea, calling me back, but summoning me more urgently still to other countries not yet visited. Even the screeching of brakes in the rain can be the talisman that opens me up to the enchantment of a garden I thought I had already seen but which next time − for I always hope there will be a next time − I shall have to see in a different way.

6. A Sooty Adolescent

> I was 17 on 14 September 1943
> it was the war and more precisely the Occupation
> and nobody knew at all when it would end
> the curfew the misery the cold that would return with the winter
> was so cold we were shivering in midsummer

I had just taken my philosophy bac I was preparing
with no enthusiasm to work for the entrance exams
for a grand and sarcastic school
just as people had spoken of a funny kind of war
I was having a funny kind of gloomy holiday

I was skinny shy and rather dirty
I looked for solitary places to meditate and yet
deep down nothing frightened me like solitude
wanting to be somewhere else yet wanting to be near
staying where I was I was always a long way off

I was tormented of course by my sex
turning in every direction like a crazy compass
throughout my well-behaved childhood rather sly
I was like the young king of the Indies in the 1001 nights
half my frozen body poisonous black marble

Very few books even fewer magazines
lies and ignominy everywhere worse than it is today
yes decidedly worse than even today
in this terrible *fin de siècle* where so many hopes
are crumbling by arrangement of the warmongers

I hid from my fellow prisoners to build
clumsily not having the wings of Icarus
with the encouragement of one or two accomplices
a frail raft of sentences on which
to glide under the chains of death stretched out from bank to bank

7. After the Party

Confidential:
Xmas on the balcony
Easter by the embers
many spent the festival wrapped up in bed
with a particularly bad dose of flu

Into the dirty clothes basket go the silk shirts, scarves, towels and elegant socks. You brush your waistcoat off with the flat of your hand, put the crease back in your trousers, hang up long dresses on their hangers, pack the kimonos back into their presentation boxes. You pick up the champagne corks from under the armchairs, collect the empty bottles for the bins, sort out the gift wrap: in one pile the pieces good enough to use again, in the other the ones only fit for the fire. You untie and retie the ribbons, especially the coloured and most especially the gold ones, stack the cans, empty the dishwasher a first time and refill it immediately; there'll be at least another load.

You rinse the teapot and the tea infuser, you filter out the tea leaves with the sieve, wipe the ashtrays, scrape the candlesticks, work out the number of meals you will get out of the leftovers, moan about the people who didn't turn up, regret that others couldn't, make fun of some, congratulate yourself on others, envy the appearance or talent of some and the elegance or wit of others. You stretch, your joints crack, you yawn, look in the mirror at the little veins which make the whites of your eyes go red, search for the fizzy tablets in the medicine cabinet and plunge them into a glass of water.

> Echoes of dancing
> folds in the cushions
> dregs in the glasses
> crumpled tissues
> stains on the tablecloth
> smoke gone cold
> crumbs on the carpet
> red cigarette ends
> forgotten gloves
> women's scent

You go over what people have said, the conversations, all the flitting to and fro of last night's butterflies. But what a complete blur it is already! We should have taped it. Was it the young duchess or the surgeon who told us about the sculptor? But wasn't it actually the musician, because they were talking about a concert the architect had been to who told us about the strange goings-on at the ornithologist's house? And, incidentally, was that architect there or not? Each time we wonder if we ought to ask guests to write their names in a book, as some people do. What is absolutely certain is that his wife was there, having a very animated discussion with the ambassador – which Latin-American country was he from exactly? He had been brought along by the publisher with a rather exaggerated idea of how happy that would make us all. You learn something interesting every day, even about people you think you know quite well. I remember now, it was the musician. As for the sculptor, it wasn't the surgeon who was telling us about him, it was the biologist. In any case it couldn't have been the duchess, for however smart she is (and what an appetite!) she has never been able to show much enthusiasm for any work of art later than Louis XVI. As for the two centuries before that, she knows her stuff, but by the Empire she's already having problems. So it must have been her cousin the countess, who looks the spitting image of her (the inbreeding of these old families!) although she's a bit older, and is unsurpassed at spreading tales and gossip. What's more, she picks her victims carefully, only attacks the best. And without the least malice either, though the consequences may sometimes be rather dramatic, which she is the first to regret.

Aldebert can't bear Julien, and far from hiding the fact, shouts it from the rooftops. Julien gives as good as he gets, which does not stop them guffawing together in company like the two chums they once were in a prestigious Jesuit college. On the other hand, Eustache's hatred for Gustave is more veiled. They belong not only to the same political party, but have the same leanings and sympathies and have always helped each other along with lavish mutual praise, so that people have begun to talk, which is what they intended. It's often the way, we shall be told. However, there's no mistaking the looks they give one another when, in ill-lit corners, they suppose themselves unobserved and after a glass or two of wine their guards are down. How clear the hatred then that suddenly flares up! It has been brooded over, simmered and fed. Most people observing it believe its root to be jealousy; their two wives, it is true, are both very beautiful, have admirable taste in make-up and clothes, are excellent hostesses and have brilliant careers, one a harpist, the other a psychotherapist. Surely enough there to organise a few delightful foursomes, say those who don't know them very well. But people who have known them longer imply not so much by stories but by strange silences that there has been some very intimate relationship and that one day we must inevitably expect a bloody outburst.

Glad you could come. – We must do this again. – So pleased to meet you. – Don't forget to remind me of what I said I'd do. – If I can be of any use to you… – So we shall expect to see you next week then… – We simply must introduce him to you… – When you think that we've been hearing about you for such a long time and that we've had to wait till tonight to finally let you know how much we admire you and are grateful to you and… – Take care of yourselves… – Let's be in touch soon… – Don't leave it too long… – You haven't changed… – Nor have you… – He hasn't changed… – He's put on a bit of weight… – She hasn't changed… – A few grey hairs… – She dyes it… – They haven't changed… – As young as ever… – How they've changed! – Couldn't recognise them… – It's true it's been a long time… – I must say at first I thought it was her mother… – I can't remember her name, but we met her at that party, you remember, it'll come back to me.

It was yesterday. No, you can't even say that. It was this morning. It was a few hours ago. But there is a rift, as if a sudden chasm has opened up between it and us. All the host of worries whose murmur was stifled by the busyness of the evening come creeping and swarming back again, firing here and there salvoes of alarm in all the tangle of discomfort and gnawing pain. It is approaching the time of tax returns, consultations with accountants, first payments, and all those absurd administrative worries, entirely harmful, which come around again and again, ever more complicated, embedding themselves in our botched society, and all to preserve the privileges of a few bosses and underlings who defend it fiercely but are in fact as miserable as we are.

And everything to do with our bodies also functions so badly. The diary is already full of appointments with the dentist, the physio, the cardiologist. And if it were only us. But there's the family, friends, you get the feeling that the whole world has begun groaning again, shivering, cursing, counting its money, losing heart, looking for oblivion until the next celebration.

What are your plans for the summer? – What are you writing at the moment? – How are the children? – And your parents? – And your friends we met in Brazil? – Weren't you talking about going to New Zealand? – Are you moving soon? – You must give us your new address. – Where do you think we are heading with the electronic revolution? What's your opinion of the yen? – Between ourselves. – Of course. – You understand me. – Of course. – I shouldn't have said that. – I'll be as silent as the grave. – You're wiser than you know! – You old idiot! – Not so old as all that! – A few good years still to stagger along. – To keep your head above water. – To get things done. – If ever I have a good tip I'll let you know. – You can't be too careful. – Cunning old devil. – Charming old rogue. – Someone to keep in with. – He has his good points. – You can't trust anybody.

All this while in the East the great promise is falling apart for ever, in dust, stink, cold, enthusiasm and want, because of foolishness, routine, lack of culture and imagination, pretentiousness, jealousy, fear, the police, the sclerosis of officialdom and armies, lies and even sometimes wickedness, folly and madness, torture and blood, whilst those who for years have had nothing to fear from it stand up and applaud. Certainly it was a relief. And we all shared in that gladness, we breathed again, along with them, yesterday's convicts, we too were freed. But how could we let it go so badly wrong? What laziness on our part too. We lean, as so many do, on the old texts which are no doubt very worthy and sometimes admirable but claim to be scientific, as if there were any such thing as science, as though it were not always utopia, as though scientific discourse were not always, and fortunately, in the future tense. We cling to the old texts instead of continually questioning them and placing them side by side with so many that are just as worthy, and sometimes even more admirable. Masters we have so loved, how have you so betrayed us?

It is not only a new year that we need
but a new century even a new millennium
and certainly what we have had from this decade
will not enable us to turn the page that is crushing us
all the paper in the world has turned to concrete
which must be ground into fine wheat flour

Translated from the French by Helen Constantine

The taste of apricots

– une histoire de fantômes –

Erica Wagner

'Back again, eh?'

When he speaks I am reaching into my wallet to pay but he waves his hand in front of his face and wrinkles his nose as if, perhaps, I had farted rather than offered him a couple of 20-franc notes.

'Who'll know? Anyhow, I can't take keeping money from a scholar. As long as I get a mention in your acknowledgements. Paul. Paul Lecomte.' He grins. He is missing one front tooth, and the rest don't look in such great shape. Today is the first day he's told me his name, although this is only one version of a conversation we have been having now for a good few weeks. 'How do you do?'

'Acknowledgements,' I say. 'Why yes. Of course.'

'I'm sure it will be an important work. I have faith in you. You have a kind of – gravity about you. An interest, I might say, in the grave.' I stand there. What else am I to do? He is always guessing. I don't mind. 'Perhaps you are a medical man. Old bones tell tales, I reckon.' He holds up his own hands and, now he keeps them still, I can see his knuckles are swollen with arthritis, although he is surely not that much older than I. 'You see? How much you could learn from me, once I'm like the rest of them.' And he glances downward towards the spiral stairs that lead down into the Catacombs. 'Of course, you could be an historian. Maybe you speak Latin and Greek – one day you'll take me down there, tell me what all those carved letters are trying to tell me. Fill my head with something worthwhile, for a change.' He is reading a movie magazine, some cheap rag. I can see, upside down, a half-naked woman, the neat meringues of her breasts.

'I'll do my best. I'll have to see –' and I give him a thoughtful pause, mustering what I fancy is an intellectual smile, just the tips of my teeth to show – 'what I discover.' So with my books and papers held tight to my chest, down I go, underground.

Once I am deep in the earth, I lean on the cool spine of a stone pillar and roll a cigarette, by touch alone in this near darkness. The match's flame makes a mockery of warmth. When the smoke begins to curl up towards the low ceiling from my mouth and between my fingers, it blends with the damp that exists here almost as a vapour, the moist breath of the dead. 'Want one?' I said once, holding out my smoke. It seemed he was staring at me, I could imagine it, just that fellow there, hedged in by his mates, his greening brain-box the transept of a tidy cross of eye-sockets and nosebones.

He didn't answer me. I suppose he'd gone without for a century or so: they say the craving lessens. I do like to smoke. *Défense de fumer*, it says just outside: a little, neat-lettered sign. Why? Who is there to harm? Those who come here surely aren't afraid of death. Surely this should be the place of licence, a place beyond law. For it says this, too: *Arrête! Ici c'est l'empire de mort*. I kept watching him, sucking the blue fug deep into my lungs. Who'd blink first? I guess it had to be me.

There is a long tunnel, before you get here, to the bonecave. The place was built by mining engineers, and the neatly winding path has the sturdy hunker of the coalface. You think you have to duck your head, but you don't, quite; you walk nearly a kilometre, the gravel's growl, breath through your nose and mouth the only sounds, each sharp turn, each mysterious blank doorway cut in the rock and gated with iron offering the possibility of terrible surprise. What will I see round this corner? Or this? It is a journey both tedious and suspenseful: but I like it. It helps me to imagine what the real journey will be like, the last journey. Yes, the thought preoccupies me. Is it wicked? They said so in the church I went to as a boy. I don't go any more, so I could say I don't remember. My mother would think it was wicked. But she is long gone, and sometimes I think of her in this corridor, with her neat handbag, her hair twisted tightly into a plait, her mended stockings, venturing cautiously along its length lit with plain caged bulbs: she can never quite see the end.

I grind my cigarette out beneath my heel. I will have another in a moment. It is a Monday morning: quiet. No one here but me. I bought myself a coffee before I came here, after another sleepless night: standing at the zinc my exhaustion ebbed away, or flowed into something else, a kind of absence in my head that's better than sleep. At least there are no dreams. I hate my dreams. You wouldn't be frightened down here if you had dreams like mine.

The taste of apricots

Couvent de Carmes, Place Maubert. 25 janvier, 1814. The allied armies about to enter Paris; Napoléon about to desert his forces; what were they thinking, those St Germain nuns? Which of you died of hunger, or cold? It's you I should offer a cigarette, not that robust-looking fellow from St Nicholas; though perhaps you would tilt your eyes downward, so sweetly, and refuse, the blush spreading beneath your habit, down your cowled throat and breast. And now a whole row of you staring back at me, prisoned by the heads of your sisters, doubled up over your own legs and your modesty gone, unable to look away or even blink. That's what I need, a girl like you.

'Excuse me,' she says. I am about to light another cigarette. I don't jump, but I drop the butt and my book of matches. She bends to pick them up and when she puts her hand into mine she smears my fingers with earth. Big grey eyes and her hair twisted into a plait behind her ears, tight. As if something might escape. A white dress, too cool for underground, and a spot of translucency where the ceiling has dripped lime water on to her shoulder. The down raised on her arms. She glances down at what she's given me. 'No smoking, I think it says.'

I don't want anyone. I want to say, piss off, but I'm too tired for that. Still, there is a dull ache of anger in my neck and shoulders.

'It's not good for you.' Smiles, tries to make it light. No way. She's lost me.

'Look around you, lady. What do you think it matters?'

'It matters to me,' she says simply.

I can't think of what to say to this. She is looking at me as if she has a right to.

'That's the way out,' I say finally, pointing away from her, down deeper into the Catacombs.

'You can't go back?' At least she seems willing to take a hint.

'Takes just as long, from here. But you won't get to see the rest.'

'What more is there to see?'

The point of the place isn't just the fact of itself. It's quantity, too. Six million, they say. When the nuns came here that number meant nothing; things are different now. But I don't say that to this girl. She has a mole at the corner of her mouth. I wouldn't exactly call her pretty. But the light here, you know, is flattering. 'All the rest of them.'

'Them?'

I jerk my head again, around me. 'Them.'

'Oh,' she says.

I light my cigarette. I take a drag. She's watching me. Because I don't know what else to do I hold it out to her and she takes the butt from my hand, sucks in the smoke. I give up. 'I was meant to meet someone down here,' she says.

'Stood up?'

She shrugs, and stares at the nuns' headbones, and then at me. She looks down at the notebook and clipboard tucked under my arm, the pen in my pocket, the books in a plastic bag at my feet. 'You study, in this place?' She hands the cigarette back to me. She doesn't wear lipstick, leaves nothing on the butt. I finish it, drop it.

'You could say that,' I reply.

'What?'

'What, what?'

'What do you study?' She is tall, but still she lifts herself on her toes to peer at my notes, narrowing her eyes in the yellow gloom, though you'd think, with all these shadows, she'd want to open them wide to see. I pull back.

'Oh, go on,' she says. 'Tell me.'

I feel heat creep up my chest. My heart expands a little, flutters. She is smiling now, with her wide, pale mouth.

'It's so boring down here. Only dead people. So quiet. But you've found something interesting. All those books and papers. Won't you tell me what it is?'

'It's just – it's not important. It's not finished.'

'Which? Not important, or not finished? If it's not important, why would you want to finish it? If you're going to finish it, it had better be important. I think you need to make up your mind. Here, let me decide.' And before I know it, she's reached out, her strong, ringless fingers grasping at my notes, her hold light at first when she thinks she could just snatch them from me, but I hang on, and she pulls, so I can see the cords in her arm tighten and flex.

'Stop that!' Let go, I am thinking, go away, who asked you to be here? And I feel the fear again, taste the yellow bile I've managed, somehow to keep at bay, by coming down here, by scribbling God knows what, reading in the half-light till my eyes hurt and my head's too full of facts to think.

I think she is stronger than I am. I think she would win this fight.

There's no anger in her touch, though: our fingers meet again, grappling over the fruits of my labours, and something in her cool flesh makes me yearn – for her? No. But for something. To speak again, to someone, anyone. Why not this girl? Or this girl particularly. Yes. So that when she lets go, stands with her palms open towards me, waiting, I feel more lost than I ever have, and yet as if I might still be found.

'Christ,' I say. She doesn't speak. 'I said it was nothing. I meant it, all right? It's nothing. It's just – time. It fills the time.'

She tilts her head. It's a question. She doesn't need words.

'There's too much time. You know? The usual story, maybe. Like everyone else's. No girl, no job – no life. Not lately. Again. And down here is just – I don't know. Quiet.' Did I mean to say it? But I have.

'You're not writing a book. You don't study.'

'I suppose it depends what you mean. But no, not like the ticket collector up there thinks I study. I've promised to mention him in my acknowledgements. Sure, I write things down, but – sometimes I think it's just to please him, now. At least it keeps one of us happy.'

'I'm sorry,' she says.

'Don't be,' I say. 'I can do that for both of us.'

So we stand together, for a moment. She looks at me. Most people don't, you know. Look at you. But she does.

'I could show you the way out, if you wanted,' I say at last.

'All right,' she says, and we turn away from the convent dead and start to walk.

There are switchbacks, cul-de-sacs, detours you don't need to take if out is where you're headed. The dead don't mind dark corners, obscurity, the stony face of a wall. They are used to being shoved out of the way. They are dismissed before they're barely cold. I think of my mother again: one day she was there, the next she was not. If I had imagined anything at all – I was ten at the time – I suppose I had thought there would be some journey involved, some preparation, but there was not. There was only absence. And that was the language, too: 'Your mother is gone,' my father said. Sitting on the edge of my bed. He was not a demonstrative man. I remember his smell: fuel oil, smoke, something bitter and lemony, but only because it hung about him like his own particular weather, not because he had ever, to my recollection, taken me in his arms. Now it looked as if he had rubbed his eyes with salt.

He wouldn't say where. Only that she was not coming back. There was a funeral – there must have been – but I didn't go to it. I recall a quiet afternoon with a neighbour, who, instead of shouting at me and flailing and trying to thump me from over the garden wall as she usually did when I disturbed her washing or made the dog bark, brought me an apricot tart on her good china (a chip on the corner of the plate) and a bowl of milky coffee and sat in silence watching me, as if I might fly into pieces or spontaneously combust before her very eyes. I did not. I ate the tart and drank the coffee. Today I recall my mother's death and all I taste is apricots.

The woman follows me. We walk in step, our pace so well-matched there is only a single echo. 'You know your way,' she says. 'You are a student of the dead.'

'I suppose I am.'

Now she looks at me, and the way she looks makes me wonder, for an instant, if I haven't met her before. Or perhaps just seen her, in the street, in the Métro. Maybe she lives near me. And then I think: she has a kind face.

'There's too much noise and confusion up there,' I say at last, as if it explained things better.

'Too much to want?'

I want to pull back from her. But that stare again. 'You don't know what I want.'

'No,' she says, 'I don't. Only I imagine it isn't much different from what everybody else wants. You said it yourself: look around you.' She waves a white hand. *Hôtel de Brienne, rue Meslée. 29 Août, 1788.* Rioters. Behind the mossy wall of empty heads, tidy as a row of stones rimming a country garden, there are real relics of that night, not so orderly: skulls stove in like earthenware bowls, thick splintered femurs, broken prisons of ribs, a pelvis sharply cracked as if it had been halved with an axe. 'They're all the same. You can't tell them apart now. You probably couldn't when they were alive.'

Her 'probably' seems a courtesy, her tone is so certain. 'Maybe not,' I hear myself say. 'But I don't think that makes them – any less.' I remember that grinning fellow I offered a smoke. Suddenly wished I'd known him long ago, when he could have taken the cigarette from my fingers, held it to his lips.

'I didn't say that it did.' We stand in silence a moment. 'Weren't you going to get me out of here?'

'Yes,' I say. I feel, somehow, as if I have just woken up. 'Yes of course. This way.' And I march forward. Still she follows me exactly so I can hardly hear her. But I feel her cool breath on my neck.

I know I do. I can smell her, a faint, sweet, cloudy scent. How many stairs, spiralling up? I counted once, but now I forget the number. The air gets heavier as you go up, warmer, and when there is a pale spill of sunlight staining the last steps you can breathe the outside air, the silver-blue scent of the stone fading into a dusty verdure of early autumn leaves, coffee, bread. It occurs to me that I am glad it is not yet winter, that there is still a little heat from the sun. Perhaps it is darkness that is tiring, perhaps what you read is true, that there is energy in light. This is a new thought.

I turn to tell her this, to say something, now we are in the light. But she is gone.

I run down the stairs again. All the way to the bottom, my hand warming the cold iron bannister with speed. On the last step I open my mouth to call her name – until I recall that I don't know it. 'Miss?' I shout. 'Miss?' Only my own voice comes back to me.

I imagine her fallen on the stairs. But I would have heard her, seen her.

I imagine her fled away from me, slipping quietly away back to the bonecave – but why? I thought – she seemed so certain – she wanted to come out. To come out with me.

All the way back up again I run, I am not used to this, my heart is trying to escape from the cage of my chest as I reach the top again and have to slow down, have to drag myself on the bannister. At the top, at a dusty little desk, sits a boy, not one I've seen before, waiting to check visitors for stolen bones, but I run by him before he can speak. I don't think to ask him if he's seen her. She couldn't have *passed* me.

Now even the grey daylight seems bright to me and I squint and I run – well, sort of skip, or hobble, a trickle of sweat between my shoulderblades and my false papers blown out of my hands down the street like escaping doves – back to the entrance, where Paul Lecomte sits quietly turning the pages of his magazine. At first I am so breathless I can't speak, but he hears the roar of my lungs and looks up, startled.

'My friend!' He says. 'My scholar! What's the matter?'

'Did she come this way?' I ask. 'Did you see her?'

'See who?'

'The girl. There was a girl down there. I was coming up the stairs with her, talking, and then – I don't know, she turned and left me.' I try to control myself. It is only my beating heart making me feel this way, I say to myself, feel this physical urgency. My blood would slow and so would my head. 'I wondered if she came back out this way.' I shrugged. Nonchalant.

'A girl?' Lecomte says. 'I didn't see a girl.' He closes his magazine. 'A real girl, anyway. No,' he says, 'it's early, still. No one down there but you.'

'She was wearing white,' I say. As if it will conjure her. 'Her hair was dark. In a plait on her head.'

Lecomte shrugs. 'I didn't take her money,' he says. 'Are you all right?'

'Yes,' I say. I can feel a flush in my cheeks. I wonder if the run up and down stairs hasn't done me a bit of good. 'I'm just – well, if you see her.' If you see her: what? Will I be back tomorrow? Somehow, I don't think so.

'I'll tell her you were looking for her, Professor.' And Lecomte winks. 'Good to know you intellectuals are flesh and blood like the rest of us. But – hey!'

I have turned to go. I stop and look at him.

'Not thieves, though? I wouldn't have thought that.' There is a disappointed line drawn in the flesh between his eyes.

'What?'

'In your pocket. What's that? I must say, Professor, I wouldn't have marked you for a bone-snatcher. You must get carried away with your researches.'

I suppose it might have looked like a bone from where he sat: something small from the wrist, or the broken-off end of a femur, neatly rounded at the vanished knee. In my breast pocket, buttoned over it. I'm no thief. I stood in front of Lecomte and undid the button, and when I reached in my fingers found an apricot. Small and round and a little warm, just too ripe and slightly bruised, scented with summer. I pull it out to hold it in my palm, and when I do a breeze like a whisper passes over the nape of my neck.

'No, Paul,' I say, 'No stolen bones. You don't have to worry about me on that account.'

He smiles to say sorry, and I turn to go, and feel the daylight warm my head.

The storm

Patrick Smith

A move to Paris had been on the cards for Gerry Cahill even before his marriage broke up and when the time came he was glad to get away. Once there, though, Paris disappointed him. The streets and cafés swarmed with tourist groups in a way you didn't notice when on business trips.

Alone one dispiriting Saturday afternoon he wandered into a small art gallery across a courtyard off the rue Bonaparte. The paintings were acrylic, a medium he didn't normally care for, but one of them, called *Images de Paris*, caught his eye. The young woman behind the table came across and murmured something inaudible. Cahill had to ask her to repeat it. 'Okay, we speak English,' she said, a condescending phrase that annoyed him. But her face was friendly, and her perfume hung fragrant as chocolate in the warm air.

'It interest you? You know, you can make a reservation,' she told him.

'I'm just not sure where I'd hang it.'

'Sometimes one must think with the heart.' *Wizze art.* 'Your reason alone cannot hear what the painting says.' He wondered if she really believed that. It sounded fatuous, like an American send-up of French intellectuals he'd just read.

He looked again at the turbulent reds. What *did* they say? Game birds outside the butchers' shops? The ivory gleams could be the shiny streets slicked white with car lights. The twisted blacks, the water churning past the quay walls. And then, with extraordinary force, it struck him that the painting was about something quite different. What it showed was an interior. He was certain of that now. The colours were erotic. The ivory gleams were the startling brilliance of a girl lying naked on the artist's bed in candlelight.

'You see?' the young woman said encouragingly.

Three evenings later he took her out to dinner.

Nadia Berthot too was new to Paris, straight from La Roche-Bernard, a small town on the Bretagne coast, and lived now in a suburban *studio*, far out of town. 'Rents in Paris are horrible,' she told him. 'So who but foreign businessmen will be here?' Her smile across the starched tablecloth stayed friendly and bright.

At their next dinner he learned that Nadia had a degree in art history. After years of collaboration, the antique dealer with whom she lived in La Roche-Bernard had wanted her out. 'He meet someone,' she said simply. 'I come to Paris.' Cahill nodded. It was a story that felt familiar. 'I was romantic then. So? I spend seven years of my life with a man who discovers he does not love me.'

'And now?' he asked, half afraid of the worst, maybe a cynical boring remark about reality.

'Now?' Her eyes opened wide and she burst out laughing. '*Bonjour métro, boulot, dodo*. Do you know that phrase? The *antichambre* of death, Sartre used to say. But what life isn't? Could he tell us that?'

Cahill encouraged her to go on. Her age was somewhere short of thirty, about thirteen years younger than himself, and he was curious to know what her life consisted of. The gallery owner on the rue Bonaparte turned out to be a cousin of her mother's. The family tie didn't stop him exploiting her, though. The hours were long and the pay mainly commission. 'During the weekend *nocturnes*,' she said, 'we are open until midnight for the suburban couples coming from the cinema or the restaurant. Young couples from the provinces. Like me. They think that buying a modern painting will make them Parisians. Sometimes, you know, I want to say to them, Count your money first! But a city without commerce is what? Nothing.'

'Did you think of saying that when you saw me?'

'Count your money? No!' She stopped the lightly loaded fork before it reached her lips. 'It is evident. What is six thousand francs to you?'

Cahill was a man easily discomfited by such talk and he was afraid it showed. Looking at him she delayed her fork another instant and then she put it down while she burst into laughter again. She had her hands on the table edge and her dark eyes creased until the surface glittered. He laughed too. At that moment he saw that what might otherwise be leaden in his life here could dissolve in her presence. It would flash and run like quicksilver if she wanted it to.

During the following weeks, whenever he could, he took her out and drove her home to Courbevoie afterwards. She would stand waiting for him by the railing in front of the church wall, slim in a long dark raincoat over jeans and a cashmere sweater, with her black hair tied back, and her face of toffee-coloured skin looking so calm and mysterious that it made his heart thump as he approached. Behind her would be the emerald stain of night-lit grass and the granite wall of the church of St Germain-des-Prés, warm and tawny-looking beneath the floodlights.

Whenever she saw him arrive her face would brighten, as though there had been a risk that he might not come, but she showed no interest in what he did outside of their time together. Cahill had told her he was a currency counsellor. 'A gambler,' he said modestly, 'with other people's money.'

'And it is amusing?'

'Like playing the casino.' He wasn't sure she'd see the excitement of tracking micro-second switches. 'It can have its moments.'

'*C'est bien*,' she said, and that was that.

They slept together. Two or three times a week, after a restaurant or the cinema, they would spend the night in his apartment on the rue Monceau, overlooking the park. She made love skilfully and Cahill was happy to try skills in return. Sometimes he surprised himself with his own confidence.

'Is that good?' he'd ask.

'*Oui, mon amour, oui, oui.*'

'This is even better, isn't it?'

Towards the end of November Catherine, his ex-wife, rang from Dublin to make plans for their twelve-year-old son's Christmas holidays. Charlie was due to come to Paris and Cahill decided the boy should be forewarned that his father had met someone.

'Well, *that's* nice,' Catherine said. But her voice sounded hesitant. He knew she was uncertain of how serious he was. 'Someone recent?'

'About two months ago.'

'Will she get on with Charlie?'

The question annoyed him. There was a burst of canned laughter from her television set. It sounded like two men whinnying at each other. 'I hope so,' he told her shortly.

When the time came Nadia went home to La Roche-Bernard for Christmas. Cahill expected a call but none came, and Charlie's holiday was almost over when she got back. They had one day to share, all three of them. Nadia suggested they spend it at AquaCulture. Cahill watched uneasily while she took the boy up the ladder to the high toboggan slide. Down they came, face first, screaming into the water. For lunch Nadia suggested hamburgers. 'Why not?' Cahill said. Charlie gave a whoop of delight. 'Just don't tell your mother,' Cahill warned him.

Four months later, in early March, Catherine asked if he could take Charlie again for the Easter break. 'I have to fly to New York.' Cahill assumed from her brisk tone that it was to do with her job, which, like so much else in her life, was new. But when he asked her she told him no. 'As a matter of fact,' she said in a voice that sounded brittle, 'I'm going to meet my fiancé's parents.'

'You're getting married?' The news struck Cahill like a blow on the head.

'Hasn't Charlie mentioned him?'

'No,' Cahill said. 'He hasn't.'

'Well, it's not someone you know. He's a New Yorker called Dennis Kushner.'

'It seems abrupt.' His voice was accusing, which was the one way he didn't want it.

'On the contrary,' she told him, assertively, he thought. 'It's thoroughly considered. I've been taking instruction from a reform rabbi for the last three months.'

'Instruction in *what*, Catherine?'

'Well, Judaism, of course. Dennis doesn't practise but his parents do. We want to make it as easy as we can for them when we marry.'

'And what about Charlie?'

'Charlie doesn't have to be involved.'

'I don't see how he can't be.'

'Can you take him? Easter's the only time Dennis and I both can get away.'

'I'm not sure,' Cahill said. 'I'll have to think about it.' He could see curious slopes of change looming up in all their lives.

Five weeks after that, driving down the boulevard St Germain with Nadia en route for Cherbourg and Ireland, he told her for the first time about the situation. She shrugged.

'So? She wants to become a Jew, she becomes a Jew.'

'It's not that simple, Nadia.'

The storm

The day was cloudy with a spring wind that sent the bright arcade of leaves billowing up and down the boulevard above their heads. They were on their way to pick up Charlie and spend the Easter week together, all three of them, in Connemara, which Cahill wanted Nadia to see.

'It's not the marrying part that bothers me,' he said slowly. 'It's the taking instruction.'

'Do you not ever have a religion? My mother still goes to mass. It is not so awful.'

'Sure. I was brought up Anglican, which is about as close to voodoo as you can get without actually slitting a chicken's throat. And Catherine's parents were both Roman Catholics. *They* wanted an RC priest to marry us. They even asked me to sign a paper saying our children would at least be baptised.'

'Did you sign?'

'No.'

'Why not?'

'Charlie can do what he likes when he's old enough but until then I don't want his mind clogged up with superstition. Catherine and I agreed on that. She never thought anything else.'

'*Oh là là!*' Nadia laughed. It was a warm full laugh and it made him happy to hear it. So happy in fact that he too was laughing, although he wasn't sure at what. He certainly didn't like the idea of his son being exposed to dark beliefs in genital mutilation and swaying back and forth to call on God for dead spirits. Or, worse, seeing grown men wear shiny boxes on their foreheads like they did, eerily, in a documentary he'd seen about the Marais.

Far over to the right they could glimpse La Défense now, and Courbevoie where Nadia had her *studio*. The sun made a galaxy of brilliant light on the high-rise blocks. Freckled water rocked past beneath a fountain. When he put an arm around her shoulder she turned her face to kiss the back of his hand. By stretching his fingers down he could touch her nipple. He let his fingers rest there.

'Your wife learns a new religion to marry another man,' Nadia said. 'Does it make you jealous?'

'No.' He gave thought to it. They had entered the concrete canyon leading them into the A10 and away from Paris. 'How would it make me jealous? I have you.'

'That is good,' she said. But her voice trailed off and when he looked at her again, she was asleep. The light gave a lambent sheen to her hair, a silken softness.

About an hour later Nadia woke when Cahill stopped in a small town to fill up before the service stations closed. When he came out from paying, she was standing beneath a row of trees, smoking. On the other side of the trees was a public parking area. A church bell clanged in the town. He counted the strokes while a cloud of swallows swooped out into the sky above him. Their balaclava heads were close together until, with a strange chattering jubilation, they rushed down and split off across the parking lot where four caravans stood in a half circle. Four large cars were lined up along the narrow gravel road. A blackened mattress and two car tyres smouldered around a gutted washing machine. Dirty-haired children ran amongst the empty tins and bottles that littered the area. The faint beat of a guitar flowed across the landscape, hanging like a pulse beneath the trees. It mixed in with the scent of the leaves and the dry settling dust of the parking area. Nadia took Cahill's hand when he came across.

'All set,' he told her cheerfully. They were only about an hour away from dinner now in l'Auberge de l'Evelot, a romantic spot he intended to surprise her with.

A chord exploded. There was a brief intricate phrase before the same insistent rhythm returned. In dark, brutal strokes the beat continued. The sound remained absolutely clear and as hard as steel. Then it stopped.

'Time for the road,' he said as a single chord sang out.

'Wait. They will play again.'

'It'll soon be night,' he told her gently. It wasn't that the music didn't affect him. The dark beat hung on even now in his mind, but he knew that once the light went they'd risk missing some sign or other on the small roads they had to take from here on.

He'd already opened the car door and was waiting when Nadia started to applaud. Her hands clapped slowly and loudly like a shutter banging in the wind. An old man with heavy hips manoeuvred out from behind a caravan about fifty paces away. He stood watching her a moment. Then he made a sign and disappeared. When he came back he was carrying a three-legged stool in one hand and a guitar in the other. He walked with slow inflections, stiff and stabbing, like a marionette, then placed the stool and lowered himself on to it until his flesh pooled softly around his hips. The children crowded forward. He struck a chord and looked up. Nadia waved. The man said something to one of the children, a girl of twelve or thirteen, but she shook her head. The guitar kept repeating the same insistent notes while he spoke to one of the others. Adults had come out between the caravans. The man spoke to the first girl again but still she didn't answer. Instead, with eyes that were huge and wary, she turned to look at Nadia and Cahill beneath the trees. In the evening sunlight Cahill saw that her bare feet were pale with dust.

The guitar reiterated the phrase, over and over, urging a rhythm until, hesitantly, her heels hit down in a series of small thuds. At once the guitar whirled into a flurry of notes, coaxing her, and now her hands rose above her head. She turned once, standing on the same spot. This time there were murmurs from between the caravans. The girl waited, letting the voices fade. Again there was only the guitar and the mute bump of her heels when, with a fierce and sudden defiance, she swirled free, moving out alone into the open space. Her hands rose higher. The small fingers opened and clasped and opened, exposing palms notched black with dirt. The beat she danced to was her own, at once powerful and exquisite. A few minutes later, with a single flourish, she stopped dead. The guitar fell silent. She remained still, as though taken by surprise, and then she turned away and ran back in amongst the caravans.

Nadia applauded again and after a moment Cahill joined in, although he knew that whatever the girl danced for, it wasn't their admiration. He was about to say this when, to his astonishment, Nadia called something to the man and began a dance of her own. With her arms straight down by her sides she did a series of quick, toe-kicking steps vaguely reminiscent of an Irish jig. The movements were deft and firm but they had none of the gypsy girl's fluid passion and Cahill thought there was something embarrassing about a woman like Nadia trying to follow such a performance. Nadia danced on. With a series of low chords the guitar picked out the tempo and accompanied her. When she finished the man stood up to give a small bow before he applauded.

'Isn't he sweet!' Nadia cried. She clapped back at him and Cahill smiled.

At that moment her face looked soft and desirable, and he would have liked to kiss her, but the man was still watching.

'What fun it was!' she said excitedly in the car. 'I have not danced like that since I am her age.'

Cahill peered ahead. They were seriously late now and the light was beginning to go. Darker clouds had appeared. In between, the sky was pale as faded denim.

'We look for somewhere to eat here?' Nadia asked happily. 'I am starving.'

'Just a few more kilometres.'

'Why not here?'

'You'll see,' Cahill told her. They were due to exit soon, north of Chartres, and head for Lemeré. He looked at Nadia but she stared straight ahead to where sunlight splintered off a distant farm.

'Catherine asked a while ago how you and Charlie will get on,' he said.

The windows in front flamed into a single glare, their edges cut with scalpel clarity.

'What do you think?' he asked.

Nadia had eased off her shoes and put her bare feet up on the dashboard. Her hands clasped her knees as she considered the question.

'It is a pity for him being a lonely child,' she said. 'I hated when I was. I see that now.'

'Charlie isn't lonely. What makes you think he's lonely?'

'You do not see it?'

'No,' he said, 'I don't.' He realised she was tired and hungry and not at her best just now. Fragile light streaked down and her hair looked briefly luminous. Ebony shot with resin. He reached over and stroked it, giving her a tender smile. Soon they'd be at Evelot, in a warm room, undressing before dinner. 'There should be a *route départementale*, D27, somewhere off to the left here, *chérie*. Can you see it on the map?' He began to hum an old Piaf song. *Oui, je suis de Paris*. Nadia gave him an uncertain glance. He didn't know what was behind it and he didn't think she did either, but it excited him. She put her hand on his thigh and let it rest there.

'I love you,' he said suddenly. 'Do you know that?' These words spoke themselves – he certainly hadn't planned to say them – but once they were out he felt that they were the simple truth. She was a sweet, attractive woman who'd been waiting for the right man to turn up and there was no reason why he shouldn't be that man and be in love with her, as he knew, here and now, he was. Instead of responding though, Nadia asked, 'What does love mean to you?'

'I'm not sure I can answer that.'

'You do not know what love is?' she asked.

'It's a feeling, Nadia. Apart from that I don't know quite how to express it is all I meant.'

'Well, that is probably true,' she said pleasantly. 'You are not good at expressing.' She leaned over and kissed him on the mouth. Her tongue was warm and wet and he could feel the surface of it clearly. The springiness of her body pressed into his and made the blood rise from his stomach in a powerful flow. He had to keep his eyes on the road though and he was glad when she pulled away.

'Maybe actions are what count when it comes to love,' he told her thoughtfully. It was what he felt right now. 'Not words. Anyone can say words.'

'But there has to be a belief, doesn't there? A belief that something exists between two people that is not just material?'

'A belief is only worth the action you're willing to put into it. Wasn't it Sartre who said that?'

'Sartre said so many things,' she said with a small laugh that sounded hard to Cahill. The car stuttered, as though in sympathy.

By seven the weekend traffic out of Paris had thinned. A faint drizzle started. The light was beautiful though, shafts of bright yellow through chinks in the dark mass of cloud, sharp as arrows through openings in a castle wall. The leaves ahead began to shine like fish scales.

'Do you think we should tell Charlie straight off that we're lovers?' he asked.

'Will he want to know?'

'Catherine's probably said something about it.'

'Then tell him.'

'He'll take it seriously though.'

A momentary thinning in the clouds left the dying sun almost visible, a dark plum that hung above the trees. He listened to the skim of the tyres on the wet road as they took off towards the hills, heading for valleys as soft as wrinkles in a crumpled cloth. To the west he could see the clear horizon beneath a band of blue sky. With any luck the clouds would have passed before they got to l'Auberge de l'Evelot and the sun would set in glory.

'How long more do we have to go?' Nadia asked

'Half an hour or less.'

They passed a narrow crossroads. Cahill stopped and backed up.

'Somewhere along here it should say Lemeré and then Evelot.' There were no signposts. He took up the map from the floor at Nadia's feet and studied it.

'We should find some place now before it is too late,' she said.

'We will. A very special place. I promise you.'

'You do not even know where we are,' she accused.

'Then trust my judgement.' He wanted her to be optimistic 'Maybe all we need is a little sunshine here.' At that instant the sun slipped through the black clouds far over to the left and pocked the hills with shadow. 'What do you say to that?' he laughed. He was on top of the wheel, hunched a little, peering into the evening.

'We should look for a town now,' Nadia told him stubbornly. Far ahead were whiter clouds and beyond them the blue sky was smiling.

Fifteen minutes later came the next crossroads. Still no signposts. He wasn't sure if they'd missed a turning. The fields were splotched with dark.

'What do you feel it's important to teach a child?' he asked to distract her as he looked at the map again. 'Supposing you had to teach someone like Charlie?'

She thought over the question briefly, setting her head askew as though to catch the call of a distant bird. It was a movement of delicate fleeting grace.

'To *céder*,' she said.

'To give way? In what?'

'Just give way. To adapt so he will co-operate. Is that possible, do you think?' she asked good-humouredly.

He composed his voice to ask the next question, which was one he had been planning to put to her.

'Do you ever think of having children?'

Grassy slopes ran up the hills. There were oaks, daintily leafy, at the top, outlined against the sky. But he had to keep his attention ahead now. The road grew narrower as they climbed the hill. When he glanced at her she pursed her mouth and shrugged, a Parisian mime she'd picked up, a way of not giving a straightforward answer. It was a gesture he disliked.

Climbing, the car began to hack again. He pumped the accelerator and raced the engine in neutral, hoping to free the supply line, but it didn't help. They'd reached the top, a small plateau, when something stumbled and gave up. Again and again he tried the starter but the engine didn't catch.

'What now?' Nadia said. She didn't sound worried but she clearly wanted to know what plans he had made. He could understand that. It was no weather for failed surprises.

'I have a romantic little *auberge* lined up for us,' he told her. 'Not far away. We'll soon be there.'

'That is nice.' She reached up and kissed him on the cheek. This was the loveable side of her coming out and he knew that all he had to do was keep it there for a little longer and they'd be home and dry. He got out in the grey light with Nadia's raincoat over his head and opened the bonnet. The battery connections looked all right. He checked the oil gauge. Touched the sparking plugs. These were ritual moves. He wiped his hands clean on the wet grass and got back in the car. The plateau ahead lay bare. The soil looked thin and dank and he heard rainwater gurgle through the dyke nearby. They discussed the situation calmly, joking to the extent it seemed to require. When the light began to go he switched the headlamps on and off to attract attention. Rocks shone against the dark fields. A long time passed and there was no sign of life around them.

'What will happen now?' Nadia asked again.

'There must be a house with a telephone somewhere nearby. It can't be hard to find.'

'In this weather?'

'You can stay in the car if you like,' he said amiably. He tried to give her a wry smile.

'In the car? Here?'

'Why not?'

A moment later, for no reason that he could see, she said, 'You don't have a lot of imagination, do you, Gerry? That is something I have noticed.'

'And when did you notice it?' he asked her.

'The first time I see you. In front of the painting, demanding your-self where it will hang.'

'I had six thousand francs' worth of imagination then. That was the trouble. And I *still* don't know where to hang it.'

She stared ahead to where the headlights gleamed on the wet grass beside the road. He made his voice patient. 'I have to go and find a telephone now and get a breakdown truck to come. Will you be all right here?'

Without a word she opened her door and stepped out of the car, not caring if it was into the worst of the roadside mud. She had a hold-all with her. Cahill's suitcase was in the boot and he decided to leave it there. He locked the doors and took her hold-all.

'Let's not make a thing out of it, *chérie*. We'll be all right.'

'*Nom de Dieu*,' she muttered. Her eyes seemed filled with aggression. Side by side they walked along beneath the thin raincoat, angling apart to avoid puddles and rejoining after. He realised how tired she was, and how much she had been looking forward to a good dinner soon, just as he had been. He touched her cheek.

'What's the matter, Nadia?' he asked gently.

'What is the matter? Everything is the matter. You don't hear what I say, do you?'

'That's not fair. You know I do.'

'Then there is a language gap,' she said. She made it sound final, as though it explained everything, but it didn't. It didn't even begin to. He decided to let it be. With any luck they'd find a house and a tele-phone and soon they'd be having warm baths and going down to sit before a wood fire and sip a glass of cool Muscadet while they studied the menu like the millions of other city-dwellers who wanted to get away to a quiet weekend in the country. Her mood would have changed by then. He knew that. She was someone who was quick to see the bright side of things when you gave her half a chance. Far up a lane, he glimpsed the outline of a small building.

'There's a farmhouse,' he said. 'I'll ask if we can use their telephone.'

The farmhouse turned out to be abandoned. The entrance door had been stripped pale by the rain and the hinges hung askew from rotting jambs. When he pushed at the sagging door a bat shot out beside his head. It was so close that he saw its thin teeth and tufted face before it whirred away and was gone in the rain. Nadia shivered beside him.

'It's all right,' he told her and he put his arm around her shoulders. The night, bad as it was, could still bring unexpected gifts. He even said that to her. 'We're together. And who knows what we'll end up sharing? No matter what, this time tomorrow night we'll be somewhere else. We have a good week ahead of us.'

Instead of answering she stamped her feet. Her city shoes and the bottoms of her jeans were soaking wet. He took his arm away. She was under stress now, and in that mood, like all the Parisians he knew, indigenous or not, she was liable to snap.

As they walked away from the house there was a crack of thunder. The drizzle thickened and almost at once became heavy rain. He took her hand to run back to shelter but she didn't want to because of the bat and they made for the barn instead, where one of the big doors was ajar. Inside the rain hammered against the tiles high above their heads.

'As soon as it eases I'll find a telephone,' he said. 'I'll get a taxi to come and take us to the *auberge*. It can't be far now.'

Nadia opened her bag. He caught an egg-white gleam from her eyes in the shadows as she handed him a towel. She shivered again and said, 'Take it. I must change my clothes. They are cold.'

Handing him the towel was a small, thoughtful gesture that he appreciated though there wasn't much he could do with it except dry his face. He heard her undress behind him, pushing everything off in one go, jeans, underpants, socks. The air had gone very still. She walked to the door in her dry clothes, and lit a cigarette and stood looking out as the lightning flashed above them. A moment later thunder rolled across the plateau.

The next flash lit everything in white. Cahill felt the shock when the thunder exploded. The ground shook, sending tremors up through his feet. It was as though the sky had broken within these four walls and his ears were filled with it.

The flash showed again, this time with a walloping crack right above their heads. A huge rock looked like a face staring in the window at them. The thunder redoubled, rattling the pile of tins in the corner. After the flash it was pitch dark and he heard Nadia come back from the door and search around for something.

'Gerry, we should lie down,' she said. 'We lie on my raincoat.'

'It'll be gone in a few minutes.'

'We also if we do not lie down.'

He listened to the rain until an explosion blasted his eardrums. There was an awful glare afterwards. The worst of it was the way the noise hung on and on, vibrating through the ground. Tiles clattered down and he heard them smash on the big rock outside. The lightning stitched the sky repeatedly now, leaving the doorway outlined so that he could see the rain hiss past.

'Gerry, please. Come and lie down. You worry me standing there.'

At that moment the pile of tins in the corner exploded. Pieces of metal slammed against the walls and fell to the floor. A huge ball of fire, two or three feet in diameter, was where the pile had been. The roar grew deafening as the ball began to roll, slowly at first, then rushing along, bouncing off the floor. He looked at it, fascinated, until a new roar cracked all around them. It filled the air with electric discharge and gave off an acrid sulphurous smell. The last thing he saw was a spurt of white. After that he was blind.

He really was blind. Then his legs and arms were disconnected and there was nothing he could do with them, or with any part of his body. It was as though his will had leaked away, leaving his limbs behind. So this is it, he thought, this is death, and he was amazed that they were right after all, you go through it and come out in something on the other side. Again there was the awful crack, and again and again, and then even his spirit had gone.

When he woke he was flat on his back and he heard the storm far off beyond the grey opening of the doorway. There was a soundless flicker of light like a vague memory and long afterwards the rumble of the thunder. Warm breath fell on his face and he was surprised to find Nadia on her knees, leaning over him. 'Gerry? Answer me. Can you hear?' He could hear all right but there was a vestige of something he was trying to hold on to, a phrase almost grasped when you pass an open window. His arms jerked once, a reflex gesture as he tried to snatch at it. But whatever it was it had vanished and for a second he was overwhelmed by the futility of having thought he could hold it in his hands at all or, worse, in his dumbstruck brain. He listened to the rain outside soften to a spatter.

'Gerry? Answer me! Are you all right?'

She put her face down until her cheek was against his. 'Gerry?' she said in his ear. He couldn't move or speak although there was something he wanted to say to her, something he felt with all his heart. While he searched for the words, it too slipped away. She raised her head again and murmured and he realised that she was praying.

'Nadia, I'm all right,' he told her.

'Gerry? Oh, Gerry!' she cried. 'Thank God!' She kissed him all over his face. He was still thinking of the graceless passage of the evening, the drab sky, the rain ceaselessly falling, then the explosion, the paralysis, the dream of death, and it seemed to him again that he might, with more heed, in that one brief flash, have grasped something from it before it was gone for good.

'Why do you not answer? I thought something awful happens to you.'

'No. I'm fine. I was dreaming but I don't remember what.'

He took one of her hands in his. She let her head rest against his shoulder and they lay there together on the ground.

'You are not going to sleep now,' she said, 'are you?'

'I'll look for a telephone in a moment.' The storm had vanished and he couldn't hear the rain any more. 'We'll soon be on our way again.'

'We should go now.'

'Just a few minutes more.' He felt in control, a wonderful assurance, and he thought that what he'd do was kiss her, a warm kiss in which she would co-operate, and they'd make love. They'd make love and lie in each other's arms and then go on from here.

Familiar fragrances emerged from beneath her sweater. He searched for and held her breasts. But when he unzipped her skirt she said no.

'Why not?' he asked. The question sounded plaintive, not at all what he wanted. He unzipped the rest and started to bunch the skirt up around her hips until she put her hand down to stop him.

'Gerry, let us go now. Please?'

'In a few minutes. I promise.' He saw another, stronger version of himself making love to her. She had her arms around him, her hands on his back. 'Why if I do not want to?' she said. But a moment later, when he caressed her vagina, he knew he had her body on his side. He felt a wonderful elation as he leaned away from her, redistributing the stresses. He had his hands beneath her buttocks, holding her as though for the first time. And in a way it was for the first time. They were here alone, where they might as easily have died, and for this moment she was his as he was hers. She cried once and pushed against him, saying *'Non, non, non.'* But these were not words that had any literal meaning now and, in fact, she gasped even as she said *'Non, non'* again and he felt a brief steadying of the pressure, the convergence that had been massing all evening between them. Their arms and chests and thighs were tight up against each other. As soon as she came he ejaculated. When he did, she made a small whimper, tender and devouring. They lay there silently in a vast shift into collapse. Her body fitted easily against him. He felt life slip by, like an eel in water.

He woke to hear her say his name. There was a distant growl across the plateau.

'The thunder is back,' he said sleepily.

He listened to the rumble like a far-off storm until it stopped and started again and the silence in between made him aware of what it was. Now it went very slowly, with a peaceful throbbing through the dark. It was a very old lorry set to climb the hill.

'What time is it?' she asked him.

He tried to make sense of the phosphorescent dots on his watch. 'After four, I think. I must have fallen asleep.'

'Me also.'

'I'm sorry about the *auberge*, Nadia.'

'It is not your fault.' She seemed resigned to that fact and, truth to tell, he didn't feel it was his fault, not in any real sense.

'Have you been awake long?' he asked her.

'No.'

Now the noise had stopped. They strained to listen for it but there was nothing. Then, above the rain, a bang.

'We'd better get dressed,' he said quickly.

A voice called out and another voice answered and the barn door opened. Two men came in, talking some kind of patois. Cahill saw them silhouetted against the moonlight outside. They were lost again but he heard them make their way across the floor. One of them struck a match and Cahill stood up. The one with the match spoke to him in a thick voice. Cahill said, *'Pardon?'*

'Anglais?' the man asked. Nadia said something to him. Cahill caught enough of it to understand *de passage* and *en panne*. The match went out. One of the men said something else. *'Moi aussi,'* Nadia said.

The first man put something on the ground. When he lit another match Cahill saw that it was a little oil stove. The second man unscrewed the cap from a bottle and poured spirit into the cup. The first one put the match to it and then pumped up the oil until the flame was strong. *'Voilà,'* he said with some satisfaction. He looked towards Cahill and said, *'Bonsoir, M'sieur, M'dame.'* Nadia moved out, still in her bare feet on the raincoat. Both of them stared at her. One of them, the one who lit the match, had a thin black moustache. The other wore a leather jacket. He was carrying a cloth bag and while he unzipped it he said something to Nadia.

'They are on their way to Paris,' she told Cahill. 'They stop here to eat something. He says it is expensive to eat on the *autoroute.'*

They talked, all three of them. When Cahill asked her, Nadia said they were talking Breton, although in fact it was a mixture, for he recognised French words and phrases even if he didn't understand them all. Nadia said the men were on their way to work at the open market on the rue Montorgueil. 'They are farmers who make *biologiques* vegetables for markets. One is married to the sister of the other. They must drive to Paris every Saturday night to sell on the street on Sunday morning.'

'Ask them if they have a telephone in their lorry.'

Nadia asked them. The man answered Cahill in French but because of his accent Cahill understood nothing except the word *camion.* 'It is an old truck,' Nadia said. 'Small.'

The man with the leather jacket spoke to her again. Patches of shadow jumped to the roof when he moved. The other bent down and put a pan on the oil burner. His moustache was no thicker than a pencil. His small head leaned forward as he looked up at Nadia. He regarded her with open curiosity and then he stared at Cahill. A ring glinted in one of his ears. He looked as if he was smiling, but Cahill wasn't sure it was a smile. His face seemed tight as if his lips had pulled apart and left some of his teeth showing like a terrier's. Without saying anything the other one squatted down and picked out two fat *andouillettes* and a plastic box and then two beer bottles from inside the bag. He put them one by one on the ground. The man with the moustache put the sausages in the pan. They worked together without talking and Cahill watched them all the time, searching for signs.

The pan began to sizzle. Nadia said something and the one with the jacket offered her the fork he was holding. The two men laughed. 'What are they laughing at?' Cahill asked.

'I tell him the pan is too hot, it smokes. He says that if I want to take over, go ahead.'

The man said something else. This time the laughter seemed ready in their mouths as though it was an old joke they knew by heart. Again Cahill had to ask Nadia what it was.

'He talks about Bretagne where the men do the cooking because a woman's place, he says, is not in the kitchen. It is in the bed.'

The two men laughed again. They looked at Cahill expectantly but told at second hand the joke didn't seem funny. Nadia had begun to stir the food around. She appeared tense and he wondered if she was wary of the men. He had the feeling that something was happening but whatever it was he didn't know what he could do about it except be prepared for the worst.

'Maybe we can ask them to send someone back from the first garage they pass,' he said.

Before Nadia answered the man with the jacket spoke to her. She shook her head. When he spoke again it was with some vehemence. She began to spoon the contents of the pan on to the two plates. The man repeated whatever he said. She walked over to Cahill and handed him the pan. It was about one-third full with stir-fried vegetables. One of the chitterling sausages was still in it.

'We can't eat their food, Nadia,' he said quietly.

'Try telling them that.'

She went back and got one of the two bottles of beer and gave it to him.

'They want us to have it,' she said. 'I argue but they insist.'

'Well,' he said. 'You and I can share it. All right.' And he felt it probably was all right. Nadia looked down at him and smiled, encouraging him to eat. He took one of her hands in his. Despite missing the *auberge* they'd got through an important night together. He hoped she saw it that way.

'Eat while it is hot,' she said.

'You first.'

'I am past the food stage now.'

'I don't know how anyone gets there,' he said cheerfully.

'No?' Her voice was sweet and light and she smiled at him again.

While he was eating she talked to the two men. From her gestures Cahill understood that she was telling them about the lightning. At first they didn't seem to believe her. Then the one with the jacket got up to examine the tins, which were fused into lumps of metal. After a moment he whistled softly. His shadow shrank and jumped on the wall. The other got up too and looked and said something to Cahill.

'He says it must frighten us a lot,' Nadia translated.

'Tell him no,' Cahill said. 'It didn't.'

When he had finished, the other two still had their plates in front of them. They were pushing the last of the food together with a piece of bread, silent now, as though thinking over what they had just seen. Nadia clasped her shins, with her chin on her knees, watching them. The one with the jacket raised his head to speak to her. He made a single movement towards Cahill and waited.

'He says to tell you they stop at the first open service station they see and send someone back.'

The one with the jacket stared while she said this. He leaned forward, his eyes moving over her.

'How soon does he think he can send someone back?' Cahill asked.

'He said the garage at Château Bourgal will be open. You wait in the car, he said. They won't find you otherwise.'

'Do you want to wait here in the barn?'

'I go back with them. They will be in Paris by seven o'clock.'

Cahill was dumbfounded. The one with the jacket got up and took the two plates and put them in the plastic bag.

'You're really going to go?' Cahill asked her. He couldn't believe it. 'What about our trip?'

'We should never have started out. I can see that now.'

The one with the moustache took the pan and the burner. Nadia put the towel in her hold-all. The two men had already gone out. The sky was black and full of stars. Cahill called after her.

'Nadia? You can't just walk off like that.'

'What?' She sounded unhappy and he thought that maybe what she wanted was for him to hold her, to take her in his arms right now before anything more could come into her life. They stood there and he realised that she didn't know what to say. Or maybe she did and was afraid that whatever it was, it would not be enough. He was still waiting for her to answer when one of the men called out.

'J'arrive,' she shouted back.

'Are you sure this is what you want to do?' Cahill asked.

'Yes.'

The other two were waiting in the lorry.

'Nadia, listen —'

'Please. Just let us say goodbye. Can we do that?'

He wanted to argue with her but he couldn't find the right arguments to use.

'It is not your fault, Gerry,' she told him. And she actually smiled.

'I know it's not. That's what I'm trying so hard to understand about it.' He had planned their trip weeks ago but something had come between, something unforeseeable that wasn't his or anyone's fault but was there and had to be taken into consideration. That was what he wanted her to see, that these things arrive out of the blue and together you have to make the best of whatever new situation they give. Instead he felt bitterly betrayed.

'I think it's wrong,' he said. 'Badly wrong.' He was angry with her. 'If you leave now it's all over.'

There was a long, cold silence when he said that. Then she put her hand on his arm.

'Say hello to Charlie for me.'

Cahill didn't answer. He felt her heartbeat when he put his arms around her to hold her tight against him. She stood there without moving until he let her go.

Speak to me

Linda Lê

I was expecting you. I knew that you would come. You left my messages on the answering machine unanswered. So I wrote to you and
you came right across Paris to visit my studio, or eagle's nest I should
say, perched at the top of this tower block. The view is nothing
special. The window reveals nothing but more tower blocks similar to
this one. I've lived here since leaving my wife, Elena. I came here to
paint. But the studio has remained empty. Nothing springs from my
brushes. I bite my nails, my hair is turning white, I'm developing a
stoop. At night, rather than sleep, I sit for hours at my window watching the lights go on and off in the tower block opposite. Sometimes I
imagine that a woman, alone in one of the neighbouring apartments,
dials a number at random and gets me. I would hear her breathing
down the line. In my imagination I would embrace her body, which
smells of solitude and crying in the dark and waking up in cold sheets
– the space beside her is empty, she drags her slippered feet to the
kitchen, pours herself a coffee that she'll drink alone, the new day begins and she covers her body, on which the loneliness hangs heavily,
with a dress she bought the day before, looking in the mirror at her
reflection, which lacks even a shadow, after a visit to the cinema that
was intended to make the day, Saturday, seem not quite so long. I always
recognise them, these sisters of solitude, by their walk, by the line of
their mouth, by their floating, somewhat fearful expression. I end up
following them through the streets of Paris. They like busy streets and
the smells of the men who brush past them, perhaps bumping into them,
giving them the impression that they're not so alone after all, that their
body can attract others, that the bed of humanity will welcome them
to its orgy of the senses. I recall one woman, middle-aged, wearing a
blue dress, whom I followed last spring along the rue de Rivoli. She
had the hesitant walk of those who have gone out merely to sniff the
air in crowded streets, leaving behind them the traces of solitude that
adhere to the walls of their apartments. She had bought a bouquet of
jasmine from a street vendor. She held the bouquet timidly, lifting it

occasionally to her lips. She stopped in front of all the shop windows, lingered over the displays. The hem of her dress hung down between her bare legs. She bought an ice cream, which she ate standing up opposite the Tour Saint-Jacques, then she went and sat down at a café terrace and ordered tea. A lone woman with a forlorn cup of tea – a phrase I remember reading somewhere. Her face bore traces of age and suffering. She was constantly raising her hand to move the lock of hair that kept falling over her right eye. Her lips trembled slightly as she drank her tea. She was the perfect incarnation of the Unknown Woman, that lonely sister from the past – a past that we no longer even remember – half child, half mother, whom we seek and are happy to view from afar, as if by addressing a single word to her we would shatter her as an icon and tear away her aura, that nimbus of tiredness and despair turning her into a young Iphigenia climbing the steps to the sacrificial altar. My Iphigenia had hazy eyes, on the edge of tears. She sat at her table as if on an island, words flying about but not affecting her. I watched her and thought of a pile of ashes concealing a smouldering fire. You would only have to reach out your hand and the fire would spring back to life. But there I leave my Iphigenia, who, beautiful in her solitude, makes me resemble an old dog looking for a bone to gnaw… You are cold, huddled up in your coat, wondering why I've summoned you here so late at night to talk about these lonely characters. You're lonely as well – I knew that when I approached you on the *quais* of the Seine. But yours is a haughty kind of loneliness, a form of entrenchment. You were hurrying across the Pont des Arts, not looking at other people, and in your expression there was neither expectation nor nostalgia. Seeing you, I told myself that you were the one I was looking for, someone who would listen to my tale without condemning me. Your hair floated in the wind, a flag declaring your freedom. I envied you your self-assurance. I said to myself, She comes from the same country as me, from the same Vietnam that we both left, she as a child, I already an adult. But while I wander about like an old dog sent away to die far from home, she walks like a princess who carries her kingdom in her heart and for whom exile is a challenge. I ran after you, knowing I mustn't let you escape. On the steps leading down to the *quais*, a guitarist played a plaintive melody. I come across him often on my nocturnal wanderings. He always plays the same fado melody, an exile's lament, its droning notes slipping into the waters of the Seine, which holds up a mirror to all the lonely people, their scuttled lives and shipwrecked love affairs, faces drowning in tears, silhouettes cast adrift. The guitar player watched you go by. You held in your hand a book, *Liberté sur parole*. You were an escapee; I heard, as I ran behind you, my chains rattling, chains of anxiety, of remorse, of softly approaching old age, of the bitch that is solitude scratching her fleas. Out of breath, I approached you. I said to you, Speak to me. You slowed down. Your face registered neither surprise nor annoyance. You gave me your full attention. I felt wretched with my four-day-old beard, my dishevelled hair and my eyes that betrayed the miserable intoxication of the insomniac. Speak to me, I said to you. It seemed to me as if the whole of Paris rustled with these words. All those lonely people without a voice spoke through my mouth. All those people muttering away to themselves in their hovels, all those people whose windows reveal carcasses scorched by the pyre of loneliness, they all formed a murmuring choir whose voice – Speak to me, Speak to me – swelled up like a river in flood. You said to me, Speak, I am listening. And you're listening to me now, huddled up in that armchair. It must seem to you as if you have been locked up in a cemetery at night with a phantom who rises from his tomb to make confession… Don't look at me like that. Your eyes are boring into me. Delving to the depths of my soul. I am going to switch the light off. I will talk more easily in the dark. It will be like talking to myself. Like I've been doing for more than thirty years. Thirty years ago I lived in that city you know well, Saigon. All my life, I have cherished only two cities, Saigon and Paris. Saigon, the scene of the crime. Paris, the place of atonement. I have haunted the streets of both cities. I have known all their figures of misery, I have rubbed shoulders with all those rendered destitute by the night. I grew up in Saigon; I grew old in Paris. I had friends, wealth. I no longer feel I have any affinities except with the winos I see on certain evenings on the corner of rue de la Boucherie in the shadow of a building where their prophecies have taken up residence. I had a name, I no longer wish to acknowledge it. Every time it rings in my ear, I think I hear that voice calling me and accusing me with its dying breath. Can you hear it, that voice that's barely a whimper? It's haunted me for thirty years. Some nights, when I was still living with my wife, Elena, I'd be woken by that voice coming out of nowhere. I'd get up and go out walking in the deserted streets around Père-Lachaise, I'd wander around the railway stations, but the voice would pursue me, chilling me to the bone. Paris became an enormous hall of mirrors. Wherever I went, I saw my own murderer's face; the shadow of the unpunished criminal that was me bulked large in every polished surface. The whisper of the Seine swelled into the murmur of a courtroom. The bare branches in the Jardins du Luxembourg pointed their accusatory fingers at me. Passers-by on the Pont Neuf spat in my face. I thought that coming to Paris would wipe out my past. But the city is a prying mother. She condemned me to aimless wanderings and sleepless nights. I cling to her breast like an outcast child. Her signature is scrawled across my forehead. She isolates me for disgrace. If Paris is a prying mother, Saigon was my accomplice, my accomplice in nights of pleasure that led, inevitably, to my crime. I remember when I was twenty. I had just discovered two passions: a woman and gambling. I was happy, I got married and spent my nights in gambling joints. My wife, a delicate, silent beauty, was like an angel at my right hand, while on my left grimaced the gambling demon. I lived for the evenings, when I entered smoke-filled back rooms. The dice, the cards, the ivory ball – they all danced their saraband. Broken man that I am, I can still remember the fervour that took hold of me as I rolled the smooth surface of the die in my hand or as I watched an ace of clubs fly across the baize. Lost man that I am, I still sometimes feel the sweat breaking out on my brow when I hear a sound similar to the clinking of dice as they roll across the table. I won, I lost – whatever. I paid with fever, heart palpitations, the shakes, expectation. There was an emptiness inside me that needed filling. And I would have continued to lead this life if an envoy of destiny had not come along to propose another way to amuse myself. I met the man during a game of dice. He won and walked off with the stake. He contrived to be leaving the place at the same time as me and accompanied me home. His face was painfully thin and serious. The dim lighting of the gambling den had made him look younger than his years. He spoke about the country, about the war that seemed to be going on for ever and about the Yankees trampling all over the soul of the homeland. His manner became increasingly intense the nearer we got to my house. Certain words – 'American imperialism', 'freedom', 'patriotic fervour' – sprang from his mouth like little balls of fire. The country was bleeding, it was grovelling under the boot of a foreign oppressor, and meanwhile, he said, spoilt children lost their heads over a game of dice. He left me at my doorstep, asking me to think about what he'd said. I saw him the next day and the following days. He no longer entered the gambling dens, but waited for me at the exit. I gathered that he was an agent from the north, a Charlie, as the Yankees called them, a communist recruiting for the resistance. Charlie's proposition to me was that I exchange the thrill of the gambling table for that of the underground. Young man as I then was, all I wanted was to alleviate the boredom of existence one way or another. I possessed no convictions. I had played with dice, I was ready to play with bombs. I agreed to enter the network, although I couldn't say if it was patriotic pride that inspired me or merely the need for entertainment. He gave me a little present to welcome me into the fold: a phial of poison, as carried by all members of the net-work, who were enjoined to swallow its contents in the event of arrest, to guard against the possibility of turning informer. Which was how I came by the idea of gambling with death. I committed my first offence: instead of carrying the poison about with me, I put it in the drawer of my bedside cabinet, forbidding my wife ever to touch it. Next I waited for orders from Charlie. Nothing came. I started hanging around the gambling dens again. My wife was waiting for me when I got home. I could see that her eyes were swollen from waiting up and crying. I saw her face as a mask of suffering, heard bitter reproaches in her silences. I vowed to myself never to go back to the gambling dens, but as soon as night fell, the dice began dancing before my eyes and I ran to fling myself into the arms of my demon. From the moment Charlie appeared, it seemed as if everything was conspiring to produce my downfall. I lost every night. Soon I was left with no choice: I stole my wife's jewellery and sold it. I remember that night as if it were yester-day; it was teeming with rain in Saigon. I was stupefied when I left the gambling den. I had played with the money I'd got from the sale of the jewellery and I had lost. Charlie was waiting for me. He didn't seem to mind that I clearly hadn't given up my past life after all. He had a mission for me. Listening to him, I was seized by blind panic. Coward, coward, said an inner voice. But I had no conscience. Still, I was haunted by the idea that I had lost everything that night while the rain poured down on the city. At that moment I had no need for the homeland or the resistance fighter by my side. But I had no choice:

Charlie was resorting to threats and I thought of my wife who by then must have discovered my betrayal. I told Charlie that I would meet him the next day, then returned home slowly through the wet streets. A whispering voice told me that there was only one way out: to swallow the poison in the drawer of my bedside cabinet. I was too much of a coward to devote my life to my country. I was going to die having known nothing outside of the gambling dens and the excitement that possessed me whenever a six was rolled. Softly I pushed open the door. The house was quiet. I made as little noise as possible so as not to wake my wife. I entered the bedroom. She was lying across the bed, curled up in the foetal position. I approached the bedside cabinet, opened the drawer. It was empty. Then, between the clenched fingers of my wife's hand, I saw the phial… Now you know my life story. It is not glorious. Bits and pieces of it I would surrender to derelicts when they weren't even listening. Seeing you, the other day, on the Pont des Arts, I wanted you to hear it. I offer it to you like a confession. I thought that in coming to Paris and marrying Elena I would find a way to forget that night of pouring rain in Saigon, that night when I betrayed everything – love and my country. Ever since, I have been a phantom haunting the streets of Paris seeking forgiveness in the eyes of the dispossessed. By day you can see me on the rue de Rennes, searching for that thin old woman dressed in a torn raincoat, who stalks past agitatedly, insulting passers-by, targeting foreigners in particular. I pass her coming the other way, she hurls insults at me and I walk on, satisfied. I head for the rue de Sèvres, where a man in a tattered grey suit with spectacles on his nose strides along the pavement demanding: Poetry, are you interested in poetry? On rue des Blancs-Manteaux I insinuate myself alongside a blind man who plays the mandolin. In the Jardins du Luxembourg I follow the two grey-haired sisters in ragged coats who walk in close formation, pressing close to each other like nervous animals. The elder sister carries a bag in her hand which she stuffs with pebbles, coins and autumn leaves that she picks up furtively as she walks along. In rue des Jeûneurs, an overweight drunk sleeps it off in the doorway of a deserted house. He is sitting down, legs apart, his shirt stained with vomit. He mumbles in his sleep. I stop and listen to him. Paris is full of such unhappy talk, snatches of meaningless chatter, words infused with loneliness to the point of madness, sad hiccups, bored stutters, confessions that nobody hears. City of ragged speech, city of drowning stares, city of hands reaching into the void, city of midnight moans and first-light laments, city of pain and corruption, of exiles whose only shelter is the stars, city of huddled bodies without even past joys to remember, city of wretchedness like a weeping wound, city of corpses in the morning beneath the majestic arch of a tranquil bridge, city of imbeciles wandering dazed through the mists of dawn, searching for the key to a lost paradise, city of metaphysical drunkenness, city of haughty decline, Paris turns her warty face to the watching world. Her leprous beauty touches me by day, moves me deeply by night. I slip into her like into an incestuous embrace. Paris my sister opens her arms to take and hold to her breast the exile whose tears, that bitter liquor of twilight, have not made him forget his homeland. Paris the cruel mother chases the son who came from nowhere, to be tormented by the wind and crucified by the stars, towards her shadowy corners. Paris is the place of my atonement, where I plough my remorse and harvest my solitude. On the pavements of Paris I scattered words whispered to myself, words of hate and regret, words snatched from the inertia of the passing days, words marinaded in sleepless nights, words stolen from the silence that has settled in me and in which resounds only one voice from the old days, the voice of a woman I killed and who used her last breath to call me. When I am here, in this empty, dusty studio, when I look out of the windows at the tower blocks that rear up cold and proud, I hear the moans of a woman in agony, a phial of poison gripped in her fist... Now, having come here to see me, you listen to that voice, as it prowls around the studio, rises like a song. The whole of Paris is filled with it. I hear it wherever I go. Every hour of my life I spend in anxious thrall to this voice, which spins around me and flies away then returns to envelop me. I flee. I go out in search of a soul in whom to take refuge. But Paris turns away from me, Paris remains silent and it's in vain that I beg, Speak to me, speak to me and make this voice go away. Accompanied by this ceaseless melody, I advance into the night and, groping my way, hopelessly astray, stripped of the possibility of redemption, I join the choir of the lonely.

Translated from the French by Nicholas Royle

The great book

Ismail Kadare

I

When my friend KV told me about his latest obsession, feeling certain that, like most of his ideas, nothing would come of it, I forced myself to look attentive, but I confess that my mind was on other things…

'So are you with me?' he asked abruptly, noticing that my thoughts were elsewhere.

'Of course I am,' I answered, avoiding his eyes.

It wasn't the first time we had discussed artifice in literature. More and more often recently he had remarked that in his opinion works of literature were so stuffed full of artifice he was surprised people didn't get sick of them and keep away from bookshops, deciding enough was enough. Books like that, he went on, are artificial adaptations of stereotypes, full of embellishments and tricks of style that are all too obvious. We laugh nowadays at novelists who see fit to begin a chapter with such sentences as 'And now, dear Reader, let us leave our hero to his sorrows and follow the fortunes of our heroine etc etc.' We make fun of such techniques without realising that what we ourselves write is no less artificial and that succeeding generations will smile when they think about us just as much as they do about our predecessors.

So we had lengthy conversations on this subject. He insisted there was a need for radical reform, especially in the novel, a need for innovation or Renovation, in the fashionable critical jargon, which would mean the rejection of all artifice, cliché or convention, of all the tedious trappings which prevented literature from getting anywhere near real life.

I disagreed. Looked at like that, writing itself was artificial. Letters and signs on paper, which man struggled with interminably, like a maniac. In the end, wasn't all literature both innovation and convention, a technique no doubt, but certainly the most important ever invented by the human mind and compared with which a possible renewal of the literary genres was of very little importance?

For a moment he appeared to be lost in thought, but, much more quickly than I'd have thought possible, he recovered himself and reminded me that Flaubert, when dissatisfied with what he had written, dreamed of writing a book 'about nothing', which would simultaneously be a book 'about everything'. For so many creative writers had cherished the idea of a book that would contain everything, a total book, in other words a Great Book. The Bible had aimed at being that, but had fallen short by a long chalk. Other writers, even in our own day, Ezra Pound or Borges to name but two, had pursued the same ideal without being able to realise it. There were even whole institutions working at it, notably in the United States where the names of every human being who had ever been, or was still, alive on our planet were recorded in notebooks and on countless tapes in a huge underground bunker. And he went on: 'Don't you see, it's tremendous, all the terms ever used by humankind and found in documents, books, memoirs, from age to age and generation to generation. The idea is very beautiful in itself: the conception of humanity as one big house, one big family with its living and its dead. A beautiful idea, no doubt, but it leaves you with a feeling of a perfection beyond reach. The project is too grand. The mind is not capable of tying it all together. And if you read this book you would not understand the world any more profoundly than if you were to read a dictionary or encyclopaedia; whereas the book I have in mind would be something totally different... I imagine, for instance, that the world, this celestial body, in which generations of humans one after the other have come and gone, one day becomes extinct, and that one man, by the vagaries of chance or fate, survives. He alone escapes death, extinction, and being therefore the only remaining witness of what was the terrestrial globe, believes it is his duty to describe to the universe what has died out on this little blue globe, and what has happened on it for thousands of years, how generations of creatures, human or otherwise, have been born and have died, how states and peoples, pictures, dreams and sounds have perished. He has not succeeded in saving anything from the planet, not a statue, not a crystal object, not a file, nor a woman's limb, a photo, a map, a mineral sample, no object whatsoever, not even a handful of earth. Of all that, nothing. But he has a little book in which you have done your best to collect the whole world, a book conceived precisely for this untoward eventuality.

And, with that under his arm, he comes before the universe as witness.

'You can imagine the difficulties of writing such a book. There must be nothing superfluous in it, but nor must anything be left out. And the problem is compounded by having to decide the relative importance to be given to various facts, ideas and phenomena. For it is not so easy to judge the relative importance in this world of oceans, laws, sex, big department stores, the symphonies of a certain Beethoven, the Pyramids, electricity, the howling of the wind, mankind's remorse, the overthrowing of states, the anxiety when an expected letter is late, the sleep of millionaires, divinities, madness, alphabets, the Chinese, the suicide's knife, hell, human sperm, nuclear fission, the crucifixion, evolution, curses, the sadness of autumn when the first drops of long-awaited rain start falling, the cruelty of tyrants, moonlight, Macbethian nights, so-called because of a certain Macbeth, earthquakes, the solitude of Don Quixote (the knight errant), communism, bank credit, deportation, obsessions with the dead coming back to life, etc.'

His long speech was punctuated by the question 'Do you see what I mean?' And I had to nod my head constantly and ever more enthusiastically so that he wouldn't tire himself out asking the wretched question.

For years that was how I had known him: worried, anxious, seeking after the impossible.

'Perhaps you think it can't be done, writing a book like that?' he asked a moment later. 'Don't say it, I bet that's what you were thinking.'

'Your project is not in itself inconceivable, but I think you would do well to stop at this stage…'

He shook his head.

'I want to go further. That glimmer of an idea means that something is about to take shape.'

'I'm sure you're right,' I answered wearily. 'But perhaps humanity doesn't need this total book and no doubt that's the reason it hasn't been written.'

But again he shook his head in disagreement.

'No, it's not that. There are a lot of things humans haven't done yet which would certainly be useful to them.'

I concentrated on not irritating him, realising that each new outburst was more of a strain on him than on me. In fact, when he regained his composure, I enjoyed listening to him. Many of his ideas I liked, even if they seemed fanciful. A year before, he had told me he wanted to write a book that was truly out of the ordinary: the history of the Ottoman Empire as it would be written in the age of television, an imaginative book about what its history would have been like if a television network had existed at the time, which events would have taken place earlier, which ones prevented or allowed to run their course, and so on. Luckily he had soon abandoned this project to devote himself to another which this time seemed to me a reasonable one. He would write a book about the street he lived in, a little book in the style of Flaubert describing the people who lived there, their dwellings, the minute details of their lives, their passions, worries, as well as their illnesses, lawsuits, even their savings, and not forgetting the drains, the water mains, telephone lines, bills, damages and a whole host of other facts which seemed futile, repairs, visits, and even the numbers of the gravestones in the big register in the town cemetery.

Such a piece of writing, even if it were to include things that were completely ridiculous, seemed to me useful to him in that it would bring him closer to people and to real life. But I had not supposed it would act as a step up towards a new objective: the total book.

II

When I heard his serious voice on the phone, asking me to come for a drink, I thought, 'I hope to goodness it's not that.' I had an uneasy hunch it must be about his famous total book. I was not wrong. I had scarcely entered the café where he was waiting for me when I guessed that not only did the book exist, but that he had brought it along with him.

We kept the subject out of our conversation for as long as we could; I because I was hoping, though it was only a faint hope, that in the end he would give up the idea of showing it to me; and he, no doubt, because he wanted to savour the pleasure of anticipation; and so it went on until he could contain himself no longer.

I felt a dull anxiety, so much so that at his very first words I broke in.

'How did you manage to put everything you mentioned – the living, the dead, the whole boiling hotch-potch that we call the world – into one book?'

He stared at me.

'I haven't,' he said slowly. 'I have done the opposite of that.'

'The opposite?'

He managed a smile.

'Yes, my book is total not so much by virtue of its *wealth* of information as by the *scantiness* of its information.'

'I don't understand.'

He smiled again. He seemed resolved to judge the originality of his book by the degree of astonishment or even wonder displayed by the person he was talking to.

'That's just it, the silence, the stripping bare, especially where the last three or four thousand years of humanity are concerned, precisely the period in which humans have been most active, that's the basic characteristic of the structure of my book.'

No doubt he expected me to make another astonished or sceptical remark, but not wishing to give him this satisfaction, I had quickly regained control of myself. So without taking my eyes off his black briefcase, which seemed, by the slight bulge in it, to contain something diabolical, I said, in exactly the tone I would have used to ask him to show me the devil himself: 'Well, go on then, show me your book.'

He opened his bag and very cautiously took out what I thought until the last moment might be a crab, a bottle of brandy, a broken old clock, or God knows what, but surely not the book he had told me about.

III

For more than an hour he set himself to explain how he had gone about writing it, and I must confess I thought it very strange.

It was in effect a complete book about the world and humanity in the last hundred thousand years, that is from Neanderthal man to the present day. There was nothing specially original in that, there already existed hundreds of works on the subject. If this one stood out, it was for another reason. Its strangeness was this: that the number of pages and even lines devoted to each period was in exact proportion to the length of time it covered. According to this criterion, as the two hundred pages of the book covered one hundred thousand years, only two pages were given over to each millennium, allowing each century about six lines. Still dividing it up like this, all the known history of civilisation – that is some three or four thousand years – was condensed into eight pages, while the twentieth century got scarcely five lines.

He was doubtless waiting for me to ask 'And what about the rest, the other hundred and ninety-two pages, what are they about?' But when he saw that I wasn't saying a word, he lost patience.

'I'm sure you're wondering what the rest of the book is about. Well I'll tell you.'

I was even more flabbergasted at what he said next. In the other hundred and ninety-two pages, the ones which dealt with the period before the dawn of civilisation, he described the long dark monotonous age of mankind, and not by way of ideas, judgements or analysis, but simply by chronicling it. Therein precisely lay the key to the book. Where, according to his chosen criteria, he could only make over a third of a line (that is, one, two or three words) to the Second World War, he devoted tens of pages to the labour of making bones into tools, or rubbing sticks to make fire, or to other similar acts of primitive man, all with tiresome repetition and wearisome, monotonous writing which somehow reproduced the lengthy unfolding of these works throughout the centuries. It was no use pointing out that whereas to the invention of atomic weapons and other important discoveries he had only allocated one or two lines, he was devoting ten pages to the fashioning of a knife out of bone.

'You realise what it has cost me, don't you?' he said. 'You wouldn't believe how exhausted I got reproducing the endless, infernally fatiguing repetitiveness of the slow progress of mankind. And it was just as hard, if not harder, to depict modern times in the densest possible way, as I explained.'

He then added that it would certainly have been possible for him to increase the space given to the recent past but that would have involved further complications. Thus, if he had multiplied the space allotted to modern times by five, by devoting not six but thirty lines to one century, which already seemed a luxury, that would have meant writing a book of several hundred pages.

'So that's the dilemma I found myself in,' he said. 'Difficult, don't you think?'

We ordered another coffee and I tried to work out from my small knowledge of psychiatry into what category of madness such a view of the world might be placed.

'However,' he added, 'compared to my first plan, which I abandoned, I admit, because I didn't feel able to carry it through, all that is not so very complicated. I had in fact at first thought I would describe human life not from Neanderthal man on but from the very first human beings, in other words, not for the last hundred thousand years, but the last million. As a result, the work would have been a lot more concise: not six lines devoted to one century but ten times less, hardly more than half a line, roughly forty letters…'

I don't know what made us look each other in the eye, but to my amazement, instead of a glint of madness, I thought I saw a huge sorrow in his. He vainly tried to avert his gaze, as though trapped, and then suddenly took his head in his hands and his whole body shook with sobs.

I decided it would be more discreet to let him regain his self-control and refrained from asking him what was wrong. His voice still weak from crying, he said abruptly: 'My wife doesn't love me.'

We both remained silent, not taking our gaze off the black briefcase containing the book, the work which he viewed as a safe refuge from the meanness of life, his ultimate reference book, in relation to which everything else was to seem slight, fleeting or futile, his consolation, his safe haven, his solace, the thing that would make him an object of envy and admiration to others (his mind was at that time on a higher plane, in ethereal spheres), in short his drug, which, perhaps for the first time, did not produce its effect.

I don't know how long we remained thus, I with my eyes riveted on the black bag, he wiping his eyes from time to time on the back of his hand, till the waiter came up and, in some surprise, took our order for a third cup of coffee.

Translated from the French by Helen Constantine

Paris noir

Marc Werner

I shoot people for a living. It's my job. It's a job I could do just about anywhere, but I happen to do it in Paris. I line them up against the wall and shoot them. Sometimes they're further away and time is a luxury I don't have. But I still shoot them. As many times as it takes, and sometimes more. I shoot people. I shoot people every day.

With a camera, obviously.

I am a photographer. Studio stuff and paparazzi jobs. Yes, I was there that night in the Tunnel de l'Alma. Who wasn't? But that's another story.

I do my own stuff as well. Not for the money, but for my own entertainment, although I'm not sure that's the right word. In fact, I know it's not the right word. For my own satisfaction, perhaps. No, still not right. I do my own stuff because I have to, pure and simple. I have no choice. I'm not claiming to be a tortured artist, struggling, sacrificing myself for my work. You don't see me cutting off my ear. But it's true to say I have certain demons with which – with whom? – I wrestle.

They call it the City of Light. Really? Tell that to the victims. Tell that to businessman Roger Le Blond, found under a tarpaulin in an abandoned car in Neuilly in October 1937. Shot through the back of the neck and robbed. Tell that to Saint-Cloud estate agent Raymond Lesobre, shot through the back of the neck and robbed on 20 November the same year. Tell it to Eugen Weidmann's *first* victim for that matter, Joseph Couffy, a private hire car driver. Shot through the back of the neck and dumped beside the Paris–Orléans road on 8 September. Tell it to Weidmann's other victims as well.

Weidmann was tried for murder, found guilty and guillotined on 18 May 1939.

The City of Light? I don't think so.

My pictures of pop icons and movie stars have filled pages and pages in *Paris Match* and *Hello!*, my snaps of Diana and Dodi reached millions of people. Yet when I exhibited my Roger Le Blond series –

an abandoned Citroën just off boulevard Maillot, an old tarp and myself as Le Blond – in a little gallery off rue Laugier, no one came.

The police came, and one or two badly dressed ghouls, but the rest of Paris stayed away, muttering something about *mauvais goût* – bad taste.

Bad taste? I had sleepless nights – *nuits blanches* – in my apartment on rue Le Sueur, imagining what Le Blond and others had gone through.

In January 1999, I had two jobs on. One of them would make me a lot of money but didn't interest me in the slightest – photographing Kate Winslet around the Paris release of *Hideous Kinky*, her new film after *Titanic*. Although she's a very striking and attractive woman, most people will agree she looks best when caught off guard without the chance to adopt a sultry pose and certainly without the chance for wardrobe, make-up and stylists to muscle in and force her into their fantasy-figure template. I spend half my life in the company of stylists and stylists' assistants and I've yet to meet one who can make me think, even for a moment, that what they do is at all beneficial to the human race.

The other job was one of a type that comes along once in a blue moon, and it was not actually a job as such, in that I wouldn't get paid for it. If I was lucky I'd get to show the results somewhere and in the meantime I would find it a lot more satisfying than the Winslet shoot. I was working on a series of self-portraits taken at night. Using a tripod and the bulb setting on an old Pentax, I'd take a long – very long – exposure of myself while I was asleep. The idea was to take one a night over a period of a month and show them in sequence. Working under strict blackout conditions, I expected to find that, blackout conditions or not, more light penetrated the thick shutters and blinds on the night of the full moon than on any other night, rendering the shot much lighter than on nights when there was no moon.

The thing about January 1999 was that there would be a blue moon, as the English call it. A phenomenon that occurs once every three years or so. Two full moons in one month, the second one being referred to as blue, possibly deriving from a corruption of the French, *la double lune*. Either way, it had little chance of coming out blue in my pictures since I was working in black and white, naturally.

It was heralded as a major revolution when printing technology changed to allow the use of colour in newspapers. But it seemed to me an unnecessary development since my eyes, and, I suspect, most people's eyes, are sufficiently adapted to the sophistication of grey-scale printing for me to identify most colours in a black and white photograph, including blue, as in moon. Red, especially, leaps out at you in black and white, so to speak. It's softer, less dense – redder. Try it. I did.

I did a sequence of pictures in rue Princesse on the Left Bank. In January 1869, a restaurateur in rue Princesse discovered part of a human leg in the well from which he obtained his water. The police were informed and they had a look, finding another leg. Questioning a tailoress who had lived above the restaurant, they discovered that she had often been visited by another tailor, Pierre Voirbo, who numbered among his acquaintances a retired craftsman by the name of Désiré Bodasse, who had been missing for some time. The legs in the well had not only been finely, professionally sewn into lengths of calico, but one of them was still wearing an old stocking with the letter 'B' stitched into it with red cotton thread.

Further investigation and some ingenious detection led to Voirbo's inevitable confession (and subsequent suicide using a concealed razor while awaiting trial).

For my series of photographs, I wrapped an artificial limb in the stocking of an old girlfriend. I'd stitched into it a rough 'B' with scarlet thread and rolled the whole thing in a piece of calico salvaged from a dustbin on rue Blondel, a side street between rue St Denis and boulevard de Sébastopol shared equally and equably between the rag trade and the shag trade.

There's not much of a slope in either direction on rue Princesse, so little call for the drain-stops you see in abundance in Paris's hillier districts, but that was how I shot my updated version of poor Bodasse's leg. Insubstantial though it was, the cotton forming the initial 'B', the vital clue, was clearly red – even, as I say, in black and white.

Clearly to me anyway. Few other people expressed an opinion either way and the exhibition – on the rue des Beaux Arts, a nicely ironical touch – closed within a week.

January came to an end with the blue moon, the second full moon of the month, shining brightly in a clear sky on the night of the 31st.

As predicted, the shots taken on the nights leading up to the end of
the month got progressively lighter, just as they had become darker as
they approached the mid-point from the beginning. The 15 January
picture was almost completely dark, and virtually nothing could be
made out, as only an infinitesimal amount of light had been able to
enter the room during the night (my alarm clock, chosen for its lack
of a liquid crystal display, woke me each morning before dawn). In the
shots around 7 and 22 January, there's enough light to make out the
shape of my body in the bed and my head on the pillow. The form is
pleasingly fluid, representing movement in my sleep, but the bias shows
that I remain on my left side facing out of the bed for longer than I
stay in any other position.

The pictures taken at either end of the month are almost completely
white. In the 2 January photograph, the night of the first full moon, I
can make out nothing at all apart from an indistinct variation in the
whiteness where the left side of the bed would be.

The 31 January shot, however, troubles me. In theory it should be
more or less an exact copy of that from the beginning of the month,
given that on both nights the sky was clear throughout (I checked).
On this night of the *double lune*, I can just make out, in addition to the
vague form bulking just to the right of centre, ie the left side of the
bed, a different shape altogether on the other of the picture. It had to
be a trick of the light, I told myself as soon as I saw it, but it looked
like a human figure standing or stooping over the bed.

Could I accept the obvious explanation, that it was a freak exposure,
an accident of the light? Or would I torment myself with the possibility that it was either myself, sleepwalking, or an intruder? Was it
conceivable that something a shade more substantial than the light of
the full moon had entered my room while I slept?

I had to get out of the apartment and go for a walk to clear my head.
The first thing you notice when you turn right out of my building is
the unusual view of the Tour Eiffel poking up above a row of beautiful old buildings on the south side of avenue Foch. As you walk down
the street towards the avenue, the tower sinks lower and lower until,
just before you reach the end of the street, it dips down below the
rising level of the buildings, like the sun setting below the horizon.

The other thing you notice if you are walking down rue Le Sueur
is that mine is the only modern building in the whole street. It has

been designed sympathetically and blends in well, but you can see that it is much newer than the buildings around it.

I walked around the edge of the place Charles de Gaulle and down avenue Marceau to the place de l'Alma, where I stood and watched people reading the thousands of handwritten messages to Diana and Dodi. There were, as always, several bunches of fresh flowers around the base of the Flamme de la Liberté. I knew, in a way, what these people were feeling, both those who left the messages and those who read them. Sometimes, you could see, someone would read for a while and then, encouraged perhaps by the simple, open-hearted naivety of many of them, would shyly add one of their own.

I crossed the place de l'Alma and wandered up avenue Montaigne, where I had wasted the odd hour or so waiting for Roman Polanski to come out of his apartment building. Or return to it. Whatever. He never showed.

I retraced my steps, returning home via the place des Etats Unis and rue Paul Valéry. The poet, I reminded myself by reading from the street name, had died in 1945. Around the time, no doubt, that they knocked down my original building on rue Le Sueur and replaced it with the one that stands there today. The one in which I rent my apartment. They might possibly have waited before rebuilding – I don't know, I've never checked. And I'm only assuming they knocked it down in '45, or the year before, but it's a pretty safe assumption given the facts.

The house was the home of Marcel Petiot, a respected doctor and member of the Resistance. In March 1944, someone noticed smoke coming from Petiot's chimney that didn't smell like ordinary smoke from a domestic fire. The alarm was raised and the police investigated, finding a furnace in the basement of the building and the dismembered remains of twenty-seven bodies. When Petiot was tracked down several months later, he boasted that he had killed many more than twenty-seven people, but claimed they were all Nazi collaborators. It was alleged that he helped wealthy Jews escape from occupied France; in his house were also discovered forty-seven suitcases containing clothing that had been stripped of any name-tags or labels. Petiot continued to maintain he had killed only traitors and Nazis, but the jury believed otherwise and convicted him of twenty-seven murders. He was guillotined on 26 May 1946.

I do not know who I would rather the intruder in my apartment turn out to be: Petiot himself or one of his restless victims. They might have knocked down the walls, ceilings and floors of the old building and run up new ones, but who's to say that when the exterior is taken away, the interior goes with it? Do buildings have souls? I should have asked myself that question before moving into rue Le Sueur. I'm wondering, I'm bound to wonder, if what my camera has caught – if anything at all – is an after-image printed on the air itself. An indelible stain of terror or guilt, or both. And what makes me increasingly anxious is the fact that this year, because of January's blue moon and the brevity of February, there is going to be a second blue moon in March. A double *double lune*.

The wishbone bag

Christopher Kenworthy

If I'd told anybody about the walk home, they'd have said I was paranoid. But it seemed to me that I was followed by a dog. Keeping a discreet distance, it was barely close enough for me to hear it muttering.

It must have picked me up when I crossed the river at Saint Michel.
Myna dogs hang around in packs, usually under bridges; seeing one
alone at street level was rare and made me nervous. The origin of the
dogs had never been traced accurately, so there were more supersti-
tions about them than other species. When they'd developed voices
the previous year, a few people assumed the dogs were intelligent. Most
Parisians contested this, because the dogs spoke English, rather than
French. For the first few months, those of us living in the English
quarters were ribbed for speaking the language of dogs. In truth, the
Myna dogs weren't speaking at all. If you listened to a group of them,
it sounded like an eager conversation, but nothing of meaning was
being said. Each could only growl and hum a handful of words, and
they were mocking phrases they'd heard, repeating them without
understanding. It wasn't known how they'd been infected with the
complexity of a human throat, but they hadn't caught the brains to
match their voices. At least, that's what most people assumed.

My friend Janine had a theory; the dogs weren't picking up phrases,
but feeding off thoughts. That, she said, was why they didn't bother
so much about food. You never found them knocking over bins, or
stealing from food carts like other strays, because they weren't interested. Instead, they tracked the unwary and soaked up their thoughts;
when they spoke, it was little more than a mental burp. 'Why not
French thoughts?' I asked her. 'Too rich,' she said.

Until that dog followed me, I wouldn't have believed her. But as it
trotted along, it spoke in time with its steps – *you've gone wrong, you've
gone wrong*.

That thought had been nudging at me for three days, but hadn't
been conscious until a few minutes earlier. I'd left Ruth's late, but glad
to have stayed up late with her, pleased that we were growing more

intimate. We'd kissed before I left, which was a relief after months of build-up. So why was this thought nagging at me? I felt that I'd done something wrong. I couldn't tell why, but when the dog spoke, it was like hearing my thoughts dragging behind me.

It started raining, and the dog stopped following me, trotting off towards shelter. It was five in the morning, so the street lanterns were running out of food, the sour whiff of exhaust from their fermentation barrels making the place stink like a brewery. Beneath this, a smell of leaves and fire. The walls of rue St-Jacques were stained with smoke from the bonfires at the Jardins du Luxembourg. Occasional protests about health risks never gained much momentum because people liked the bonfires, especially in autumn. So long as it was mostly plant life being burned, it added something essentially Parisian to the arrondissement.

The same sense of romance made me decide I wouldn't go to bed when I got in. Having stayed up so late, I fantasised about spending the whole day exhausted, reading, writing, thinking about Ruth. The problem was that, even while walking, when I tried to think about her, I remembered the dog's words. *You've gone wrong.*

I concentrated on the water seeping into my boots, the trickles around my coat collar. When I reached my apartment, I was distracted by the state of my door's flyscreen. I'm not as paranoid as some people, but mites had eaten fresh holes through the mesh. If October warmed as forecast, I'd have to get those repaired.

It was good to get back to my room, but its familiarity was disturbed by the remnants of an evening I'd spent there with Janine. We'd left the wine glasses on the floor, and the book we'd been reading from was open at the same page.

I didn't tidy up at first, but watered my plants. There weren't many. People call me old fashioned, but I like to take advantage of the space I've earned. Janine called my flat spartan, because apart from the seats, I only had lamps and books. There were no paintings or ornaments, and all the walls were the same faint yellow. I wasn't obsessed with cleanliness, or anything peculiar, but liked my space to be free. It was strange, then, that I left the wine glasses and the book where they were for the rest of the day. It wasn't to remind me of Janine, but to make the flat feel a bit more lived in. The sense of confusion that had come over me made the apartment feel a bit lonely.

I wanted to call her, but wirelice were rife in this block, and the cables had been down since Tuesday. There was talk of handheld phones being issued again; pocket-sized, wireless transceivers, with a built-in food battery. Most people dismissed this as fantasy, because there was too much interference from speed growth for anything other than cables to be effective. They were faulty so often, though, that people resorted to paper messages, carried across town by friends, to be left on local boards. Janine once suggested we stay in touch by carrier pigeon; it was something she'd read about, which was supposed to be true. Trained birds were said to have carried messages across vast continents. If they could do that, taking messages across Paris should be easy, she said. I countered this, by reminding her of the French fondness for pigeon meat. Although the rest of the world ate stillborn flesh, older Parisians preferred to eat things that had some level of awareness before they were cooked.

I ate the soft part of a baguette, dropping the crust into the bin. A smell came out, making me wonder if the digestive swelling was ill again. I avoided looking in the bin as a rule. At best, the veined dome inside it looked like a peeled muscle, covered in the slime of waste food. If my bin was ill, I'd be stuck with its stench until the following weekend. The vets were taking weeks to get round to domestic call-outs, because of engineering problems in the city. The construction machines were getting sick at an alarming rate. With the reordering of space being an ongoing project, the Paris skyline was always busy with cranes and scaffolding. Apparently, it's always been that way. While the various monuments and towers come and go, the only permanent features in the landscape are the bright orange cranes. They used to be made of metal rather than bone, and used hydraulic ligaments instead of muscle sheaths, but their design was essentially the same. Being overworked, though, the latest cranes were susceptible to cramping, seeping and malaise, at a frequency the vets couldn't keep up with. And with the Métro being as unhealthy as ever, I knew a poorly waste bin wouldn't be a veterinary priority.

Looking in the bin, it was worse than I'd feared, because shreds of undigested squid were still there from three days ago. The swelling had split down the middle, its wound lined with white flies' eggs.

I wasn't too bothered that my bin had died, but I slammed the lid shut. The image reminded me of what happened to my brother when he was fifteen. We lived in England then, in an area that was still used for agriculture; we could wander around fields and by streams without being bothered. Space was barely a problem, but disease was. Stephen was prone to illness, and quite small, so that he looked more than five years younger than me. Whenever he went off on his own, I worried. He hadn't gone missing, as such, but I went looking for him because he'd been out all morning. I found him lying beneath an apple tree, not far from the house, asleep, breathing, but otherwise still. He'd been still for so long that blossom petals had landed on his eyelids. Leaning closer, I saw that they weren't petals, but eggs, which had been buried between his lids into the meat of his eye. I tried to pull them off without disturbing him, but as the first one burst between my fingers, he woke up, scratching the rest of them away. For years, I'd convinced myself it was the scratching that blinded him, but now I know the damage had already been done.

My Dad grew up at a time when synthetic adaptation was seen as an expression of personality. He tried to explain it many times, using phrases such as 'being yourself', but I never understood how replacing withered parts of the body with metal was expressive. He was old enough to think the word 'cool' could justify anything.

It began when he was young, before the technology had advanced further than artificial valves and limbs. Yearning for the cyborg, his generation pierced themselves, adorning their faces, teeth and genitals with non-functional metal. This paved the way for the metallic look, when replacement body-parts became widespread; a metal finish was used for the sake of fashion. Even though skin-friendly synthetic could integrate better, people chose metal. Dad believed the shining hub of chrome around his face was better than any piercing.

He went through a mid-life crisis in his sixties. The metal husk of his jaw had tarnished, and the flesh around it was a pale lip. Attempting to spruce himself up, he had the metal polished and engraved with Celtic swirls.

That was the year he started preaching about drugs again. He'd pestered me throughout my teens, saying I was missing out if I didn't try them. I'd read enough about the drugs from his era to be terrified of them; not for the lack of control or side-effects, but for the suppression of intelligence. The drugs depressed judgement and boosted sensation, so that a rather vacuous experience felt mystical. Ignorance was bliss. You only need to read the fiction from those decades to see the effect it had. If I brought that up, Dad mocked my interest in literature, saying, 'Why waste your time with other people's thoughts, when you can open your own mind.' It was a standard speech.

If I sound like a fanatic, it's because Dad made it personal. He was essentially a kind man, until you got on to his opinions. And sadly, it's those times that are easier to remember; the complaints, blame and hinted disgust. It came to a head when Stephen lost his eyes. Dad wanted him to have synthetic replacements, because they carried no risk of infection. It was nothing to do with fashion, he said. I put forward the argument for biological growths. I knew they had been dangerous once, when they were grown in live hosts and blood-stocks, but now they were spawned in isolation there was no risk.

'I don't want him to be a mutant,' Dad said, refusing to use the word 'bioborg'.

Stephen was so withdrawn during his blindness, that getting an opinion out of him was difficult. It was only when I suggested that we escape to Paris that he showed any interest. I was old enough to leave home, but Stephen would be running away. I enjoyed the thought of looking after him. My Dad would have blamed my love of fiction for this plan, and that made me value it even more. My hope was to steal Dad's car, taking it as far as the port; that would give us transport, while taking his away. Cars had vanished in Europe, but the habit of private ownership was strong in England, and roads were cherished until the need for space became too great. Although muscle engines had been around for a decade, efficient public transport was resisted for as long as possible. Instead, sheep were modified to excrete a fuel for combustion engines. But when we left, the reorganisation of land had begun, and maps were going out of date weekly.

Stealing the car involved nothing more than taking the keys while Dad was asleep, and rolling it out of the shed. Despite the simplicity of our plan, Dad might have been proud of us, because when he was young, petty crime attracted a lot of kudos. At the gate I fired the engine, and managed to get down our lane without the headlamps. I spent the next few hours learning to drive.

I met Janine within a few weeks of arriving in Paris. It happened on a day when I was feeling confused, which could have explained my reaction to her.

She was working in the eye clinic, on rue Manin. It was on the wrong side of the river, but the standards on the Right Bank were said to be higher. Stephen and I made our way there on the overground. The street was busy with carriages, but most were only half full, their lid-like tops drawn back because of the sunshine. When the driver pulled out, the engines made a spongy chugging noise, as flanks of muscle tugged on bone to drive the wheels. The Métro would have been quicker, but Stephen hated it down there; he said it stank like a nosebleed, and the sound was too muffled. Travelling above ground gave me more to see and share with him. I was glad of the hours I'd spent immersed in books, because the vocabulary I'd acquired helped me describe the views. Stephen prompted me eagerly, asking for the source of sounds and smells.

That day I talked more than usual, feeling anxious about the city. While the rest of Europe struggled to make plans, Paris was implementing them. As the critics pointed out, that rush for change was leading to problems. Modified life was becoming unstable. The reason was simple; they'd started using something they didn't understand. They'd found that water was responsible for transferring the patterns of life; DNA was there to read quantum information from the water, expressing it chemically. That breakthrough gave them control of life; species could be mixed, organs spawned, and life-based machines became the most efficient. The problem was that although it had practical value, water memory was too obscure for them to understand. There was no way of predicting what might happen once the locks of stability were removed. Water gets everywhere, so there was a danger that nothing would remain pure. There were rumours of complexity patterns becoming viral, spreading throughout Europe. At first only chaos was passed on, which is probably how Stephen lost his eyes. Over time, form was beginning to spread, and species were blending.

It was curious that I should worry about this, because the world is never out of danger. I'd read enough to know that there's always an imminent war, plague or technology to worry about. Especially if your own life is feeling rather empty.

The clinic was on the fourth floor, so while Stephen was giving his samples in the growing room, I looked out at the parc des Buttes

Chaumont. Vine-draped suspension bridges led from the surrounding buildings, through trees, to the steep island of rock in the centre. People filed along the walkways, gathering on the grassed verandas around the rock to eat and drink. Vendors grew meat in tanks, slicing and frying it to order.

I saw a reflection in the window; a woman closing a door gently, then watching me. When I turned round she introduced herself as Janine Larbelestier, and said Stephen would be in there for some time. Her accent was so French, I had to listen closely. 'He'll be quite relaxed, and Gloria will look after him. I'll see him again in an hour or so.'

I'd seen Gloria in reception, wearing a white uniform, even a hat, so it was peculiar to see Janine looking so informal. She was wearing a long brown skirt and top, and a small pink cardigan. It was the sort of combination that could have looked dreadful, but she wore it perfectly. I never used to notice clothes, but since I'd been in Paris, I couldn't help making an effort.

I wanted to say something that would encourage her to stay, to show that I might be interesting to know. All I could say was, 'It's an incredible view.'

She came closer, and leaned on the window sill, her blonde hair drifting forward to brush against its reflection. I'd never seen hair look so soft, and was already quite cross with myself for feeling so moved by her. It was probably because she was the first French woman I'd spoken to. I tried to ignore the sensation and looked out again.

'Everything's changing,' Janine said.

She was so melancholy that I felt as if I was being tricked, forced to find her attractive. When you're in a foreign city for the first time, worrying about the future and longing for meaning, a sad voice makes you ache. I wanted to hold her.

'You don't sound happy,' I said.

She smiled in a way that was almost a wince. 'We never just *do* anything in Paris. We always have a revolution.' When I didn't reply to that, she added, 'The worst is yet to come.'

My own fantasies about disaster had encouraged hers. Which is how we ended up in a café on Baurelle sharing coffee and lemon cake while Stephen remained with the nurse.

We'd covered the basics so quickly that by the time our drinks arrived she was telling me all about her childhood in Paris and the rush of changes. I got the impression she hadn't been able to talk to anybody openly about this for some time. Although she'd sounded apprehensive about the changes, she was clearly excited by them. I was glad to find that I liked her more when she was enthusiastic; it was healthier than being attracted to somebody who was terminally wistful.

After a while she said, 'Am I boring you, because if I am, tell me.'

Her voice would have been enough to hold my interest, so I said, 'You're not. Not at all.'

'If I do, you can talk to me about the English weather, and get your own back.'

'So tell me about the riots.'

She put her cup down and made eye contact again. I found it difficult to look back at her, because I felt as though my feelings were being read. If I smiled dumbly at everything she said, I would look stupid, so I tried to look as if I was concentrating, without pouting too much.

'It happened last year,' she began, 'after money was withdrawn. People were all given the same amount of food, clothing, the same machines and luxuries. It evened things up. But that didn't please the rich. It meant the only advantage they had left was space, and they wanted to keep it.'

'I can imagine.'

She seemed to misinterpret this affirmation, thinking I was starting a sentence, so I nodded for her to continue.

'Now that so much is catered for by machines, intelligence and imagination are more valued. A good mind will earn more space. The problem for the rich was that they had nothing creative to offer. They'd inherited their land, or earned it from the labour of others.'

'The bourgeoisie?' I suggested, half-joking.

'Yes. So when it was announced that they would be moved on, they took to the streets, threatening to riot. But they'd never really learned to be rebellious, and barely filled a single street. Their riot was limited to a few thrown bottles and restrained jeers. The crowd of onlookers was larger than the protest. They were worn out by sunset, and that was that.'

'What happened to them?'

'Most live in loft conversions in Montparnasse; they eat as well as the rest of us, but they have menial jobs now. Vendors, cleaners, waiters. It makes a change. When I was a child, all the waiters were at university. Do you think I'm bad, for taking so much pleasure in this?'

'No. I hope they do the same in England. My Dad would be delighted.'

'It's inevitable,' she said. 'There is no value in *stuff* any more.'

'You sound like an enthusiast for the changes.'

'But look at how miserable everybody is. The problems people thought they had were not the real problems. Everybody is still lonely.'

I felt exposed, and knew that if I said something now, about what I hoped for with her, she would be embarrassed. To avoid this, I asked how she came to work at the clinic.

'You want me to tell you something romantic, about my father going blind…' She trailed off, laughing.

'No, I…'

'Have you ever seen a salamander's egg?' It was probably rhetorical, but I shook my head. Her face was serious now. 'My father was a breeder of salamanders, so I saw many of them. In the evening, I would lie down next to their tanks and watch the eggs hanging from blades of grass. They are so beautiful. Each egg is like a drop of water, but inside there is a white shadow that spins slowly – the baby. All the time it spins. Nobody knew how or why for a long time. That fascinated me. Now we know the movement sets up a pattern that allows water memory to be expressed.' She raised her eyebrows back towards the clinic. 'Your brother's eyes will be spun into existence as well. And so,' she concluded flatly, apparently worried that I was bored, 'I became interested in morphology. I like to see things coming into being.'

'But you weren't interested in designing machines?'

'New ways of doing the same things. No, I'm not interested in that. We've always had transport, we've always had food. Giving sight back to people makes me feel worthwhile. And now you'll say I really am being romantic.'

'Not at all.'

There was a pause, and she looked worried, as though she was about to tell me a secret. I almost didn't hear what she said, because for a moment her face was so familiar, it was like recognising somebody I knew. I managed to catch the words, before they faded.

'Before, you said you could imagine… something. But you didn't say what.'

'It's a phrase. *I can imagine*. It means, *I believe you.*'
She looked a bit disappointed, but changed the subject.
'We'd better get back to the clinic. He'll nearly be ready.'

Stephen saw more of Janine than I did over the next few weeks, while she trained him to see again. I said hello to her at either end of their sessions and she always smiled, but so formally it was as though we'd never had that conversation. By the time Stephen could see well enough to walk, he'd make his way across the city alone, and I didn't get to see her. Worst of all, he told me that in the course of their conversations, Janine had mentioned a partner. She'd been living with him for five years.

This bothered me more than I thought it would. I barely knew Janine, and although she'd been good company, I shouldn't have expected anything to happen. But I kept thinking that a mistake had been made, and that we should have had more time together.

When I talked to Stephen about this, he was embarrassed. We were sitting on our balcony above rue Lussac, looking out over the Palais gardens. Our room was tiny, because we were still in tourist accommodation, so we often stayed on the balcony even when it was getting cold. That evening, the air felt icy before the sun had set: the first sign of autumn. Fascinated with his new sight, Stephen avoided eye contact with me, staring across the park, while I pestered him with my problems. I could always tell when he was getting anxious, because his pupils would dilate at different rates, the mauve irises twitching. Being several years younger, he was reluctant to give me advice, but I pressed him for suggestions.

'Perhaps you're taking this too seriously,' he said when I wouldn't let the subject drop. I looked so stunned that he added, 'I mean, just that you can't look for answers to your own life in somebody else. You know, maybe you should be happy with yourself first.'

It sounded so much like one of Dad's speeches, that I shouted my reply.

'So we're all meant to live in isolation are we?' Before he could answer, I said, 'People have needs.'

Dad always used to go on about the importance of being independent, of letting people come and go. Needs, he insisted, were a weakness. Which hardly made me feel like I was important to him. But of course, there was some truth in it, which is why it angered me so much. Perhaps my attachment to Janine *did* arise from weakness. It was possible I imagined the emotions, because it was better than having nobody to desire.

Janine's unavailability wouldn't have affected me so much if she hadn't seemed so familiar. Since meeting her, I'd been bothered by a sense of having forgotten something important. Logically, I knew I'd never been to Paris before, but I was troubled by a memory of it. I could remember an oak-panelled room with wooden floors and a tall window; it smelt of burning leaves, and dusty blue sunlight came through the window. I could remember somebody else in the room with me, and somebody in the room next door. But nothing more. The sensation was akin to waking from a meaningful dream, unable to recall what made it feel so important.

It was mid-September and I was anxious for the leaves to turn, but we were faced with the prospect of leaving Paris. That would destroy any chance I had of tracing the source of these memories. To stay there we'd have to give up tourist status. Neither of us wanted to leave, so we applied for new accommodation. Stephen found a good room by attending college, and I ended up one street further from the park. To stay there, I was obliged to get a job and was assigned to a careers officer. In England, I'd barely worked since finishing my history degree, so she struggled to find anything suitable. Long term, I wanted to be a writer and thought Paris would be an ideal location, but she said there were no jobs available. Writing was, she suggested, more of a hobby. She didn't sound enthusiastic about any of the proper jobs on her list, but spent most of her time telling me what was wrong with them, saying, 'I just don't know what will suit you.'

The only description that caught my eye was Untouched Spaces Officer. She looked at the list, staring at the ceiling to translate her description.

'These are rooms, houses, places that weren't changed during the reorganisation. The council sealed them off, because they are only allowed to redistribute space once the owners have been found. I don't imagine this is your sort of history. These are houses from just a decade ago. And you'd need better French.'

'But I'd get to go into the old houses?'

'Your job would be to track down the owners. You would be given access to the untouched spaces. There would be a lot of damp and infection.'

I started work the next morning.

Paris greened. For every private room, an area of equal size had to be made public, as a park, gallery or café. Graveyards were dug over and grassed, buildings razed or shifted to make space. The stone banks of the Seine veiled themselves in ivy, and the bridges were lined with poplars and lime trees, speed-grown during a single spring. Plants were unrationed, so window boxes and walls ran wild with them. Paris in the spring was so heavily perfumed, it made me feel drowsy. By July, the rotting flowers began to attract flies, so it would have been a bad summer for disease, except that autumn came early. In mid-September there were so many leaves that on windy days the surface of the river was thick with them. They were dredged out before they could rot, piled in the nearby spaces and burned. Sunsets that autumn were deeper than usual.

My own work was unaffected by the speed of the changes, because once a house or room was set aside, nobody could touch it until our department gave authority. And nobody seemed to mind how slowly we worked. I was less concerned with tracking down missing owners than with finding the oak-panelled room that I'd remembered. I didn't tell Stephen about this, because he'd say I was fixating on a dream, clinging to a hope, rather than facing reality. I knew he might be right, but couldn't abandon my search.

Nothing more tangible came to me than the tall window, the wooden floor and the sense of people being nearby. The details were exact, in terms of smell and warmth and light, but the memory was limited to one view of the room. If the memory came from a time before the changes, untouched spaces were the one place I might find more reminders. It was even possible that the room itself had been preserved.

During that year, I didn't find the room, although many were similar. In each case, once I had carried out the initial research demanded by my job – rooting through cupboards for letters and clues – I would sit quietly in the empty spaces, trying to remember more. In some rooms there was almost nothing, but others hummed with familiar impressions. It felt as though the history had been stored up when they were sealed away, and by disturbing the air I was gaining a whiff of the past. Usually, just as I became distracted or sleepy, I'd feel a brush of the memory.

It was almost a year since I'd seen Janine, and although I still thought about her, the memory of the oak-panelled room seemed more important. I doubted now that she was even associated with it, except perhaps in terms of its vaguely sad emotion. It was this realisation that made me decide to tell Stephen about the memory, on the anniversary of our arrival in Paris. He'd become a much more interesting person since starting at college. Although his opinions were effectively the same as every student's, he became less like Dad and more fun to be with. I didn't get to tell him, though, because he had news for me. We'd planned to go out, but when he came round and told me that he'd seen Dad on the Ile de la Cité, we stopped in, sharing two bottles of Beringer before it went dark. It wasn't that we were scared of bumping into Dad, but that we wanted to talk openly, without being overheard.

He said that Dad's jaw had jewels in it now, a line of amber studs along its edge. Apart from that, he looked old before his time, greying and bald.

'He wasn't at all frightening any more, but I backed off anyway.'

'What could he be doing here?'

'He could be looking for us,' Stephen said, not really believing it.

'But why?'

'I don't know. Perhaps he couldn't believe it when you took me away. You know, he might not have *forced* me to have those eyes. He was probably just mouthing off and couldn't believe it when we left.'

'I can hardly picture him being heartbroken. I imagine he was relieved.'

Stephen shrugged. 'But he wouldn't be coming to do anything bad to us. He's hardly going to gouge my eyes out, is he?'

It was over two months later, towards the end of October, that I had my first breakthrough. All the conditions were right: the sun filtering through thin cloud, the air cold enough to suggest frosty mist, but smelling of wood smoke. It was so similar to my memory of the room that I felt sure I'd find a connection.

Carriages in the Latin Quarter were in short supply, because of disease; of those that were running, many limped, one wheel dragging against the others. The Métro had been down all week, so I walked to the other side of the river and waited for a carriage. I could see dogs gathered on the bank under Pont Neuf, talking. I'd heard rumours about these dogs being seen at Tournelle, but had assumed they were another myth. Nobody else seemed to be taking much notice, which made me realise I'd not spent enough time in the city recently. I was so fascinated by the dogs' chattering that I missed the first carriage. Their words were rapid and sudden, each dog talking over the other so that it was impossible to make sense of their conversation. It was clear, however, that they were speaking English.

I was still thinking about them as I wandered into the parc Moulin. The basement flat I was seeking was all that remained of a residential block that used to stand near the windmill, before the area was cultivated. Rather than leave the building standing, they'd pulled it down and crafted their park over the flat. You can always recognise an untouched space by the zinc plates over every door and window. In this case, because the flat was effectively buried, I was simply looking for an entrance to a stairwell. The zinc sheet was set in the grass like a silver puddle. The metal looked slightly more crystalline than usual, but felt dry to the touch. The lock turned without breaking, which was a relief, because some types of metal were becoming prone to decay.

Downstairs, I struggled to see with my gas-lamp, but could tell the rooms had remained untouched since being sealed. I'd come across some houses that had been broken into by kids looking for extra space, which always reduced the purity of evidence.

The space beyond the windows on the other side had been filled in, so they were looking out on to soil. The glass had broken where white tree roots wormed through. Little piles of soil had dried on the floor. The room smelt of mulch and wasn't at all in keeping with the day above ground, which disappointed me. I checked for nests, in case anything unpleasant had made its home there, then spent an hour or so looking for indications of the owner's whereabouts.

After that, when I sat in an armchair, my eyes had adjusted enough to see the whole room at once. In artificial light, I found it difficult to gain impressions. The sound of the gas-lamp was distracting and it was impossible to imagine what this room would have been like when filled with daylight. After five minutes I gave up.

When I reached for the lamp on the window sill, I noticed a shape that I hadn't seen before; it was something dry, like the shavings from a pencil. Looking closer, I could see it was a moth or butterfly, the wings pressed together with age. I cupped it in my hand and went upstairs.

Outside, it was bright, but the closed wings looked dull, like a dead leaf. The air felt still, but there must have been a breeze, because the wings parted. Inside, they were orange, blotted with inky blue. Around their edge was a vein of gold; when I touched it, the gold dust coated my fingers. Another movement from the air, and the wing broke against my hand.

I remembered the oak-panelled room; bonfire smoke outside, making the sunlight cold; the chill of wooden floorboards warming when I stepped in front of the window. In the next room was an old man, writing at a desk. And Janine was behind me; I could see her in the reflection, sitting on the floor, leaning on one arm. I turned to speak, but as I did so, my eyes opened, and I was staring into the sun over parc Moulin. The butterfly had gone, with only the bloom of dust left on my fingers.

I planned to keep this discovery to myself, but that night I was put off guard. I'd eaten at Blanchimont, then spent too long walking, realising how tired I was only after the transport had closed down. By the time I made it back to rue Guynemer, most of the lamps had burned out, but I could make out a person sitting on my steps. I thought it was my brother from his posture; he never buttoned his coat, but wrapped it around himself from the pockets, making his shoulders slump forward. His face was in shadow, so I sparked up my pocket lamp and directed the beam at him. It was Stephen, but his eyes shone like a dog's. It looked like there was a grainy film of bronze at the back of them. He covered his face as I approached.

'You weren't in,' he said, his breath smelling of wine.

'Your eyes were golden.'

'Oh yeah,' he said, a bit embarrassed, still looking dazzled. Then moving on, he began to ramble. 'I didn't want to go home. There was a gathering near here. A few friends. I was too tired to go home. I hoped you wouldn't mind me coming here. But...'

'Stephen. What happened to your eyes?'

'Can't we go inside?'

He wasn't one for getting drunk or staying out, and this worried me as much as the light in his eyes. I wanted to talk to him and find out what was going on. His face was lined more than it should have been, with tension rather than age. Although he said he wanted to warm up and go to sleep, I guessed that he wanted to talk. When we got upstairs he confirmed this, by sitting in the kitchen and letting me get him a drink.

My immediate suspicion was that he'd seen Dad, but he denied that. 'Not even from a distance,' he assured me, cupping a bowl of coffee.

I pressed him to tell me about his eyes, and his response was to rub them, then mutter an explanation. The regrowth had made him susceptible to infection. Anything to do with eyes could be passed on to him. Not just disease, but complexities, patterns of form. He'd acquired a layer of shiny cells behind his eye, like a cat's. They reflected light back through the retina, to intensify the image. 'Helps you see in the dark. Not much use in Paris.'

'How did you catch it?'

'Flies, I suppose.'

It was coming light by the time he'd levelled out, even though he hadn't gone into much detail about his private life. He was, he said, just in need of a bit of space from his usual friends. Whatever was bothering him seemed to diffuse without discussion. When he eventually yawned, I imagined him going off to the spare bed, and felt the need to tell him about my afternoon in the basement flat. In a rush I told him about the oak-panelled room.

He shrugged. 'I've heard of things like that,' he said without elaborating, but then said, 'How old was she?'

'Who?'

'Janine. In this memory, how old was she? Only, it might be the future you're remembering.'

A visit to the eye clinic confirmed that Janine had left a year ago. Nobody knew where she lived now and their computer files had gone rotten, so they couldn't make further checks. The staff I talked to couldn't imagine that she'd left Paris, which was something.

It should have been easy to track her down, especially with the resources available to me through my job, but all the databases were suffering. Every form of storage device was prone to sickness, and many decayed before they could be backed up as hard copies. The information that remained was rapidly being printed, because paper was easy to spawn. Even though it took up valuable space, it was the most stable way of recording information. It became illegal to throw away books, in case they contained a last trace of information. Sorting through what remained was close to impossible, and much was being stored out of reach (even from my department) until new library space could be found. To make matters worse, that autumn Paris experienced the first communication breakdown. Wirelice and ceramic mites bred through cables faster than they could be replaced. Parisians adapted rapidly, because the French have always relied on word of mouth to get a message around. The real loss was music; not just recordings, but instruments of every kind were eaten away and orchestras were put out of work. Choirs became fashionable again. People whistled more. You even heard them singing as they worked. By that point, almost everything made of metal was pitted and weak and had to be replaced with a bioborg equivalent. *La fatigue du métal*, people called it. The old technology was being expunged, like grit from a sealed wound.

By New Year I was tired of wondering about Janine. My desire to speak to her was still urgent, but my inability to find her was boring me. Stephen kept telling me to get a life and let her go. Trying to pin down a future with her was more likely to limit me, he said, and I was weary enough to agree.

My forced enthusiasm for a new life was soon reduced to ennui by a sunless January. Snow and rain competed for attention, so the streets were always glossed with water. Everybody had wet feet and hair. In cafés there seemed to be more steam from people's clothes than from drinks. Perfume was masked by the smell of wet wool and skin. People went pale with the cold, then stewed themselves overnight in central heating. They became breeding grounds. Illness flourished. Wherever they gathered – cafés, parks and meeting halls – the sound of coughing was louder than conversation. The diseases caused minor physical symptoms – runny eyes, aching legs and a sore throat – but they broke your heart. Painful emotions were passed on with every wet breath.

I caught my first dose of sadness in February, which was a shame because the frost and sunshine made it my favourite month in Paris. Fortunately, the melancholy I picked up wasn't the sort that made me want to hide away. If anything, I rushed through my work in the untouched spaces, so I could get out into the sunlight. But even then I was subdued. The sadness made me feel as though something was missing, and I wandered around Paris, tired and thirsty, my lips and skin dried by the sun, looking for something I wasn't certain about.

The sensation was so similar to the loss I'd felt over the oak-panelled room that I refused to accept I'd caught sadness for a couple of weeks, thinking the emotions were my own. I couldn't imagine it was a symptom of my physical illness; conversely, I was convinced the ache in my body was triggered by feeling sad. But even on good days I was uncomfortably plaintive and could never laugh without going quiet afterwards, feeling bad about nothing in particular.

It was in this state that I came across Janine again. Being too cold to sit, I was wandering by the Seine, between Notre Dame and Pont de la Tournelle. The trees by the book-exchange carts were black with meltwater, only their shadow-sides frosted. I was watching barges trawl the river. The fish had been introduced years ago to clear silt, but now they were taking too much detail from the water and had to be removed. I'd seen the fish barges many times, but every time they built the charge (in a nerve cluster based on some kind of eel), I grew expectant. I didn't like watching the fish die, but couldn't resist the build-up. Although the edge of the river was frozen around the lilies and reeds, it was clear beyond. I could make out the fish as dusky ovals, until the barge discharged its shock with a sound like strained ice, and then the fish turned on their sides, silver, and floated to the surface. I turned away and saw Janine. She was smiling, and the man she was with repeatedly kissed her cheeks and nose. She kept pushing him away, but he persisted. It appeared to be some kind of game, and they both laughed.

If you're going to be jealous, it's best not to be jealous of the French, because they make such a big display of their affection.

I escaped from view up the steps and watched from the bridge. Even as they walked, their arms and hands constantly moved to stroke and warm each other.

It took a while for me to realise the trees were dripping and that my face was being numbed by water.

I couldn't tell where the sadness ended and my depression about Janine began, but it took until May for me to start feeling better. Meeting Ruth helped. I first saw her at one of Stephen's late-night gatherings. I'd dropped in to see him for a chat and was surprised to find there

was only standing room in the main lounge. The place hushed pleasantly and everybody listened while I explained myself and prepared
to leave. It reminded me of walking in on Dad in the evening when
his friends were there; trying to appear natural, feeling observed.
Stephen encouraged me to stay, and his guests hummed approval, but
I felt that would make me look a bit sad, so I pretended to be in a rush.
I made eye contact with Ruth and then wished I'd stayed. I'm not
usually attracted to tall women, but everything about her suggested
warmth. Her face had the calm of somebody who has woken up after
a good night's sleep, and her skin was the sort that instantly makes you
wonder how soft it would feel. She was the last person I looked at as
I left the room.

Stephen was obliging enough to ensure that I was invited the next
time he went out with that crowd, and Ruth sat next to me during
the meal. She was younger than me, and English, but somehow we
found it quite easy to talk.

We went out several times, but after a fortnight of going places
together and eating out, nothing physical had happened. After a while
I came to enjoy the pleasure of being near her, without actually starting
a relationship. It wasn't a friendship so much as a build-up.

The only time we argued was following an incident at the parc des
Buttes Chaumont. It was the first hot day of the year so the park was
busy. Being there made me unusually tense, which was strange, because
normally I loved wandering on the ivy bridges. It was somewhere that
I usually went alone, but I tried to feel good about having Ruth with
me. She was quiet, which might have been because of my mood, so I
made an effort, telling her a story about Stephen. We walked on to one
of the grassed verandas and she interrupted my story. That could have
put me in a worse mood, except that her observation interested me.

Three girls, no older than ten, were kneeling around the base of a
beech tree. Something was leaking from the trunk, and they were
pulling at the bark to find its source. I was about to shout at them to
stop, but a sheet of the bark tore away, revealing sappy wood the colour
of pine. There appeared to be some kind of fungus under there. The
girls backed off and we moved closer for a better look. Several clear
sacs were growing from the wood. Each contained a milky fluid, and
within that, the partially formed body of a bird. They appeared to be
made of scar tissue, rather than good flesh, and their feathers were like

wet spines. Their eyes were more advanced and they twitched open in response to the light. One of the sacs gave way, the body dropping out. Unable to stand, the chick struggled, coating itself in dust and grass. The others followed soon after, their beaks straining open, as though gasping. I couldn't tell whether I was disgusted, or upset that they were dying.

'Kill them,' Ruth said. Her voice became quieter. 'We have to kill them.'

The girls became aware of us for the first time, and all three began crying.

I couldn't bring myself to stamp on the birds, but felt unreasonably sad, and annoyed. Ruth said something like, 'I can't believe you,' and I snapped back at her. In a matter of seconds we'd taken on fierce expressions and were arguing. It was over in a minute, but I felt confused, because although I knew we shouldn't have argued, I was annoyed with her.

'It's not worth it,' she said. 'I'll see you tomorrow.'

It was said fondly, given the circumstances, but as she walked away, the afternoon felt spoilt and incomplete. I was left looking at the bodies of the birds, the mucus on their skin making them look as though they were melting.

It was a bad summer for plagues. Species were passed on as infections, and most organic matter was capable of giving birth to new forms. Baby snakes hatched from fruit, hairless mice were seen nosing out of dead dogs, and ants erupted from leaves. Animal faeces in the street, if left untreated, could spawn all manner of beetles by the following dawn. Most of the plagues were stillborn, but those that lived were hungry. A flock of crows that emerged from a sweet-chestnut tree in parc Saint Julien became known as the swallowing birds, because they were meat-eaters. They fed off rodents and stillbirths, but had been known to hunt down pets. More damaging to the infrastructure of Paris were sugar-stealers: birds, insects and plants that tapped into nectar supplies, leaving many lamps and transports without fuel. Culling was rare, though, because most plagues came to the end of their own natural history in a matter of weeks. More tenacious were the speed growths; wherever wood came into contact with earth, it was liable to grow rapidly. Wooden fences and benches sprouted and became knots of trees in a matter of days, often rupturing tarmac and upsetting the foundation of buildings. Even soil spilt from a pot on to a wooden floor could lead to saplings.

The Myna dogs bred rapidly. Nobody ever saw the puppies, but their numbers quadrupled.

Humans were affected less than most species; the changes were minor adaptations, rather than birthings. Mouth-like wounds opened, usually in the belly, leading to useless new organs. Moss grew in patches on the scalp, a pattern like the veins in leaves could form in your cheeks. What might appear to be a bruise could turn out to be fungus. Scabs, when scratched, released seeds. On the Métro, the smell of perfume was replaced by the odour of overripe fruit, as people greened.

Although little remained stable, there were some attractive benefits. The alder trees in the Jardins du Luxembourg picked up biolumin-escence, possibly from fireflies, and at dusk their leaves would glow. Like their insect counterparts, they didn't shine all the time, but flick-ered on and off. It made them appear to glitter, and they cast a sap-coloured glow on to the ground beneath them. The place became popular with students, but I liked it there all the same.

My favourite way to spend a Sunday evening was sitting on the east side of the park, where bird–owners brought their cages and slung them from the trees as the sun set. The birds had been taught to sing tunes that were largely lost. Each could manage only a few bars. You'd expect the competition for sound to make it cacophonous, but it was more musical than if each had been left to sing alone.

Sitting at my usual table after the sun had gone down one night in July, I saw Janine. She must have seen me first, because she was watch-ing me, to see if I recognised her. I must have looked more shocked than pleased.

'What happened to your eye?' she said.

I had no idea what she meant, but was pleased she'd spoken. After all the time, and the thoughts I'd had about her, I couldn't think of anything to say, except, 'I don't know.'

She sat down, putting her bag on the table between us, rooting through it.

'Are you well?' she said. 'Generally?'

'Yes. Are you?'

She nodded, but then looked at me; I wasn't sure if she was looking into me, or trying to see what was wrong with my eye. It was difficult to tell what her mood was. From her manner, it seemed clear that more had gone on between us than one meeting would suggest, especially as it had been over two years ago. Until then I hadn't realised she'd experienced any *frisson*, and that gave me hope. But she seemed bored, or maybe resigned.

She found a flat polished stone in her pocket and handed it to me. 'A mirror,' she said. 'There should be enough light from the tree.'

I hadn't seen my reflection, except in water, since metal became unstable. Her stone was good enough for me to see that the iris of my right eye had darkened, as though a bleed had spread through it. It reminded me of the blotting of colour in the butterfly's wing.

'What's happened to me?'

'You've picked something up. I told you this would happen, didn't I?' she said, rolling her eyes to suggest she was referring to all of Paris.

I'd forgotten how much I loved her voice, and was pleased she'd remembered our conversation.

We talked about the changes and how things were merging and changing. She didn't relax, but ran through her ideas quickly, seeming to want my confirmation. She said something in French to summarise it, because she didn't know the translation.

'The simple becomes complex?' I suggested.

'That's it,' she said. 'That is how things are in Paris. We complicate.'

She saw me smile and I thought she was going to smile back, but she said, 'Let me examine you.'

She stood on her chair and reached to pull a leaf from the alder, then held it, flickering, close to my face.

'I have no equipment,' she muttered and I felt the flutter of her breath on my face. She moved closer, and her hair touched my cheek, and then she moved away. She looked shy, as though it was too obvious that something had passed between us. 'Something minor, I think,' she said.

I wanted to tell her how much she'd affected me, what I'd thought about her, how much I'd wanted to see her, but didn't know how to sum it up. I wanted to tell her about the oak-panelled room, to see if she remembered, but knew it might sound too weird. Most of all I wanted to ask if she was still with that man, but before I could she said, 'Maurice will be here soon. I'm meeting him there,' she said, pointing to the other side of the park.

The way she said this almost implied she was doing something wrong, by talking to me. That gave me the courage to say, 'Would he mind?'

She shrugged.

I managed to say, 'Can I see you again?'

She looked cross and stood up, but said, 'Tomorrow for lunch. Le Grenier at noon. OK?'

She never heard my answer, because she slung her bag on and left quickly. The leaf on the table lit up again, its flicker becoming steady, more like a pulse.

Worn out on adrenaline and lack of sleep, I managed to arrive twenty minutes early and stood outside the restaurant trying to think of things to say. When Janine arrived, she smiled as though she was really pleased to see me, which was hardly what I'd been expecting.

I can't even remember what we ate, partly because we ate so little. We would have found it difficult to talk, except that she said she only had an hour, and that gave us a sense of urgency. Somehow, within a few minutes I'd established how I felt.

'Perhaps we shouldn't have met like this,' she said. 'I didn't want to raise your hopes, because I don't have any.'

I would have taken that for arrogance, if she hadn't sounded so upset.

She was almost whispering when she said, 'It's not that I couldn't like you, but that I chose not to.'

'But you know how I feel?'

She countered this by smiling and said, 'Perhaps you're just melancholy. You've spent too long in Paris, wandering in rain. You are attracted to impossible situations.'

'Is it impossible?'

'I think so.'

That left an opening for me, so I tried to explain the sense of recognition I'd felt when we first met.

She blinked, looking up, as though there were tears in her eyes, but then I saw it was a way of preparing herself to tell me something.

'I felt that too. Which is why I'm here at all. But I believed in it once before, with somebody else, years ago. I left Maurice for that man, because of a sense of recognition. Within two weeks it had failed. A passion I'd thrived on for three years came to nothing in a few days. All I did was hurt Maurice and confuse myself. I don't believe in taking risks like that.'

'You're young for such an entrenched view of life, aren't you?' She wouldn't look at me, so I said, 'I don't think you mean it.'

There was still no response, so I said, 'I can remember something that might be relevant. There was a room, somewhere in Paris, with a wooden floor and oak panels on the wall. It was early morning and there was an old man in the next room, writing. And you were there as well. With me.'

Throughout this Janine listened closely, but didn't react. I'd expected her to look confused, or to show recognition, but she only looked blank. Then she glanced across at the sundial-shaft, on the far wall, and sighed.

'How can I go back to work now?'

I hoped that meant that she wouldn't go back, that we'd go back to my house.

'It's too difficult,' she announced. 'I would be stupid to make the same mistake again.'

I waited a long time, my throat growing sore, before I said, 'That's a shame.'

'Not if we stay friends.'

I was upset, because she knew it wasn't what I wanted, but knew I couldn't reject her.

I imagined spending hours longing for her, feeling uncomfortable when we were together, but she was such good company that we became easy friends. We spent hours talking and laughing at ourselves, drunkenly planning how we would run the world, if it was up to us.

There were odd occasions when she would drop her guard, and say something revealing. 'I can talk to you better than anyone. Even my boyfriend. But I don't want to tell you that, in case it means more to you than it should.' I tried not to be moved by such things.

I never got to meet Maurice. She said he knew about me, and didn't mind Janine seeing me. He wasn't opposed to meeting me, but the opportunity never came up. She hardly ever talked about him, even when I mentioned him, and I wasn't sure whether that was to avoid hurting me, or to keep me separate from her other life. And yet, whenever we parted, I knew she was going back to him. He was the one lying next to her. I coped with that mostly, but sometimes she would sit in a particular way, as though she was gathering light, and I'd remember something greater. In those moments, life felt unfair, and it would be an effort to keep the mood friendly.

On a Sunday in September, when the weather was turning to its familiar warm and cool, we went for breakfast on rue Mouffetard. The sky was clear, but we went inside, where the room was warmed by sunlight. Even before our apple compôte arrived, Janine went quiet, looking at the way the light brought out blond veins in the polished wood of the table.

She brought up the subject of the oak-panelled room.

'Do you remember it now?' I asked.

'It sounds familiar,' she admitted, 'but that may be because there are a million rooms like that in Paris.'

'Maybe.'

'But,' she said quickly, 'I'd like to help you find it.'

We ate breakfast quickly, and started our research in the Panthéon library. Her idea was to use my memory of the architectural details, which direction it faced and what floor it was on, to narrow the search. We spent hours looking through files of planning designs, to find something that matched. Although there were a few near-misses, nothing seemed quite right. A couple of times we checked up on hopeful cases; it was easier when the rooms had been made into public spaces, but we even managed to persuade our way into some private homes, making excuses about childhood memories. In every case, there was no doubt we were in the wrong place, and that made me more certain the memory was real.

Some nights we sat up at my house flipping through books about old Paris, drinking until we ended up talking about anything other than the room.

At the end of an evening like that, I walked her home. She looked up at the window, saw Maurice and beamed. I didn't even try to hide my disgust, but managed to say goodbye warmly.

I went straight round to Ruth's, and told her I didn't want to go home. I made it sound like a confession, so that she would know I wanted to be with her. It didn't work out quite like that. She went very serious, as though I'd made too large a declaration. We talked for a long time, and when boredom had almost got the better of us, we kissed. In the early hours she said I'd better leave, and I went home, enjoying the cold air. It was that night I was followed by the dog.

I might not have made so much of that, except that I was followed by other dogs later in the week. The same one spoke to me on the Wednesday, this time saying its piece only once, then bolting back in the direction it had come. Another turned up, scratching at my door at dawn the next day, saying something like *wasting time*. When I told Janine she said it was my conscience speaking; the dogs were picking up my fears and voicing them. That was about the only conversation we had that week. I didn't see much of Ruth, but I made excuses to Janine and said I was too busy most nights. On Saturday, I returned from an afternoon at Ruth's to find that Janine had left a note for me. She'd brought it personally, and I'd been out. It said, *I think I might have found your room.*

It was a building on my list of untouched spaces, but I'd been avoiding it because rue Lhomond was so close to home and I preferred to see as much of Paris as possible. It was due to be examined in two weeks' time, but nobody would mind if I brought it ahead of schedule, so on Sunday morning Janine and I went there at dawn. The air was blue at street level, although the sky was lit in a way that suggested the sun had risen but had yet to clear the buildings. We struggled to untie the wooden boards. Since zinc had decayed, most entrance ways were now boarded up with old wood, secured with vines. Behind that, plastic sheeting. It took us about ten minutes to force our way in.

Inside, we headed upstairs. It was light in there, with a glow coming through the gaps between the wooden boards over the windows, criss-crossing the rooms with lines of light. On the fourth level, the air smelt familiar, even though it had been unbreathed for years. The walls were plastered, rather than panelled, and the shape was wrong, but it felt similar to the place I remembered.

Two things caught my attention at once. A grand piano was standing underneath the boarded window. To the left of it there was a locked door. Beyond that door, the windows must have been open, because bright light came from under it.

'There shouldn't be sunlight,' I said, pointing down at the door, but Janine only glanced at me, heading for the piano.

'Untouched spaces aren't meant to have locked doors.'

'Perhaps you should knock,' she said, sitting at the piano, and lifting the lid.

'We need more light.'

I went to the main window, tore off its plastic, and managed to force the shutter open.

Janine pressed a key on the piano, and it sounded. The note was cut short, as she withdrew her hand.

'It works,' she said.

It was the first time I'd heard a piano in years and I wished I'd continued with lessons when I was younger. Janine seemed to have the same thought and pressed a few keys in succession. She made the notes sound soft, though tuneless.

I felt as though we should hurry. Something felt extremely familiar, but I couldn't tell what.

I went back to the locked door and tried to look underneath it. The light in the room beyond was cooler, but I couldn't see much else. There didn't appear to be any movement. I tried the handle a few times, wondering how much force it would take to break the lock. I was about to suggest that we wait until infection got to the metal, but I heard a sequence of notes that I recognised. Janine stopped and looked across at me, confused.

She said something in French, which I couldn't take in, because I was trying to remember the notes. She played them again, a few more this time, and it was like having the memory uncovered.

'I remember,' she said, putting her hands over her mouth. 'Something. Something about that music, and these rooms.'

I wanted more, but as she started again the wire broke. The rest followed, snapping so rapidly it sounded like somebody was running a knife across them. When it was over, the wood vibrated for a while longer.

I don't remember moving closer, but I must have done, because I was holding Janine. Her face was pressed into my chest, her breath hot through my clothes. She sounded distressed.

'I can't ignore that,' she said.

Neither of us had a clue what it meant, but it was clear what we should do. We left immediately and went to my house, spending all day in bed. It was the first time I'd enjoyed sex with the curtains open, letting the light flood across our bodies, so our skin looked over-exposed. Where the air was cold, we warmed each other with touching. It wasn't happy, but potent.

Afterwards we sat on the bed, miserable. I would have to tell Ruth, and she would have to tell Maurice.

Her mood swayed as we talked. Sometimes she would hold my face and kiss me, pressing her forehead against mine to speak kindly, but other times, she would cry, saying, 'I just can't.'

Something had happened between us that was beyond explanation. My belief in the validity of the shared memory grew, but she seemed reluctant to accept it, so my voice became desperate. I ended up sounding like I was trying to convince her.

'I don't know if I believe it,' she said. 'Maybe we imagined this.'

All afternoon she put off going to see Maurice, because she said that whatever the future held, somebody was going to be hurt.

What could she tell him? That she'd fallen in love with her friend, because of a half-memory of something that never happened.

When it went dark, I hoped she'd send him a note and leave it, but she finally resigned herself to going back. Otherwise, she said, he would worry. I wished she'd gone earlier, because I then had to spend the whole night imagining him winning her over and coaxing her to bed. She'd get tired, would probably have a drink; the thought of me would seem ridiculous. I fantasised about going round there and shouting my piece, but it was pointless, because my French wouldn't match my emotions.

She didn't come back, even in the morning, and because I'd been awake for most of the night, it felt like she'd been away for a full day.

That afternoon I tried to get back into the house on rue Lhomond, to see into the locked room. I never made it that far, because as I went up the stairs I heard voices.

I stopped, and the voices stopped. I was authorised to be there, when very few people were, so I decided to continue. In the piano room, three dogs were facing me. They looked startled, but their words were angry.

fucker, fucker, fucker
why bother, why bother, why bother with that, why bother
fucker fucker fucker

They shouted over each other, the same phrases over and again. I looked behind them. The lock had fallen from the door, quite rotten, looking more like sand than metal, and a circle of light came through the hole where the handle had been.

I backed off.

That evening I sat waiting for Janine and must have looked disappointed when I opened the door to Stephen. I wanted to tell him about Janine, but he stopped me.

'I was followed by a dog,' he said. 'A talking dog.'

I urged him to come and sit down. He didn't wait to get his breath back to tell me.

'It followed me for about five minutes, talking all the time. It was telling me that I was lost.'

'Were you?'

'Well, no. But it went on and on. *You're lost, you're lost.* I thought, you know, maybe it had a point. So I followed it instead. It went back to this place – there were hundreds of them.'

'Hundreds?'

'Well, at least fifty,' he said. 'Maybe more. They're all in this house on rue Lhomond. One of your untouched spaces. The door's been forced open. I couldn't even get inside, there were so many of them. Do you know what's going on?'

'I knew a couple of them had moved in, earlier. But that's all.'

We considered going back to get a better look, but Janine came round. She said hello to Stephen then went into my room to cry. I didn't get a chance to explain, but went to see her. Even though she was upset, I was pleased she'd come back.

Our relationship didn't make much sense. We knew we liked each other, we made each other laugh, and the sex was gorgeous, but there was a nagging sense that we'd made a mistake. I put it down to pressure. We'd invested so much hope and both given up decent relationships and our friendship for the sake of something that might be a dream. It didn't take long for us to start arguing and because of the pent-up confusion we said horrible things to each other.

We both thought it had to be perfect. If we were giving up so much, the reward had to be perfection. That meant that every problem was magnified into a disaster. The arguments would usually end when one of us declared that it was all a fantasy and the other would agree.

Later, after hours apart, we'd reassure each other that something meaningful had happened. That we had met for a reason, that it was worth continuing. The next day, we'd argue again.

It was half-way through an argument that she silenced me.

'Listen,' she said.

'No, you listen to me.'

'Please,' she said, pointing at the window. 'Music.'

I could hear somebody playing a recorder. We both went to the window, but couldn't see the source; if anything it sounded quieter, but we both recognised the melody. It was the tune Janine had played on the piano.

We found a man of about thirty playing the recorder, just around the corner. He was playing the same tune, but stopped when he saw us.

'What's that?' I asked in English.

'You know this?' he said. His accent sounded German, and his English was slow. He blew a few notes of the tune.

'Yes. We remember it. What is it?'

'And you remember the room, and the woman? A man at his desk?'

'You remember that too?' Janine asked.

'Oh yes.'

I pointed at Janine. 'You remember *her* being in the room?'

'Not her,' he said, 'but somebody *like* her. Everybody remembers it differently. It's an infection. Something from flies. The memory has been passed all over Paris. Some people believe it's a real place. I think it was a dream. It bothers me. I know it isn't even mine, but it's the most beautiful memory I have.'

Stephen's estimation was probably correct; there were dogs on every floor. With so many voices, their chatter made more sense than usual, as strings of phrases passed over each other, forming half-sentences. They were more frantic, but I doubted they would bite. We managed to make it up to the fourth floor with nothing other than abuse.

Convincing Janine to come with me had been difficult. At first, she had walked away from me as though I'd cheated her, even using that word. 'I feel cheated,' she'd said. 'It felt like love.' I wasn't about to let it go, though. 'What about the dogs homing in on me? What about the way it affected us? There has to be more to it than a common infection.' She'd agreed, but said, 'We based everything on that memory.

Everything. If it isn't real, we can't carry on.' On the walk over there she didn't speak again.

Inside the locked room, there was too much sunlight to see clearly. It smelt bad, but as my eyes adjusted I saw the place as I remembered it; a wooden floor, oak-panelled walls, with a tall window looking out. There was a blue armchair in the centre, facing the window.

'This is it,' Janine said, though it sounded like a whisper over the calls of the dogs.

We moved around and saw that sitting in the armchair was a dead man, his skin framed over his bones like leaves of tobacco. Where they had caved in you could see that parts of him shone. His jaw and throat were a mesh of wire and plate, barely touched by metal fatigue. I didn't recognise the pattern of jewels in the metal jaw, but from what Stephen had told me, there was no doubt who it was.

'This is my father.'

There was a linen bag on his knees. In front of him was a dead dog, its head open. I bent to look closer. A confetti of finger-nail-coloured shells were in the base of its skull; I blew on them and they flurried. Picking one up, I could see they were the shells of dried flies' eggs. Between him and the dog were two small bones. Janine picked them up and noticed that they fitted together, forming a V.

'Wishbone,' she said. 'From an edible bird. They were broken for wishes.'

'I know,' I said.

'What would your father have wished for?'

'To be heard, probably.'

I imagined he'd been using the dog, to record his thoughts, downloading his ideas and opinions into its mind, unwilling, or too short of time, to write them down. He must have had help, getting it infected with a human throat. His one wish, perhaps, was that the dog could home in on Stephen or myself, finding us when he could not, to pass on his memories. It was strange that Dad had resorted to the technology he hated, in order to contact us. Clearly, something had gone wrong, though, and stability had been lost. The dog's brain had given way to infection, and the memories had broken free. Segments of them had been passed on complete, by flies. The rest had shattered, now being barked out at us by infected dogs.

Janine pulled the linen bag away from his lap, brushed off the skin, then passed it to me. It was full of wishbones. Some were so old they were white and peppered with caries, but others were yellow. All were intact, unbroken. Unwished.

'What would you wish for?' Janine asked.

People are always so unhappy, so full of hopes, but when somebody asks you to make a wish, you struggle. I'd hoped to find something else there, a clue as to why we should be together. I'd hoped that our relationship was meant to be. Instead, I saw that it was a choice. We'd looked for evidence to back up our feelings, because it's frightening to trust in something so strong and unexpected. But evidence was unnecessary. It didn't matter where the feelings came from, or what made them grow. It was the opportunity that counted.

'We have a whole bag full,' she said, pulling out the first bone and holding it out to me.

It was the first time I'd seen her smile like that. It wasn't hopeful or desperate, but pleased. We gripped the wishbone with our little fingers, and without thinking of anything at all, pulled.